C000233460

GET A FREE BOOK!

I'm a pretty nice guy once you look past the grisly images in my head. Most of all, I love connecting with awesome readers like you.

Join my VIP Reader Group and get a FREE serial killer thriller for your Kindle.

Get My Free Book

www.danpadavona.com/thriller-readers-vip-group/

FATAL MERCY

A WOLF LAKE THRILLER

DAN PADAVONA

A CHILLING PSYCHOLOGICAL THRILLER

1

The grandfather clock ticked with the grim finality of a failing heart. Kay Ramsey listened at the bottom of the stairs, but couldn't hear her husband, Lincoln. It was quiet in the master bedroom, and the silence made her wring her hands. It was just a matter of time before Lincoln passed, though she'd spent the last year lying to herself, grasping for an invisible tether of hope that someone would cure Lincoln.

She padded to the kitchen where her daughter, Ambrose, sat at the kitchen table and stared into a mug of hot chocolate. The ghosts of chicken dinner spiced the air.

"I didn't hear anything," Kay said, sliding into the seat across from her daughter.

"I swear Dad got out of bed."

"Your father hasn't risen since yesterday afternoon." Kay played with the salt shaker and set her chin on her palm. The kitchen seemed too large without Lincoln's presence. "Can I get you a slice of carrot cake? Mrs. Beadle brought it over this morning, and I can't eat it by myself."

"Why isn't he in hospice?" Ambrose asked, ignoring the offer and swiping a dark lock off her shoulder.

"Because he wants to spend his remaining time at home."

"But they can take care of him."

"The nurse comes daily. There's nothing they can do for your father that I can't do with the nurse's help."

Ambrose set the mug down and glared.

"Is that true? You're exhausted, Mom. Tell me the truth. How much sleep did you get last night?"

Kay tapped the salt shaker against the table.

"Enough."

"You can barely keep your eyes open. That settles it. I'm spending the night and taking care of Dad. If you don't rest, you'll make yourself sick."

"What about the kids?"

Ambrose tutted.

"Martin can watch the kids. He's not helpless."

"Could have fooled me. They're probably running the house by now." When the joke failed to elicit the desired response, Kay set her hands on the table. "I'm sleeping next to your father tonight, and you're going home to your husband and children. This isn't open for discussion."

Ambrose bit her lip. Kay's eyes dropped to the table where her reflection stared back at her—face drawn, gray hair disheveled and unruly, the lines in her face deepening with each heartbeat. She'd married Lincoln straight out of high school. Her parents chastised Kay, told her she was too young, that they were rushing into a critical decision. They were wrong, and Kay and Lincoln had fifty-five years of marriage as evidence. As if Ambrose saw the memories flashing in Kay's eyes, she set her elbow on the table and supported her cheek.

"You want to look at pictures, Mom? Maybe page through the wedding album over a slice of Mrs. Beadle's carrot cake?"

A hurt laugh crawled out of Kay's throat. She bit her hand and willed herself not to lose control in front of Ambrose.

During quiet times, when the house sat vacant except for Lincoln upstairs, she cried in the basement.

"Your father was the best-looking boy in his class," Kay said, twirling her hair around her finger. "I remember the first time he asked me to dance, how nervous I felt. As soon as he held my hand, the stress melted away. I always knew he was the one."

"You've had a wonderful life together."

Kay crossed a leg and swallowed the lump in her throat.

"So many good times. Some not so good, but that's life. The worst was when he fought overseas. I was terrified he wouldn't return."

"My favorite pictures are of Dad in his Navy uniform."

"He was so proud. Your father would have given his life for his country. No regrets. By the time he returned, our classmates had graduated college, settled into careers, and purchased homes. But I never felt we were running behind. We'd figure it out. When your father took the teller position at the First National Bank in Harmon, he swallowed his pride. He was more qualified to manage that institution than the people who'd worked there for two decades. His salary wouldn't pay for the tiny apartment in Harmon. But he refused to let me work. Told me we'd find a way. I never doubted him."

When Ambrose sipped the last of the hot chocolate, Kay took the mug and heated the kettle.

"How long did it take before Dad became bank manager?"

"Six years."

"That's incredible."

Kay opened the pantry and retrieved another packet of hot chocolate.

"When your father sets his mind to something, nobody can stand in his way. After the promotion, we gave up the apartment, paid cash for the house, and started planning a family. Then you came along, and your father had never been happier."

Ambrose's eyes glistened.

"Everybody loved him."

"Not everyone." Kay dabbed the corner of her eye with a tissue. "That bastard made your father's life a living hell. No sympathy, even after his health took a downturn."

Quiet poured off the walls as the women lost themselves inside memories.

"Isn't there anything the doctors can do for Dad?"

Kay leaned against the counter.

"There's no cure for COPD. He's already beaten the odds, hanging on for as long as he has."

"I can't understand why modern medicine hasn't solved this disease."

"Every day he lives, there's a chance for a breakthrough."

Except Kay had given up believing that was true. She'd lose him any day now. The walls tilted closer. She had to get out of here before the stress of being inside the house made a husk of her body. The kettle whistled. Kay reached into the cupboard for a fresh mug. Her eyes stopped on Lincoln's favorite coffee cup. She covered her mouth. Ambrose came to her and set a hand on her shoulder.

"I've got this, Mom. Why don't you sit?"

Kay waved a hand in front of her face.

"I'm sorry. Sometimes it hits me. It's best if I stay busy and stop my mind from racing."

Ambrose led her mother back to the chair and sat her down. She held her mother's frail hands across the table as night spilled down the windowpane, the stars sharp for a summer evening in Wolf Lake, New York.

"You'll never be alone, Mom."

Kay sniffed.

"You and Martin are too good to me."

"We love you, and we'll always be here for you." Ambrose

glanced down and weighed her words. "Martin and I talked. When it...happens, we'd like you to come live with us."

Kay released her daughter's hands.

"That's unnecessary. I'm happy here. Why would I ever leave?"

"We're converting the attic into a bedroom. Kyla wants it to be hers, which means her bedroom will be free."

Falling back in her chair, Kay touched her cheek.

"How can I say goodbye to our home?"

"This is too sudden," Ambrose said, waving her hands. "Don't decide now. Think it over."

"I need fresh air. I can't breathe, suddenly."

"Mom?"

"It's okay. Just give me a second."

Kay shut the back door and stared at the yard through a haze of tears. Crickets sang in the grass. Inside the kitchen, Ambrose flipped the patio light on. A pool of radiance spread into the yard and met the dark. She could make out the picnic table where her daughter's playground once stood. A flood of images rushed back to her—Lincoln pushing a laughing Ambrose on the swing, the family roasting marshmallows on warm summer nights like this one, Fourth of July with half the neighborhood talking and laughing together while Lincoln grilled steaks. A firefly lit and disappeared as if vanquished. When was the last time she saw a firefly in their backyard? They were so plentiful when Lincoln and Kay purchased the house. Nature's fireworks, Lincoln called them.

She bit back a sob and straightened her back, hearing Lincoln's voice in her head.

"You're stronger than you believe, Kay. You'll be fine without me."

Kay touched her heart and squeezed her eyes shut, wringing out the last of the tears.

A thump came from inside the house. Then a shadow crept

along the neighbor's wall. As Kay stepped into the yard, a glass shattered in the kitchen. Ambrose yelled.

Kay whipped the door open and stumbled inside. No, this couldn't be happening. Not now. She wasn't ready.

Her daughter's frantic voice carried down the staircase.

"Dad, Dad, wake up!" Footfalls racing to the landing. "Call an ambulance. He's not breathing!"

2

Dr. Ryka Mandal crosses her stockinged legs and jots a note on her pad. When she glances at Deputy Thomas Shepherd, her eyes hold concern and a penetrating understanding. It's as if she peers straight through him.

"How are you sleeping?"

Thomas rakes his fingers through the mop of unruly hair atop his head.

"Four hours per night, sometimes more."

"That's not optimal. Your body needs eight hours to heal. Without it, you're prone to sickness, lethargy, mental disorders."

When he first met Mandal in April, her thick accent distracted him. Now it soothes. Grounds him. She sets the notepad on the coffee table separating his chair from hers. They each sit in comfortable, cushioned chairs with ample back support. With the drapes drawn, the mahogany room appears bathed in caramel. An air purifier whispers white noise in the corner.

A lock of hair slides down her forehead and touches her ski slope nose. She brushes it away and sets her hands in her lap.

"How do the other deputies treat you?" she asks.

"Well."

"They're not prejudiced against deputies with Asperger's?"

"No, they accept me."

"How about your previous job in Los Angeles? Did the other officers treat you differently?"

He ponders the question and shrugs.

"The department promoted me to detective. That demonstrated faith."

"So no problems inside the Los Angeles or Wolf Lake offices."

"None."

She narrows her eyes.

"And yet you're into your third month of therapy. Do you feel you're progressing, Thomas?"

"That's for you to say."

She fixes her skirt and crosses the opposite leg.

"Last week, you told me your father is dying from stage four lung cancer."

"Yes."

"You learned this in April, yet you waited until July to speak about it in therapy. Why?"

He touches the bridge of his nose. A headache lingers behind his eyes.

"It has nothing to do with my career."

"When you came to me in April after you shot Jeremy Hyde, the county required I give you a thorough psychological evaluation."

"And you cleared me to return to work in May."

"Yes, with reservations. We discussed my concerns."

Thomas fidgets in the chair and glances at the clock. In five minutes, the questions will end. Until next week.

"My issues haven't affected my performance."

Mandal levels her eyes with his. In this setting, she can be intimidating. Yet Thomas appreciates her no-bullshit attitude. Under different circumstances, she would be a valued friend, someone who wouldn't shy away from airing ugly truths.

"You're not sleeping, and shift work provides its own challenges. I fear you'll regress, if we don't uncover whatever you're holding back."

"Why do you think I'm holding back on you?"

"For one, your father. Losing a parent is a traumatic experience, Thomas. We should have discussed this in April. How do you feel about your father's diagnosis?"

Thomas's mouth opens and closes. His eyes seek the clock again.

"It's no problem if the session runs long," she says, following his gaze. "You're my last appointment for the day."

"All right."

"Don't worry about the time. Tell me about your relationship with your father."

THOMAS SWUNG his cruiser to the curb and stepped into the humid night. His partner, Veronica Aguilar, was already on the scene and awaiting his arrival. She scribbled on her notepad as a middle-aged woman with brunette hair bobbed her head to Aguilar's questions. An older woman followed the paramedics as they pushed a gurney toward an ambulance where a female paramedic helped her inside. Thomas assessed the situation as the ambulance sped into the night with flashing lights. He winced when the siren blared. Loud noises frayed his nerves.

After Deputy Aguilar finished, she held up a finger, a signal for the middle-aged woman to stay put. The muscular, diminutive deputy sauntered over to Thomas at the curb while Deputy Lambert guarded the door.

"What's the story?" Thomas asked. "Looks like a medical emergency."

Aguilar set herself between Thomas and the distraught woman.

"The house belongs to Lincoln and Kay Ramsey. Lincoln was the man on the gurney."

"Heart attack?"

"COPD. Ramsey's condition degraded over the last decade. It accelerated over the past two months. He didn't have a heartbeat when the paramedics wheeled him out. My guess is the guy died twenty minutes ago."

"I wouldn't expect this many uniforms on scene unless we suspected foul play."

"The woman over there," Aguilar said, tilting her chin toward the female she'd interviewed. "That's the daughter, Ambrose Jorgensen. She lives with her husband, Martin, and two kids on the east side of the village. She claims someone broke into the bedroom. When she ran upstairs, she found the window open to the screen. Lincoln Ramsey wasn't breathing. She called 9-1-1."

"That's why there are three deputies here."

"Right. Sheriff Gray worked overtime today, and I didn't want to call him in."

"So what do you believe happened?"

"My theory? The guy died of natural causes, if you consider COPD natural. Had a great uncle who passed from COPD. It's not pretty at the end. Anyway, Kay Ramsey couldn't verify her daughter's concerns. The poor woman probably couldn't remember what she ate for dinner, let alone if she'd left the bedroom window unlocked."

"Warm night like this one, most people leave their windows open."

"Ramsey said someone was in her neighbor's yard. It was too dark to recognize a face."

"Did we check with the neighbor?"

"Yeah. It's an eighty-six-year-old woman, and she says she

settled down in front of the television three hours ago and was ready for bed before the commotion started."

"Okay, bring the daughter over."

Aguilar motioned at Ambrose Jorgensen. The Ramsey's daughter sloughed across the front yard with her head lowered, her makeup smeared by tears.

"Mrs. Jorgensen, this is Deputy Shepherd. Please tell him what you told me."

Ambrose folded her arms and glanced at the house, her eyes haunted.

"Mom and I were downstairs inside the kitchen when somebody broke inside."

"What makes you think someone was in the house?" Thomas asked.

"The floorboards creaked, and then there was a thud, like someone bumped against the furniture."

"Are you certain it wasn't your father?"

Ambrose rubbed at her arms.

"He was too ill to move. Mom said my father hadn't left his bed in twenty-four hours."

Thomas pictured his own father, diagnosed during the spring with stage four lung cancer. Mason Shepherd had lost weight and energy. But the downward spiral was still to come.

"I told Mom someone was upstairs," Ambrose continued. "But she waved it away and said I imagined the noise."

"What happened next?"

The Ramsey's daughter chewed her thumbnail.

"Mom had a horrible time dealing with my father's disease. She stepped outside to clear her head. While I called home, another thump came from inside the bedroom. This one was loud enough that I worried my father had fallen out of bed."

"Did you check on him?"

"Right away. On my way up the stairs, I heard something else. Like the screen opened and slid shut. When I reached the bedroom, my father had stopped breathing. I yelled for help and called 9-1-1."

Aguilar lifted her chin at the master bedroom. "Did you look out the window for an intruder?"

"No," she said, glaring at Aguilar as if the deputy had slapped her. "My priority was my father. All I cared about was calling for an ambulance." She bit the inside of her cheek, her eyes glistening. "Not that it helped. Dad was gone when I found him. There was nothing the paramedics could do."

"Your mother claims she doesn't recall locking the window."

"No, but she saw someone next door."

"We'll check for shoe prints," said Thomas, assuaging the Ramsey's daughter. "But it's possible your mother saw a neighborhood kid running through the yard. When I came down your road, I noticed a dozen or more kids chasing each other."

"If you're suggesting my mother mistook a child playing hide-and-seek for a full-grown adult..." Ambrose took a composing breath. "She can recognize the difference, even in the dark." Ambrose shifted her pocketbook to her opposite shoulder. "Now if you'll excuse me, I'd like to be with my mother."

"We'll call if we have additional questions."

After the Ramsey's daughter drove off, Deputy Lambert stepped off the porch and joined Thomas and Aguilar in the yard. Trained by the U.S. Army, Lambert stood a few inches over six feet, his hair buzzed military short beneath his hat.

"This seems like a wild goose chase," Lambert said, following the taillights into the night. "I'll dust the bedroom for prints. Between the Ramsey couple and their daughter, there must be prints all over the room."

"Concentrate on the windowpane," Thomas said. "And it wouldn't hurt to dust outside the window. Is there a way to enter the master bedroom from ground level?"

"There's one possibility," Aguilar said. "Follow me."

A porch roof stood over a side entrance. Thomas ran his gaze over the stoop.

"Could be someone climbed over the rail, pulled himself onto the roof, and jostled the screen open." Thomas scratched his chin. "But why would anyone murder a man dying from COPD?"

"Maybe Lincoln Ramsey had enemies," Lambert said.

Aguilar shook her head.

"I'm sticking with my original theory. The guy died in his sleep. He might have thrashed before passing, and that's what the daughter heard."

"All right," Thomas said. He nodded at Lambert. "While you dust for prints, I'll check the neighbor's yard where Kay Ramsey saw the shadow. Aguilar, knock on a few doors. Perhaps a neighbor saw someone."

Lambert's heavy frame climbed the stairs inside the house as Thomas swept his flashlight through the grass. He followed Kay Ramsey's tracks to the back stoop and stood where she had, gazing out at the darkness. The silhouette of a fence separated the backyard from commercial development. He flicked the light along the grass, moving with slow, deliberate strides until he reached the elderly woman's home. Gravel girded this side of the house, potted flowers throwing splashes of color along the border. The grass stood erect, undisturbed.

He circled the house, then rounded the Ramsey's home, searching for another way inside. Footsteps behind him brought his head around. He shone the beam against Aguilar's face.

"Lower the flashlight, Columbo," Aguilar said, shielding her eyes.

"Sorry."

"I knocked on a dozen doors. Of the seven people who answered, nobody saw an intruder break into the Ramsey house. Then again, it's almost ten on a Sunday night. A lot of these people need to wake up for work tomorrow morning."

As Aguilar finished her thought, Deputy Lambert swished through the lawn. Slick with dew, the grass grew up Thomas's shins. He wondered how often the lawn was mowed. Kay Ramsey looked too frail to handle the work. Would his mother fall apart after cancer broke his father?

"No prints on the outside of the window," Lambert said. "But I found thumbprints on the inside pane. I'll wager good money they belong to Kay Ramsey or the daughter."

Lambert was right, Thomas thought. The investigation seemed like a wild goose chase.

So why did he feel they'd missed something critical?

C helsey Byrd tolerated the dump trucks and shouts from the construction workers outside. But when the jackhammer started, she rushed across the room and shut the window before the clamor rattled her teeth loose.

"Now I can hear myself think," she said, settling into her chair.

She slung her tawny locks over her shoulder, leaned back in the rolling chair, and set her feet on the desk. Two years past her thirtieth birthday, she stared at the case folders spread across her desk and took a deep breath. Business had never been better at Wolf Lake Consulting, the private investigation firm she'd founded within a converted single-story home inside the village center. She could barely keep up with the work. If Chelsey didn't hire a third investigator soon, she'd have to turn down cases.

At the neighboring desk, Raven Hopkins, Chelsey's partner for the last nine months, clicked around her computer screen. The ebony-skinned investigator tied her long braids behind her neck today. The high cheekbones, fresh manicure, and sapphire nails lent a false sense of security to anyone who got on Raven's wrong side. She had the body of a sprinter. Or an MMA fighter,

Chelsey mused. Today, Raven seemed preoccupied as she called up files on her computer.

"You're talkative this morning."

Raven glanced up.

"What?"

"I said you're talkative...never mind."

"Sorry, I'm trying to wrap up the Franklin case. And I didn't sleep much, but that's nothing new."

Chelsey sipped her green tea.

"Everything all right at home?"

"Mom had a tough night."

Raven had moved her mother, Serena, into her house near Wolf Lake. Seven years ago, when Raven was eighteen, Serena threw her daughter out of the apartment. The women had been like oil and water for as long as Raven could remember. Addicted to heroin, Serena overdosed in April. Raven and her brother, LeVar, forced Serena to enter rehab. Though Serena had remained clean for three months and developed a fresh outlook on life, she had her share of bad days.

"What happened?"

Raven set her pen down.

"We got into another argument, and like she always does when she's under stress, she started talking crazy. Like how she needed a fix to take the edge off."

"Are you sure she hasn't used since she moved in?"

Raven issued a humorless laugh.

"I'd know if she had. Her ass would be back in rehab a second later." Raven dropped her face into her palms. "I'm doing my best. It's just that my place is tiny, and we're always in each other's hair."

"You might need a break from each other. Does she have any friends she can spend a few nights with?"

Raven cocked an eyebrow.

"Nobody who didn't feed her addiction over the last ten years. I'm trying to get her away from Harmon, not push her back. I'm uncomfortable leaving her alone when I'm at work. That's why I drive home for lunch every day."

"And leave me to eat by myself like a total loser."

Raven snickered.

"You only have yourself to blame." Raven raised a hand. "I'm not suggesting you go back to Ray." During the winter and spring, Chelsey had dated Ray Welch, a loudmouthed bully with alcohol issues. Why she'd wasted time with Ray, Chelsey couldn't explain. But when Raven brought Ray's name into the conversation, it reminded Chelsey of her poor judgment. "There are a hundred guys who'd kill for a date with the gorgeous Chelsey Byrd."

"Yeah, well. I haven't met the right guy."

"And you never will, if you lock yourself up in your house every night."

"I happen to enjoy binging Netflix."

"When is the last time we went to Hattie's and fed the jukebox for a few hours? We should go. What are you doing Friday night?"

"Catching up on these case files."

"Give work a rest, or hire another investigator," said Raven. "You deserve a life. Look, if I have to drive to your house and twist your arm, you're going out with me."

"Sounds kinky."

"Laugh it up, girlfriend. But you'd better be ready to party when I show up Friday night."

Chelsey sighed.

"Fine, but Friday is four days away. We need to get cracking on the Sadie Moreno case."

"Moreno...which investigation was that?"

"Sadie Moreno's ex-husband took her for a million dollars during the divorce, and now she's got a fiance."

Raven snapped her fingers.

"The boy toy. Damian, right?"

"Damian Ramos. Sadie is still worth three-million, and she's paranoid this guy is only in it for the payday."

"What's making her paranoid?"

"For starters, Ramos is twenty-five-years-old. He's thirty years younger than Sadie."

"Okay, that's a little curious. What do we know about Damian Ramos?"

"He's a market research analyst for a trading firm in Syracuse. The guy's also a fitness freak and hangs out at Benson's Barbells in Kane Grove."

Raven twisted her lips.

"I've been there. Nothing but muscle heads and steroid freaks."

"Ramos hits the gym every day between five and six o'clock. That's when the facility is at its busiest, everybody cramming inside and sweating together after the workday."

"At it's smelliest too. Okay, when do we start?"

"*You* start today. If I don't make up ground on the Bellinger case, we'll lose his business."

"Is this just a surveillance mission?"

Chelsey tapped a pen against her lips.

"Stay out of sight and take pictures. Get a sense for his hobbies and who his friends are."

"And if he's sleeping around behind Sadie Moreno's back."

"Exactly. I'll get you the address for the trading firm. It's a forty-minute trip from Wolf Lake."

"Sounds good. Let me finish this document, and I'll drive over."

"Would you prefer I stop by your place and check on your mother while you're in Syracuse?"

Raven slapped her forehead.

"Oh, shit. You're right. I'll never make it home, if I spend the afternoon in Syracuse and Kane Grove. Would you mind?"

"Not at all."

"Thanks, Chelsey. I owe you one." Letting out a breath, Raven clicked out of the document and shut off her screen. "It's hard enough sharing my place with my mother. I can't believe I almost moved LeVar in. Where would any of us sleep?"

LeVar Hopkins, Raven's brother, abandoned the Harmon Kings, a notorious gang in the city. Chelsey had investigated LeVar for murdering Erika Windrow, a prostitute working for a rival gang. Chelsey still harbored guilt for suspecting an innocent teenager. That LeVar was Raven's brother only complicated matters.

"What's going on with LeVar? Last I heard, he was taking classes at the community college and working on his GED."

"He has one more class this summer."

"You must be excited for your brother."

Raven's eyes lit with pride, and Chelsey spied the warmth in the woman's smile.

"He was always the smartest member of the family, and by the end of August, he'll have a high school diploma. After, he intends to stay at the community college and earn credits toward an associate's degree."

"Has he decided on a major?"

"Not yet. He's interested in everything from public relations and marketing to criminal justice."

Chelsey widened her eyes and tossed the pen on the desk.

"How does he go from the lead enforcer for a Harmon gang to criminal justice? I figured he hated the police."

"Ever since Deputy Shepherd invited LeVar to live in his guest house, he's rethought his position on cops."

Chelsey bit her lip and glanced at her hands. She dated Thomas Shepherd through high school before falling into a deep depression. Chelsey cut Thomas and her friends out of her life and hid inside herself. After years of therapy and medication, she crawled out of her hole and rejoined humanity. While Chelsey traveled the United States, staggering from one dead-end job to the next, Thomas moved from Wolf Lake to Los Angeles and joined the LAPD.

Raven rose from her chair and sat on the edge of Chelsey's desk.

"Enough with the sad puppy eyes. Why don't you climb off your high horse and call him? It's obvious you still have feelings for the man."

"I don't have...I mean, I care about Thomas and want to see him succeed. But a relationship? That was twelve years ago. Who dates their high school sweetheart?"

"Lots of people, I bet."

Chelsey had followed his career through the newspaper and internet. It warmed her heart when her old boyfriend made detective. The feat was no small accomplishment. It was rare for people with Asperger's syndrome to work in law enforcement. But he'd overcome prejudice and moved up the ladder. During a raid, Thomas was shot in the back when a rival gang ambushed the DEA and LAPD joint task force. Chelsey hadn't realized Thomas returned to Wolf Lake until she encountered him in a parking lot three months ago.

"Fairytale endings are for Disney movies. Besides, why would he be interested in someone with my baggage?"

"Now you're feeling sorry for yourself. If you're looking for pity, you won't find any here." Raven rapped her knuckles on

Chelsey's desk. "I'm leaving for Syracuse. When I return, I want the old Chelsey back."

"You never met the old Chelsey."

"All right. The one I met last winter." Raven kissed the top of Chelsey's head. "And thanks for checking on my mother."

4

MONDAY, JULY 13TH, 6:10 P.M.

W olf Lake, shimmering in cerulean perfection, filled Thomas's windshield as he turned his silver Ford F-150 onto the lake road. He chewed a piece of beef jerky. Aguilar was trying to get Thomas to eat more protein.

He'd spent the day with his fellow deputy, mired in paperwork. The emergency room doctor declared Lincoln Ramsey dead on arrival last night, surmising the man passed in bed at home. Remembering the family's pain forced him to fold the beef jerky wrapper and stuff it into his pocket. Would it be weeks or months before his own father succumbed? Mason Shepherd would die at home like Lincoln Ramsey, not in some antiseptic hospital room.

By choosing law enforcement over Shepherd Systems, the business which made their family wealthy, Thomas became the black sheep of the family. His father demanded he leave the Nightshade County Sheriff's Department and take over Shepherd Systems, and neither parent would return his calls until he quit law enforcement.

He was lost in thought when movement in the woods caught his eye. A trail ran from the state park down to the lake. His friend, Darren Holt, held the ranger position at Wolf Lake State Park. Darren had worked for the Syracuse Police Department before choosing a simpler life, managing the forest and ensuring his campers stayed safe.

Thomas slowed the truck and pulled along the shoulder. The shape struggling through the brush looked like a lost dog. He trotted through the field bordering his property and caught the trail fifty feet from the shore before he lost sight of the dog. Cupping a hand over his eye, he squinted into the sunlight and scanned the undergrowth. A hundred feet away, the brush rustled. The dog yelped as Thomas pushed a branch aside. He couldn't see the dog, only patches of silvery-black and creamy-white hidden behind the flora.

"Here, boy."

Thomas whistled, and the dog yelped again. Stepping over a fallen tree, Thomas cut through a stand of pines and rejoined the trail down the hill from the ranger's station. He wondered if Darren was in his cabin or walking the trails as he liked to do during the warm season. A bee buzzed at Thomas's head. He brushed it away and followed the whimpers.

When he stepped within ten strides of the dog, the animal lowered into a crouch and growled.

"Easy there, buddy. I won't hurt you."

He took a cautious step forward. The low growl rumbled through Thomas's bones. His heart hammered with the possibility the dog was rabid. Even if it wasn't, a cornered, injured animal demanded caution and respect. Thomas dropped to one knee. Through the tall grass, he could see the emaciated dog, patches of fur missing, the animal's ribs clearly defined.

"I'm coming closer, all right?"

The dog disagreed. Its hackles rose, fur standing erect as Thomas shimmied through the weeds. His eyes followed the ridge, hoping Darren was close enough to help. Dogs escaped campers all the time, so there was a fair chance the ranger kept an extra leash. Except Thomas didn't see a collar on this dog. No tags to identify the owner. Even if he convinced the dog to trust him, how the hell would he get it back to the truck?

Thomas remembered the beef jerky pouch. He fished the package out of his pocket and tore off a piece. Crept closer.

The dog bared its teeth. The fangs were long enough to rip Thomas's throat out if the dog lunged.

"Here you go, boy. You look hungry."

He tossed the jerky at the dog's paws. The canine locked eyes with Thomas. After a tense moment, the dog sniffed the jerky and gobbled the food in one bite. A split second later, its head shot up, orange and black eyes burning at Thomas. Then it sniffed the air, its focus on the package in Thomas's hand.

"Oh, you want more?"

Thomas tore a small piece and tossed it half a foot in front of the dog, forcing the animal to crawl out of hiding if it wanted to eat. The dog eyed the bait for a heartbeat as the wind played through its coat. Now that he was close, Thomas saw the dog was only a pup despite its impressive size. Large paws with sharp talons. Siberian Husky? When the dog shifted forward, it issued a high-pitched squeak and lifted its front paw. Thomas eyed the thorns piercing the padding, the dried blood. The same leg had a nasty gash down the front.

"That's an easy fix, boy. Let me help, and you'll be on your feet in no time."

Right. How could he remove the thorns without the dog taking his head off? It settled on its belly, paws splayed out. As it snapped up the jerky, Thomas ripped another piece. This time he held it in his palm, arm extended. It took all his will to stop his arm from shaking. He loved dogs, felt more comfortable around canines than he did people. But this was no ordinary dog.

The snout edged closer as the monstrous pup sniffed the air. No growl. That was a good sign. Thomas was mid-blink when the dog snatched the dried beef off his palm. His heart leapt into his throat as the dog chewed. That could have been his hand.

Thomas didn't recall moving toward the dog with the last of the jerky. Before he knew what he'd done, one hand was stroking the dog's fur as his other held the food, palm-up as before. To his shock, the dog licked his face before turning its interest to the jerky. With the dog distracted and eating, he plucked two thorns from the dog's paw. A yelp and a growl. Then another lick across his cheek.

He worked the last of the thorns out of the padding. Beneath the summer sun, he stroked the pup, careful not to touch where the dog lost its fur. The exposed skin looked pink and irritated, and the gash needed attention—a cleaning, antibiotic, and a bandage. Easier said than done.

When Thomas rose, the dog stood with him and nuzzled his thigh.

"Are we friends now?" Thomas patted the dog's head and searched the trail. "Whether we choose the ranger's station or the truck, it's a five-minute walk. But I don't have a collar or a leash. How should we handle this?"

The dog cocked its head.

"What if I run to the truck and grab a rope out of the back? You wait here, okay?"

As Thomas turned down the trail, the dog limped after him. Thomas held up, and the dog stopped at his feet.

"So you want to come with me. I suppose that makes things easier. Follow me, boy."

Dragonflies hummed along the path as the man and his new best friend trekked back to the lake road. The F-150 rested on the shoulder where he'd left it. Thomas opened the door, and the dog sat on its haunches and stared up at him.

"Good thinking. Better not test that leg until we fix you up."
He closed the door and locked it. "See that A-frame over there?
That's my place. Let's you and I take the easy way home, and I'll
come back for the truck after you're settled."

Windows covered the bulk of the A-frame, letting in brilliant
light. This was the house his Uncle Truman built when Thomas
was a child. He spent many nights sleeping in the guest house
beside the lake to escape fights with his parents. Now he
followed the two-tiered ramp he'd installed during the spring to
accommodate Scout, Naomi's wheelchair-bound teenage daughter. His neighbor's car sat next door. He'd also paved concrete
pathways so Scout could wheel around the backyard without
getting stuck in the soft earth. One path led from Naomi's back
door to Thomas's guest house.

The dog's talons clicked the bare wood floors when Thomas
led him inside. One glance at the steep staircase told Thomas to
leave the dog in the living room while he retrieved medicine and
bandages from the cabinet upstairs.

"I'll be back in a minute. Don't do anything I wouldn't do."

He worried the wild-looking dog would tear a hole in the
sofa or take a chunk out of the kitchen cabinetry. But when
Thomas descended the stairs, the dog sat where he'd left him,
curious eyes gazing around the downstairs.

The dog whined when he dabbed a sponge against the
wound. There was no helping it. Thomas needed to clean the
wound before disinfecting it. After he applied ointment, he
wrapped a bandage around the dog's leg and sat back, assessing
his work.

"No running for a few days. Leave the bandage alone, and
you'll be fine by next weekend."

The dog barked, a booming sound loud enough to rever-
berate off the ceiling and walls. What had Thomas gotten
himself into?

5

A hip-hop beat thundered out of the guest house as Thomas crossed the backyard. Thomas didn't plan to take the dog outside, not until he bought a proper collar and leash. But the massive pup wouldn't leave his side.

When he knocked on the door, he spotted LeVar and Scout beside the window looking out at the lake. Since LeVar moved in three months ago, the eighteen-year-old former gang member had forged an unlikely friendship with his fourteen-year-old neighbor. They shared a love for rap music, Scout arguing old school hip-hop acts like Run DMC and Erik B and Rakim marked the pinnacle of the genre. LeVar disagreed, favoring new rappers like Pusha T and Freddie Gibbs. Whatever they were listening to today, it was heavy and loud.

Sweeping his dreadlocks back, LeVar hopped off the chair and turned down the music before waving Thomas inside. Though the guest house belonged to Thomas, he respected LeVar's privacy and gave the teenager space.

"Hey, Deputy Shepherd," Scout said, pushing the glasses up her nose as she swiveled the wheelchair to face him. Scout lost her ability to walk two years ago after a violent car accident.

When the dog padded inside, LeVar stopped mid-stride and stared.

"My apologies," Thomas said. "I didn't realize you were afraid of dogs."

LeVar leaned back on his heels.

"I ain't, Deputy Dog. But I don't think that's a...uh..."

"He's a Siberian Husky," Thomas said, ruffling the fur on the dog's neck.

"A Siberian Husky?" LeVar met Scout's gaze. The girl lifted her palms and shrugged. "Looks like he got into a scuffle. I'd hate to see what the other animal looks like," he said, nodding at the dog's bandaged leg. "Where did he come from?"

"I found him a half-mile up the ridge trail."

"Where's his tags?"

"He doesn't have them, so it'll be difficult to locate the owner. Judging by the missing patches of fur, he's been in the wild for a long time. I'll take his picture and post it around the village. Maybe someone will recognize him. Isn't that right, buddy?"

The dog's tongue lolled as he panted at Thomas.

"And if you don't find the owner?" Scout asked.

"Then he stays with me. I always wanted a dog."

Mason and Lindsey Shepherd forbade Thomas from owning a dog when he was young.

"Flea-ridden monstrosities," his mother called them. "Why anyone would bring a wild animal into their home is beyond me. It's uncivilized."

"Does he have a name?"

Thomas tilted his head at the dog.

"That's a good question, Scout. I guess I should give him one. What do you think, big guy? How's Rex?"

LeVar laughed.

"Rex? Why not call him Snoopy or Rufus?"

"You have a better name, Mr. Hopkins?"

"How about Koda?"

Scout palmed her face.

"Everybody names their dog Koda these days." She cocked her neck and studied the pup. "How about Jack?"

"Why Jack?"

"I don't know. He looks like a Jack, doesn't he?"

"More like Wolfman Jack," LeVar said.

"I'm impressed, LeVar," Scout said. "You're becoming a pop culture historian."

They glanced at Thomas.

"Jack, it is," Thomas said.

The dog looked back and forth between his three new friends. Scout wheeled toward Jack.

"Is that a good idea?" LeVar asked, moving protectively to Scout's side.

"He's a big, gentle baby," Scout said as Jack nuzzled the girl's leg. "See?"

LeVar moved a cautious hand toward Jack. He flinched when the dog swung his head around. But Jack remained still as LeVar stroked his fur,

"He's thin as a rail," said LeVar. "I don't suppose you have dog food."

Thomas scratched his head.

"Can't say that I do. Do Sloppy Joes count?"

"I'm grilling steaks for dinner." LeVar had a key to the A-frame and cooked in the kitchen. But since summer hit, he preferred the charcoal grill beside the lake. "How about I toss an extra steak on the fire for Jack?"

"Sounds like a plan. That gives me time to run to the pet store later."

A honk brought Thomas's head around. He recognized Chelsey's green Honda Civic idling in the driveway. LeVar's older sister, Raven, hopped out with a pile of clothes under her arm.

"Be right back," Thomas said.

Thomas rounded the house to meet Raven, Jack trotting alongside, while LeVar stayed with Scout. Raven dropped the clothes and covered her heart when Jack bounded up to her.

"What the hell is that?"

"That's Jack."

"Oh. Well, that explains it." Raven bent to retrieve the shirts and blue jeans and handed them to Thomas. "I'm sure LeVar won't mind a few grass stains."

"How many times do I need to tell you? LeVar's welcome to use my washer and dryer."

"I know, but I feel bad. You're doing too much for our family. At least let me wash my brother's laundry."

"Your choice. If you change your mind..."

"So, where did Jack come from?"

Thomas recounted finding the Siberian Husky along the state park trail.

"Well, he's cute," said Raven, exercising the same caution her brother displayed. "But those jaws could swallow a bowling ball. Are you keeping him?"

"I'd welcome the company."

Raven glanced over her shoulder at the running car. Chelsey sat behind the wheel, purposely studying her phone.

"I take it Chelsey doesn't want to say hello," Thomas said, shifting LeVar's laundered clothes under one arm.

Rolling her eyes, Raven said, "She's stubborn. I can't decide what to do with that woman."

Thomas couldn't read Chelsey. She'd opened up to him the night he shot serial killer Jeremy Hyde, crying into his shoulder as she apologized for cutting him out of her life. The next morning, she turned frigid and refused to speak to him.

"Leave her be. She'll say hello when she's ready. How's your mother?"

"She's living with me now."

"Rehab worked?"

"It seemed to." Raven's eyes trailed toward the west side of the lake where her house stood. "But I don't prefer leaving her alone. She gets lonely, and I worry she'll do something stupid while I'm away."

"She's welcome at my place anytime, Raven. Bring her by the house. I haven't seen her since she was in the hospital."

"Mom would like that."

"Give me a day that works for you, and I'll invite everyone to dinner. How's that?"

"Everyone?"

Raven gestured at the running car.

"I don't expect she'll say yes. But sure, invite Chelsey."

"Yeah, don't get your hopes up." Raven stared at her watch. "Listen, I'd better bounce. Chelsey's driving me back to the repair shop. They're putting new tires on my Rogue." Raven hesitated, then knelt in front of the dog and patted his head. "It was nice to meet you, Jack."

6

Thomas set his fork down and patted his belly. He had to give it to LeVar—the kid grilled a mean steak. Thomas skimmed the documents from the Lincoln Ramsey file. Nothing caught his eye. Like Aguilar and Lambert, Thomas chalked the death up to Ramsey's disease. They found no evidence of foul play, and the shadow Kay Ramsey saw along her neighbor's house was probably a kid from the group Thomas passed when he responded to the call.

At his feet, Jack gnawed a bone. He'd wolfed the steak down in record time, and already the dog had filled out. The deck door stood open to the screen, inviting a warm breeze to search through the house. The wind ruffled the papers, so he clicked them together and put them inside a manila folder. In the yard, LeVar threw his hands around animatedly as he grilled his last steak. Scout leaned her head back and laughed. Thomas couldn't hear the joke. But their laughter was infectious, and he felt his lips curl into a grin. He reached for his water when someone knocked on the screen. Naomi, wearing a pair of cut-off jean shorts and a pink Finger Lakes t-shirt, waved from the deck.

"Come on in," Thomas said.

The screen slid open and Naomi stepped inside. She wore her dark brunette hair in a ponytail today. The second she entered the house, Jack jumped up. She stared at the dog and froze in her tracks.

"Easy, Jack. She's a friend."

Thomas doubted the dog had been to a trainer. But Jack took his cue from Thomas's calm demeanor and lay beside his plate.

"Scout told me you found a dog," Naomi said, eyeing the Siberian Husky with wariness. "But I had no idea he was so..."

"He's something, isn't he?"

"You're sure he's safe?"

"He let me bandage his leg and pull five thorns the size of wood screws out of his paw."

Naomi's eyes softened, and she dropped to one knee beside the dog.

"Is that right, Jack? Did Deputy Shepherd make you feel all better?" Jack panted and opened his mouth in a doggy grin while Naomi spoke to him in baby talk. "He needs a flea and tick collar. The ticks are terrible this year."

"I'll put it on my list. I'm running to the pet store after I wash the dishes."

Naomi sat across the table from Thomas and folded one leg over the other. Thomas respected the woman for raising a teenager in a wheelchair by herself. After the accident, Naomi's husband, Glen, blamed himself for the crash and drifted away from his family. The Mournings separated, Glen living in Ithaca where he worked as a supervisor for the electric and gas company, while Naomi moved Scout to Wolf Lake. The settlement paid for Scout's initial medical bills and a down payment on the lakeside house, Naomi setting aside the rest for Scout's college fund. But Naomi struggled to pay the mortgage. Her last employer, a technology firm in Auburn, downsized and cut

Naomi from the payroll. Now she bounced between temporary jobs to make ends meet.

As she set her chin on her palm and gazed out at LeVar and her daughter, she smiled. It had taken a few weeks before Naomi accepted LeVar. These days, Naomi treated the teenager like her adopted son.

"I wonder what they're laughing about," she said. "With teens, laughing equals trouble."

"I'll keep my eyes open," Thomas said. "Can I get you anything to eat or drink?"

"No, I'm fine. Hey, I need to talk to you about Scout."

"I'm all ears."

"She's looking at the teen sleuthing website again."

During the spring, Scout investigated the Erika Windrow murder case on the Virtual Searchers forum, a website devoted to teen amateur sleuthing. Scout corresponded with the serial killer, Jeremy Hyde, who disguised himself as a teen girl named Harpy.

"Are you worried?"

"After what happened in April, I'd be a fool if I wasn't. But she's interested in crime investigation, and she has a mind for it. The problem is, the school doesn't offer classes in criminal justice or investigative work. Didn't you tell me you interned with the sheriff's department while you were in high school?"

"I interned under Sheriff Gray. But I was seventeen."

"Scout is a little young."

"It wouldn't have to be a formal internship. What if Scout came to the office for a tour?"

"She'd get a kick out of it."

"I'll check my calendar, and we'll set a date."

"Thanks, Thomas. As always, you're a lifesaver."

"Would you like me to speak to her about the amateur sleuthing?"

Naomi peered out at her daughter.

"No, I should give her space. She's a lot more careful about who she talks to after the Harpy incident."

Her face twisted when she spoke Jeremy Hyde's faux user name. Another knock brought both of their heads up. Darren Holt peeked inside, and Jack's tail thumped against the floor.

"Am I interrupting?" Darren asked.

"I was just leaving," Naomi said, rising from her chair. "Thanks again, Thomas. Scout will be so excited."

"Anytime."

When Naomi crossed the yard toward her property, Darren set his hands on the table and shot Thomas a wry grin.

"What?"

"Getting friendly with the neighbor, I see."

"Nothing like that. She wants Scout to tour the station sometime."

"Well, you're missing out, Thomas. Naomi's interested—"

Darren's mouth dropped open when he laid his eyes on Jack. He took an involuntary step backward.

"Is that a...uh..."

"Yes, Darren. It's a dog."

"Thomas, that's a—"

"Siberian Husky, I believe. He's a pup, so I figure he has some growing to do."

Darren stammered.

"Well, he's damn big right now. Where did you find him?"

"His name is Jack, and I found him a half-mile from your cabin."

The ranger swallowed.

"*That* was hanging around my cabin?"

"Down the ridge, yes. It appears an animal took a chunk out of his leg, and he was starving."

"He looks healthy now."

"Amazing what a warm meal will do for you."

Darren eased himself into a chair, one eye fixed on Jack, who watched the ranger with a mix of curiosity and amusement.

"Like I was saying, Naomi has eyes for you."

"I doubt that."

"Her eyes grinned like you were her knight in shining armor. You don't believe me? Ask her out on a date. I guarantee she'll accept in a heartbeat."

Thomas tossed the case folder aside and feigned indifference. Had Naomi flirted with him? If she had, he'd missed it.

"Is there a reason you're here, Ranger Holt? Or did you walk all the way from the cabin just to break my balls?"

Darren removed his baseball cap and wiped his hand across his forehead. At forty-two, the dark-haired ex-cop looked like a grizzled model, his face covered with stubble.

"The state installed new grills to replace those rusty monstrosities. With Independence Day behind us, it's not as busy. I had an idea for a party. No big deal, just beers and steak. Everybody is invited, of course."

Thomas leaned back in his chair and set an ankle on his knee.

"And by everybody, you mean me and the Mournings."

"Interested?"

Thomas stared into the yard. Two canoes drifted across the lake as LeVar pushed Scout along the concrete path to Naomi's back door.

"Definitely. But I want you to invite LeVar and his sister."

Darren tapped his fingers against the table. In his eyes, LeVar was still the feared enforcer of the Harmon Kings. After last April's murder, Darren theorized LeVar trafficked drugs through Wolf Lake and killed Erika Windrow.

"He's a good kid, Darren. Sit with him and talk, and you'll see I'm right."

"You sure he didn't kill anybody? The Kings have a reputation."

"Not a chance. LeVar gave me his word."

"And you believe him?"

"See how good he is with Scout? Does that look like a cold-blooded killer to you?"

"Looks can be deceiving."

"Ruth Sims hired LeVar at the Broken Yolk. She harbored prejudices about his background. But now she swears by him, says the boy works harder than anyone she's hired."

Darren scratched his neck and set the cap on his head.

"Fine. If you vouch for LeVar, then I trust your judgment."

"He's part of the family now."

"What family?"

"My family—LeVar, the Mournings, Jack. And you, I suppose."

"As long as I get to be the ragtag member of the family."

"I wouldn't have it any other way."

"What day works best for you?"

"Probably Wednesday or Thursday. Let me make a few calls, and I'll get back to you."

Darren rose and stopped.

"Hey, I read about Lincoln Ramsey in the newspaper. I take it you responded."

Thomas nodded.

"Did you know Ramsey?"

"Met him a few times. I have an account at the First National Bank. He seemed like a fair guy. Shame he got sick." Thomas rubbed his chin. "That's what killed him, right? Because I've seen that look in your eye before."

Thomas pulled his lips tight, lost in thought.

"The daughter swears someone broke into the house and murdered him."

"Any evidence to support her claim?"

"Nothing. No fingerprints, no sign of a struggle. She heard a thump upstairs and claimed the window slid shut. But she was distraught and could have mistaken the noises for her father dying. As far as the department is concerned, Lincoln Ramsey died in his sleep."

"That's good to know. After the Jeremy Hyde case, Wolf Lake can't handle another murderer."

7

TUESDAY, JULY 14TH, 3:30 P.M.

Cecilia Bond checked her tow-colored curls in the mirror, gave up on brushing the disorderly locks, and threw a baseball cap on her head. The exhaustion grew each day and threatened to cripple her. Yet she refused to confine herself to the house another day. As she turned out of the bathroom, Duncan set his hands on his hips and blocked the staircase.

"You can't leave again."

"Move, Duncan."

"Not until you come to your senses. You're not in any condition to walk by yourself."

She strode up to him.

"Then come with me," she said, poking her index finger into his chest to stress each word.

"If you get sick, I can't carry you back to the car. Stay home. There's a chance someone will—"

She blew out a frustrated breath.

"We've waited for a donor for fifteen months. Even if we find one, there are no guarantees."

"You can't think that way. I pray every day, and Father Fowler is praying too. You have to believe, Cecilia."

Cecilia bit her tongue so she wouldn't yell. Since her diagnosis, Duncan had spent more time at St. Mary's than at home. Though Duncan attended church every Sunday, she'd considered his faith reserved, thoughtful. Now he burned candles throughout the day, draped rosaries over the bed, and prayed as if he had a direct line to God. He'd become unhinged. It scared her.

She squeezed by and descended the stairs, clutching the rail when her head spun. He noticed the wobble and hurried to her side, hooking her elbow with his.

"This is lunacy. If you won't return to the bedroom, I'll call Doctor Singh."

Cecilia chuckled.

"What will the doctor do? Place me under house arrest?" Finding her footing, Cecilia rested against the rail. "I just want to feel sunshine on my face and breathe fresh air."

"We can do that here. Come with me. We'll sit together in the yard."

She touched his arm. The hurt coursing through his eyes tightened her throat.

"That's all we've done since winter. Duncan, I'm not getting any better. I want to live while there's time. Kidney disease hasn't stolen my ability to walk. All I want is to see the river, hear birds, and smell flowers. Is that too much to ask?"

"And all I want is for you to get better so we have more days together."

She reached into her pocket and dug out the keys, dangling them in front of his face.

"Last chance. Come with me. I'll even let you drive."

He folded his arms.

"You're making irrational decisions. Doctor Singh said your mental faculty could degrade once the—"

"Oh, enough with Doctor Singh. I'm perfectly capable of making sound decisions, and right now I want to take a walk and live for a change. Are you coming with me?"

His eye twitched, a nervous tic he'd developed since spring.

"I won't be party to your downfall. One of us has to care about your future, and that's why I'm driving to the church to pray with Father Fowler."

The cross around his neck glimmered, catching the light beaming through the dormer windows. Cecilia was angry enough to scream. Rather than fight Duncan, she rounded the hutch and whipped the door open. His shouts followed her outside and pulled Mrs. Gaverson's attention while she weeded her flower garden.

Cecilia aimed the key fob at the car and pressed the button. The locks didn't respond, a sign the fob's battery was on its last life. She moved closer and tried again when the bushes rattled beside the house.

"Hello? Is someone there?"

She circled her car and stood upon the blacktop walkway. Shadows poured off the bushes guarding the house's west side. When she came within a step of the shrubs, expecting a cat or squirrel to burst out of hiding, something moved in the dark. Cecilia's heart pounded.

Pulling the branches aside, she glared at the white siding. Nothing lay hidden from view, though she noted the mulch had been disturbed and scattered across the walkway. The mess wasn't her concern. Let Duncan take care of it for a change.

A horn blared at the end of the neighborhood as Mr. Hendrik's pulled into his driveway. His daughter pedaled past on her bike, legs pumping in excitement as she raced to see her father. Somewhere down the block, a family grilled chicken. Everyone enjoyed the day except Cecilia.

As she unlocked the car and slid inside, the flora pulled her eyes again. The hairs on the back of her neck rose, and the sensation that someone was watching her set Cecilia on edge.

While she backed the car into the street and checked the mirrors, a shadow shifted behind the shrubbery.

8

Mortar fire appeared to have blown holes in the rutted blacktop outside Benson's Barbells. Raven parked the black Nissan Rogue near the back of the lot between a delivery truck and a sports car. Raising binoculars to her eyes, she scanned the gymnasium. On the other side of the glass, Damian Ramos finished a set of overhead presses and wiped his forehead with a towel. At five o'clock on a Tuesday afternoon, half the city of Kane Grove packed Benson's, the after-work crowd blowing off steam and burning calories.

When Damian moved to the leg press machine, Raven placed the binoculars on the passenger seat and sifted through the boy toy's dossier. Twenty-five-years old, Damian held a degree in economics from the University of Buffalo. After working construction for eight months after graduation, Damian caught on with a trading firm in Syracuse, where he served as a market research analyst. Raven didn't know much about finance careers, but assumed a market research analyst commanded a high salary. It made no sense. Why swindle a rich, older woman into marriage if he didn't need the money?

Inside the gym, Damian cranked out a heavy set of leg

presses. Raven preferred free weight squats. But she admitted Damian worked harder than the other gym rats. He had a teenager's complexion, minus the acne. A guy like Damian wouldn't have difficulty finding dates.

Raven hadn't dated in two years, and she spent eight to twelve hours per day investigating for Wolf Lake Consulting. The rest of the time she took care of her mother.

She dug inside the greasy fast food bag and snatched two fries. Stuffing them into her mouth, she savored the salty goodness. Though she prided herself on eating healthy, she ate fast food when she felt depressed. Raven was adrift at sea, the waves pulling her in random directions. Is this what she wanted to do with her life? She loved Chelsey and enjoyed the challenge of investigative work. But private investigation seemed like a compromise.

Raven sipped her shake and pushed the bag away, forcing herself to stop binging. She raised the Canon camera and focused the zoom lens on the front windows. A quick pan found Damian beside the Smith machine and talking to a twenty-something blonde. The woman's baby blue crop top showed off her rock-hard abdominals. Her shorts touched the tops of her thighs and left little to the imagination. The blonde's ponytail bobbed and swayed as she laughed with Damian.

Raven snapped three photos of the chummy couple as Damian leaned one arm on the Smith machine, one leg casually folded in front of the other. When the blonde said something funny, Damian leaned his head back in laughter and touched her arm. A minute later, they scrolled through their smart phones, and Raven imagined them exchanging numbers. She zoomed in on the blonde's face and snapped another picture, cursing when a muscle head walked in front of her shot. She framed the picture and took another photo, this one catching the blonde's face as she turned toward the window. Perfect. Now all she needed to do was learn the woman's name and figure out if Damian was cheating on Sadie Moreno.

She was about to send the images to Chelsey when a loud knock on the window made her jump. Focused on Damian and the woman, she hadn't noticed the man sneaking up on her vehicle. He leaned toward the window, his white handlebar mustache puffing with each angry breath. His biceps stretched the sleeves of his t-shirt as he motioned for her to lower the window. Raven fumbled with the keys and turned on the engine. After the window slid down, the man poked his head inside, invading her space. His breath smelled of cigarettes.

"You a cop?"

"No," Raven said, not wanting to reveal she was a private investigator and blow her cover. What if this guy knew Damian?

"Then what the hell are you doing in my parking lot? This is for gym members only, and I don't see a sticker on your car."

"Excuse me, but who are you?"

"Mark Benson. I own this gym, and I can have you arrested for loitering."

"My apologies. I was actually here..." Raven scanned the storefronts beside Benson's Barbells and focused on a salon. "To get my hair done. I guess I pulled into the wrong lot."

He rested his forearms on the sill and nodded at the passenger seat.

"What's on the camera?"

"The camera? Oh, nothing. Just nature shots. I'm an amateur photographer."

"Is that why you're taking pictures of my clients? Don't look surprised, Missy. My security cameras miss nothing. Now, hand me the camera, or I'll call the police."

"Slow down. I screwed up and drove into the wrong lot. Give me a second, and I'll get out of your hair."

He tapped a meaty finger on the sill.

"You're not going anywhere until you show me what's on the camera."

She'd played nice until this point. But this guy was pissing her off.

"Sir, I'm raising the window. If you want to keep your arm, you'll step away from my vehicle."

"I got your plate number. The second I get inside, I'm calling the police. You can explain to them why you're photographing my clients."

He didn't remove his arm until she raised the window. When she gunned the engine, Benson shot her a glare. Her body trembled with fury as she navigated the busy lot. She could see him in the mirror. The jerk hadn't budged.

When she turned onto the thoroughfare, Raven called Chelsey.

"I got pictures of Damian talking to another woman."

"So he's cheating on Sadie," Chelsey said.

"I can't prove it. But the girl was young and drop dead gorgeous. They were still talking when I left."

"You aren't following Damian home?"

Raven tossed the braids off her shoulder.

"The owner ran me off. We might have a problem, Chelsey. He recorded me with the security cameras and caught me photographing Damian."

"Is he calling the police?"

"He claims so."

"Don't worry about it. Chances are he's bluffing and trying to scare you. I know a cop inside the Kane Grove PD. If this guy makes a stink, I'll call the office and explain. This won't be an issue."

A laundromat with a purple hatchback in the parking lot stood on the opposite side of the roadway. Raven pulled the Rogue into a parking space and idled.

"I'm sending you the pictures now," Raven said, toggling the camera's transmission screen.

"Where are you?"

"Louie's Laundry. It's a quarter-mile past Benson's. I'll wait until Damian drives past, then follow him."

"Don't let him see you."

"I'll be careful. Before I forget, Deputy Shepherd called this morning."

Silence.

"Chelsey?"

"I'm here."

"He's hosting a cookout with Darren Holt at the state park Thursday after work. You're invited, if you're not busy."

Chelsey shuffled papers in the background.

"I can't Thursday. My central air is acting up, and the repairman is stopping by between five and six."

"Uh-huh."

"Hey, stop by if you don't believe me. The upstairs is like a sauna."

"Okay. Well, I'd better watch for Damian. See you at the office tomorrow morning."

"All right, Raven. Terrific work as always."

Raven ended the call and pushed her tongue against her cheek. Another lame excuse from Chelsey. If her friend wanted to be alone for the rest of her life, Raven couldn't change her mind.

It was five-thirty. Damian probably wouldn't leave the gym until six. She shut the engine off and paged through her phone. Bored, she snatched the fast food bag off the seat and palmed another fistful of fries. They were lukewarm and soggy. She crumpled the bag and tossed it out the window into a garbage can.

As she leaned the seat back, prepared for a long wait, a red

Kia shot past the laundromat at twenty mph over the speed limit. The windows were down, and Raven recognized the athletic blonde from the gymnasium. Raven gunned the engine and swung the Rogue onto the road, theorizing Damian might drive to the girl's house after his workout.

The Kia darted through traffic like a pinball, then sped up at the intersection. The light turned red as Raven raced to keep up. Slamming the brakes, she slapped the steering wheel and watched the Kia shrink in her windshield. A tractor trailer crossed in front of her.

She'd lost the girl.

9

Two hours before sunset, Cecilia Bond stopped beside the river and set the walking stick on the grassy bank. Water chuckled over rock, the level high after the rainy spring. Across the way, two trees lay uprooted where May's flood chewed up the bank. She caught her breath. Ten years ago, she'd run a 10K in Kane Grove. Since the diagnosis, even a leisurely walk winded her.

If Duncan could see her now, he'd say, "I told you so. I begged you not to go out on your own. But you didn't listen. You never listen!"

The echoes of his shouts made her flinch in quiet times like these. The kind man she fell in love with in her thirties had changed. She no longer recognized Duncan. Did her disease cause his anger, or had the church brainwashed him? Something ugly hid beneath Duncan's skin, and she didn't believe religion had anything to do with his psychosis. A part of her wanted this moment in the sun to never end. She was a free woman. Nobody could stop her if she just kept walking and never turned back.

Worried someone will see, she scans the trail before pulling her shirt up. The rash from her belly to her chest rises into welts. She shouldn't scratch the rash, should wait until she can apply cream at home. But there's no helping the infernal itching. Her nails dig into the rash. It's getting worse. Every day a little worse.

Using the walking stick, Cecilia pulled herself to her feet and steadied herself. A moment of vertigo. Then the fog cleared out of her head, and she followed the dirt trail paralleling the river. She climbed over a rock pile, fatigue heavy on her chest. When she cleared the obstacle, the winding river opened to a straight-away. A man sat upon the bank a hundred feet ahead. He held a fishing pole, the line cast into the deep middle and pulled taut. A voice in her head urged her to turn back. Something about the man unsettled her. She caught him staring as she approached.

Tall grass partially concealed his face. The wind shoved the flora aside, and she recognized the fisherman as Garrick Tillery. She pulled up and considered her options. If she turned around, he'd realize she was avoiding him. Tillery attended St. Mary's. He drank himself sick at Hattie's on the weekends, and he had a sexual assault charge on his record. Cecilia didn't know the details. Whispered rumors at church claimed Tillery raped an underage girl.

Cecilia lowered her head when Tillery glanced at her. He chewed a piece a grass and held a beer can in one hand. Two empties littered the bank.

"Afternoon," he said, nodding as Cecilia passed.

His gaze slithered over her skin and violated her.

"You too good to answer me?"

She flinched and looked over her shoulder.

"Afternoon, Mr. Tillery."

He cursed under his breath, yanked back on the rod, and reeled the line in. As she dropped out of view, he recast. The baited hook plunked into the river and sank beneath the reflected light.

His stare pierced her back as she emerged beneath the ridge. She exhaled after she put distance between them. But she wouldn't look back. Not until she made it to the tree line, where the trail weaved through forestland before depositing hikers beside the river again.

Cecilia quickened her pace. Inside the forest, she turned and parted the leaves. Ran her vision along the faraway bank. Where was he? Not seeing him sent a chill down her back.

She reached for her phone and checked her messages. None waited. The signal strength fluttered around one bar until she lost coverage inside the forest. Duncan was right. She was stupid to come out here by herself. Turning back wasn't an option. Not with Garrick Tillery fishing along the river. She'd finish her hike and wait for sunset, then return after he'd packed his gear and left.

Beams of light cut through the canopy ,and painted a checkerboard pattern across the forest floor. Dead leaves crunched underfoot. The temperature dropped ten degrees inside the woods, and she chided herself for not carrying a jacket.

Cecilia was halfway to the river when a whisper pulled her head around. She turned in a circle, the forest looming over her like silent guardians.

"Who's there?"

She searched for kids, expecting to find a teenage couple strolling down the trail. But there was nobody.

Cupping her elbows with her hands, she fought the growing fatigue and continued down the trail, her eyes darting between the shadows.

"Cecilia."

There. That hadn't been her imagination. Someone whispered her name.

She whipped around and searched where the voice had come from. Saw only darkness hiding among the trees.

"Duncan? Is that you?"

Or was Garrick Tillery following her through the forest? Would he rape a dying woman?

She quickened her pace and rushed between the trees, the phone held at arm's length as she struggled to read the screen without her reading glasses. Placed a call to Duncan. No service.

A branch snapped like a gunshot behind her, just beyond view. Footsteps approached.

Cecilia tossed the walking stick aside and ran. The river had to be close, no more than a minute ahead. Once she reached the bank, she'd be out of the dark and into the sunlight. Safety was close. Except few people walked this section of the trail.

Her lungs protested as she picked up speed. No way to tell if the footsteps were her own echoing off the trees or her pursuer's racing up behind her. Light grew beyond the branches. Precious light. Her legs were rubber bands, arms hanging at her sides as she neared the river. Leaves rustled as someone pushed through the forest. Her pursuer was a heartbeat behind.

When she burst into the light, she searched the trail for help. Deserted. She was the only person walking this length of the river. An idea formed when she spied the plank bridging this bank to the far side. The river rushed past, speeding up as the width narrowed. Shooting a look over her shoulder, she assessed the dark forest. Didn't hear the pursuit anymore.

Without looking down, she balanced on the plank and stepped across. If she slipped, the current would drag her under, and she was in no condition to fight the river. Her ankle twisted halfway across. She clenched her teeth and pushed on, arms stretched to each side to lend balance. After another stumble, she leaped and landed on the opposite bank. More forest lay ahead. Picking up the plank, she tossed it into the flow and hurried into behind the trees.

Still no one coming.

Cecilia exhaled and placed a hand over her speeding heart. The dead leaves crunched behind her a second before the hand covered her mouth. A hammer crashed down on her head, blinding her. Cecilia's eyes rolled back as she pitched forward and slammed against the earth.

Her last sensation was someone dragging her across the forest floor.

"**D**o you dream about the shooting?"

Thomas glances up from his lap. Dr. Mandal sits behind the coffee table with a cup of herbal tea beside her legs. The spicy scents reach his nose and draw his attention. He struggles not to stare at the tea, lest she think he's looking at her legs.

"No."

"Never?"

He lifts a shoulder.

"Rarely."

"How often is rarely?"

"Once, maybe twice a month."

Mandal makes a note on her pad.

"Are the dreams an accurate recreation of the shooting?"

"Usually."

"What's different?"

"I'm not sure."

She claps her hands over her knee.

"Have you ever died in the dream?"

The question sends a shockwave through his nerves. He wonders if she saw him flinch.

"No, but others have."

"The DEA agents and LAPD officers?"

"Yes."

"Why did they die in your dream?"

His hands wring together and squeeze until his knuckles crack.

"Because I failed to react."

"So the car pulls to the curb, and the gang members fire at the task force before you can warn them."

"Yes."

"How many die?"

"Everybody. There's so much blood."

"So it's just you left alive. Then what happens?"

"Then I wake up."

She pauses, then writes another note.

"In your dream, do you blame yourself for their deaths?"

"They're my responsibility."

"You led the task force?"

Thomas shifts his back. He can't get comfortable today.

"No."

After Mandal writes a longer note, she says, "We'll return to your dream. Right now, I'd like to discuss how you react to stressful situations in the field. When you secure a location, do you still worry someone will pull to the curb and fire at you from behind?"

"The gang issue isn't as bad in Nightshade County."

"So you never glance over your shoulder, searching for a shooter that isn't there."

He drops his head and scratches behind his neck. The clock ticks on the wall, each second punctuated by the mechanical heartbeat.

He doesn't answer.

"I'd like to increase the frequency of our sessions."

"I can't commit to additional time. Shift work dominates my week."

"*You stand to benefit from increased therapy. Your insurance will cover the cost—*"

"I said I don't have the time." He winces at his outburst and softens his eyes. "My apologies."

"*You need not apologize. We'll pick this up at your next appointment. One week, Thomas?*"

"If that's what you want."

THOMAS DROPPED into the chair beside his desk and rubbed his eyes. It had been a long, frustrating day, and he was into his third hour of overtime. Early Tuesday afternoon, residents in an upscale Wolf Lake neighborhood spotted a man in a hooded sweatshirt climbing through a window with a computer monitor tucked under his arm. A security camera caught the intruder, and Deputy Aguilar identified the man as Chuck Meyer, a thirty-one-year-old local with a prior conviction for car theft. Thomas and Aguilar found the man in a city park on the southern border of the village. When Meyer spotted the deputies crossing the baseball field, he leaped onto the playground equipment, swung from the monkey bars, and executed a flawless back flip. Aguilar cuffed Meyer, who didn't flee.

"Why were you doing back flips off the monkey bars?" Aguilar had asked him inside the cruiser.

Meyer shrugged.

"I thought it would make me appear less guilty."

Thomas completed the paperwork and tossed the pen inside his desk drawer.

Lincoln Ramsey's family had scheduled his calling hours and burial for next week. The daughter still insisted someone murdered her father. Thirty minutes ago, Ambrose Jorgensen phoned Sheriff Gray, furious with the department for not conducting a thorough investigation. Now Gray called Thomas into his office and told him to close the door.

The last decade had been difficult for Stewart Gray. At sixty, the sheriff appeared ten years older than his age. The position had become political, and too many Nightshade County residents called for Gray to step down and make way for a younger sheriff. Four years ago, he lost his wife, Lana, to a fatal accident on icy roads. Gray believed Father Josiah Fowler, who witnesses claimed to see driving erratically, had crossed the centerline and run Lana off the road. Fowler was no stranger to DUI arrests. But the department couldn't prove Fowler caused the accident.

Gray's puffy white mustache hid his lips as he placed his hat on the desk. He slumped in his chair and watched Thomas with battle-weary eyes.

"Ambrose Jorgensen reminds me of Tessa Windrow," he said, grumbling as he stared at his hands. "I'd label her a kook, but I remember how the Erika Windrow case turned out. Did you see anything that indicated foul play at the Ramsey home?"

"I did not. No footprints outside the property, no broken windows, no fingerprints. Lambert was meticulous."

"I'd like you to take another look, if only to shut this Jorgensen woman up and set Kay Ramsey's mind at ease. The last thing that woman needs is her daughter scaring her and making her believe someone killed Lincoln. It doesn't have to be tomorrow. But I'd like it done by the weekend."

"Every day we wait, Kay Ramsey compromises the scene."

"You won't find evidence inside the house. Check with the neighbors. Find out if anyone has a security camera. I can't put the case to bed until I prove nobody approached that house the night Lincoln Ramsey died."

Thomas rubbed his chin.

"So we're ruling out murder, not gathering evidence."

"Don't look at it that way. You're putting a grieving widow's mind at ease. I don't want Kay Ramsey dialing 9-1-1 every time she hears a strange noise outside."

"And you want Ambrose Jorgensen out of your hair."

"That would be nice." Gray pushed the stapler to the corner of his desk. "How's your father, Thomas?"

"The cancer is progressing. He's still managing his business."

Three months ago, Mason Shepherd threatened to pull his donations to the sheriff's department if Gray didn't fire Thomas.

"Did my father contact you again?"

"Not since we wrapped up the Hyde case." Gray scratched his nose when he answered, a sign the sheriff wasn't telling the truth. "If you're worried about your job, don't be. You're my top deputy. How many sheriffs have a big city detective on staff? Rule out foul play in the Ramsey case, and you'll have the key to the city."

"I need to clear a few things off my schedule. But I can probably make it to the Ramsey house before Friday."

"Do your best. That's all I ask. Go home, Thomas. You've been here long enough."

Thomas tapped his hand against his thigh.

"Remember Scout Mourning?"

"The teenager who dug up information on Jeremy Hyde."

"She's interested in criminal justice. With your permission, I'd like to give her a tour."

"Any quiet day works for me. After four is best."

Thomas rose from his chair.

"Thank you. I'll set up the tour with her mother."

"My pleasure. I remember when you were an intern. If Scout Mourning is as half as smart as you—"

"She's twice as smart as me."

"Well, then. You'd better hope she doesn't steal your position."

Maggie, the department's administrative assistant, was still at her desk when Thomas left at six. It seemed everyone put in extra hours to keep up with the workload. Thomas had chosen Wolf Lake over Los Angeles, expecting quieter days. It seemed the sleepy village of Wolf Lake had run off the rails since his teenage years.

During the drive home, the Erika Windrow case clung to him. He'd shot Jeremy Hyde after the serial killer broke into his house with Naomi and Scout sleeping upstairs. Had it not been for Chelsey Byrd, Thomas would be dead. She distracted Hyde and gave Thomas time to retrieve his gun.

He stepped inside his house and automatically scanned the shadows for an intruder. His pulse rocketed when the dog's head shot up from behind the couch. The Siberian Husky padded to Thomas. Thomas stroked Jack's fur. He'd worried the dog would mess inside the house. But Jack took care of business in the backyard after Thomas let him outside, his tail wagging as he grinned back at his new owner. Jack finished his business and galloped back to the door.

"I don't know what's happening to Wolf Lake."

Jack didn't reply.

The dog followed him to the refrigerator. Thomas retrieved a ginger beer, twisted off the cap, and took a long drink. He squinted and squeezed his nose when the spices hit his sinuses. In the neighboring yard, Naomi wheeled Scout down the path toward the lake.

Thomas descended the deck stairs with Jack trotting alongside. Though he'd purchased a leash and collar, he didn't see a need for either. Jack was his shadow, his constant companion. When Jack spied Naomi and Scout, he barked and took off running. Scout swung her head around and waved, while Naomi set a protective hand on her daughter's shoulder. She didn't let her guard down until Jack stopped beside Scout's wheelchair and sat panting with his doggy grin. By the time Thomas reached the trio at the shore, Jack was bounding through the shallows while Scout giggled and cheered him on. Keeping watch over her daughter, Naomi motioned him back toward the trees.

"I spoke to Sheriff Gray," Thomas said. "Scout's welcome to tour the office any day after four o'clock."

"That's wonderful." An aqua headband pulled the hair off her forehead. Sunlight danced in her eyes. "She'll be so excited."

"Should I tell her now?"

"Wait until after. Thomas," Naomi said, her eyes dropping to the ground. "I feel terrible asking you for more favors. But I need someone to watch Scout tomorrow between two and seven."

"Hmm. My shift doesn't end until four, and the last few days I've ended up staying over. Did you ask LeVar?"

Naomi bit her lip and looked across the water.

"He's working at the Broken Yolk until five."

"Is something going on?"

"I've got a job lined up tomorrow afternoon."

"That's great. Where?"

"Harmon Associates," she said, her eyes downcast. "They're a legal firm in the city."

"Sounds promising. Why so glum?"

"It's a cleaning job." She blew out a frustrated breath. "When we lived in Ithaca, I built strategies for small businesses and analyzed their financial data. Back then, I earned more than Glen. Terrific benefits, vacation time, a retirement plan. I shouldn't have uprooted Scout. If we'd stayed in Ithaca—"

"You're talented, Naomi. Good things will come to you if you're patient."

"I can't leave Scout alone."

"Let me talk to LeVar's sister. You've met Raven."

"She's the private investigator?"

"And she's good with kids. I'll call and see if she's free."

"You always save the day, Thomas."

She touched his arm. Before he could react, she kissed his cheek and bounded back to Scout.

11

This was a bad idea.

Thomas sat in his truck outside his childhood home. Updated landscaping embellished the immaculate four-bedroom contemporary. Two flowering cherry trees greeted visitors at the walkway, and bushes sprouted from a freshly mulched row paralleling the sidewalk. The house appeared abandoned and lifeless. It always did, though he spied the vehicles beyond the windows of the two-car garage.

He braced himself. Thomas hadn't seen his father in three months. Not since Mason Shepherd imposed his will on Thomas, ordering him to quit the sheriff's department and take over Shepherd Systems. Thomas had refused before Mason told him he was dying. His parents wouldn't take his calls until he agreed to their terms, even if it meant the next time he saw Mason was at the man's funeral.

Thomas yanked the keys from the ignition and juggled them in his palm. A boy coasted past on a scooter, a welcome sight in the snobbish, self-important neighborhood of Poplar Hill Estates. When Thomas was a boy, his mother's sole concern when he returned home was he remove his shoes at the door, lest he track filth inside.

He knew how this evening's conversation would go. They'd sell him on the merits of Shepherd Systems, make him feel like a fool for hanging on to his deputy position, then order him to leave after he refused to quit. Yet he needed to see his father. Time grew short.

As he stared at the home in procrastination, he realized his father had become the estate. Stately, impenetrable, cold as the grayish-blue exterior. He wondered, after the cancer consumed Mason, if the house would crumble around him as it did for Usher.

Thomas climbed down from the cab and inhaled. The mulch scent mingled with the thickening humidity of the approaching sunset. A crow perched on a cherry tree and cawed at him. The porch grew nearer. Had he stood still, the sidewalk would have swept him up and thrown him onto the steps. The stairs groaned under his weight as he climbed. Then he pressed the doorbell and listened as chimes rang through the house.

Footsteps puttered to the door. His mother, Lindsey Shepherd, pulled her mouth tight.

"At last, you're visiting us, so I suppose this means you've come to your senses."

"Good evening, Mother."

She folded her arms and barricaded the entrance with her body.

"Well?"

"I'd like to speak with Father. May I see him?"

She narrowed her eyes.

"Remove your shoes. I just cleaned, and I don't want you muddying the floors."

Lindsey tossed her shock of gray hair over her shoulder and turned on her heels. He glanced down at his sneakers. No dirt, but he didn't relish testing her. After he slipped his sneakers off, he padded down the long corridor toward the study, their footsteps echoing off the high ceilings.

"You have a visitor, Mason," she said at the doorway to the study.

"Who is it?"

The voice sounded too frail to be Mason's.

"Your son."

She lifted her chin in challenge before motioning him inside. Thomas stepped into the study. Books on finance, marketing, and leadership lined the shelves, sharing space with classic fiction from Twain, Hemingway, Dickens, and Fitzgerald. Thomas tugged at his collar. The room felt like a wood stove, but the thin, gray man in the lounge chair wrapped himself in a blanket. Thomas sucked in a breath at the sight of him. His father had aged twenty years since the April encounter. Mason's hands trembled as he gestured at the chair across from him. Mason often listened to Chopin. The lack of music was an ominous sign.

Thomas slipped into the chair and placed his arms on the rests. He half-expected clasps to spring out of the chair and lock his wrists in place. Lindsey eyed Thomas as she leaned over her husband and kissed the top of his head.

"So you've finally come to visit," Mason said with a dry chuckle. He coughed into his hand. "Or perhaps you're here to dance upon my grave."

"How are you, Father?"

Mason waved away his son's concern.

"You already know. Enough with the formalities. Have you decided?"

The clock ticked on the wall. A march toward the inevitable confrontation.

"I'm not qualified to run Shepherd Systems. You must know this."

"I can teach you. You're trainable, I suspect. After all, you're a Shepherd."

"The business must stay in the family," Lindsey added, placing a hand on her husband's shoulder as she stood behind him.

Thomas shifted.

"If I ran Shepherd Systems, I'd bankrupt the company in the first year. I refuse to believe you don't have a list of candidates in-house. Hire a CEO."

Mason focused his gaze. Even in his dilapidated state, he could burn holes through Thomas with his stare.

"The name is *Shepherd* Systems, and it will stay that way. I won't have my legacy ruined by an outsider who didn't dirty his hands building the company from the ground up. Now, stop this foolishness. We all know you went into law enforcement to challenge me. You proved your point, Thomas, as idiotic as your point turned out to be. Stop the charade. It's time you placed family before folly."

Thomas chewed the inside of his cheek. No matter how hard Mason pushed, he wouldn't yell, wouldn't fight a dying man.

"There's no reason for me to step down from my position."

"What does Gray need with you? Tell me, Thomas. When the neighborhood boys picked sides in football, were you the first or last chosen?"

"I fail to see what this has to do with—"

"Last, always last. You always picked yourself up, no matter how many times they knocked you down. Because you're my son. Yet you were never big enough, Thomas. You spent your entire life trying to prove everyone wrong, including your parents. And look where it got you. A bullet in the back, and now you're back home because California turned out to be the foe you couldn't conquer."

Thomas stood.

"I've heard enough."

"Sit down, boy. I'm not finished."

His fingernails digging into his palms, Thomas glared back at his parents. Mason's voice reverberated off the walls and rang in Thomas's ears.

"I'm leaving. It was a mistake coming here."

"Consider your future. You've seen the company reports. You'd be rich and never worry about money again. Imagine the possibilities if you took the company public."

"Listen to your father, for once in your life." Lindsey stepped from behind the chair and strode to Thomas. A challenge flared in her eyes. "This isn't a game anymore. You could have died. Then there'd have been no one to continue the Shepherd legacy."

"Is that what this is about? Ensuring the Shepherd legacy lives on? Thank you for caring, Mother."

She covered her mouth.

"That's not what I meant. I was...we were devastated after the shooting."

"I'll be by to check on Father this weekend. Now if you'll excuse me, I need to get home. I have work tomorrow morning."

"Don't walk away."

"Oh, let the boy go, Lindsey." Mason struggled out his chair. He gripped the arm rests until he steadied himself. "He doesn't value what we've given him. So why would he appreciate this offer?"

Thomas turned toward the door and stopped. Before Mason reacted, Thomas crossed the room and wrapped his arms around his father's shoulders.

"I love you, Father," he whispered into Mason's ear. His

father squirmed. "I'm not the man to lead your company, and I won't destroy what you spent a lifetime building. If ever a way existed to dishonor your legacy, that would be it."

His father's mouth hung open after Thomas released him. Rounding the chair, Thomas kissed his mother on the forehead.

"You'll call me if anything changes before the weekend." Lindsey stood like a statue, her mouth moving, but no words pouring forth. "Mother?"

She gave a start as though electrocuted.

"Yes, I'll call you, Thomas."

"Mother, Father. Good evening."

They never left the study while he retrieved his sneakers.

12

Through a thin slit between the curtains, Suzanne Tillery tugged on her shirt and peeked out at the neighborhood. Darkness slid across the village, the shadows pouring off the houses like spilled oil. Garrick should have returned home hours ago. Suzanne expected to hear the big truck motor rumbling into their driveway. Instead, she saw children on bicycles racing each other in the last light.

They'd spent the afternoon screaming at each other. She could set her watch to their fights, they'd become so predictable. At three o'clock, Garrick had grabbed his fishing gear and left in a huff. Suzanne suspected his first stop had been Hattie's, not the river.

She sat at the kitchen table and listened to the world fall sleep around her. Lights flicked off at the Ramsey house. She kept meaning to speak with Kay about Lincoln, but couldn't find the right words. Suzanne and Kay had drifted apart after someone vandalized the Ramsay's house. Kay believed Garrick knew who caused the damage. The sheriff's department had searched Kay's property the night Lincoln Ramsey died. A short, muscled deputy named Aguilar pounded on the door and jostled Suzanne out of sleep. The deputy asked if she'd seen anybody snooping around the Ramsey's house, noticed any vehicles parked along the curb that didn't belong. And that struck her as strange. Did the deputy suspect foul play? Aguilar also asked if Suzanne's husband was home. But Garrick had pulled another disappearing act that evening, and stumbled in at four in the morning, reeking of sour beer.

A napkin lay shredded on the table, Suzanne tearing the pieces as she listened for Garrick's truck. She was losing him, and though she suspected Garrick was cheating, his true love was the bottle. Since spring, she'd argued with him to enter rehab. At least speak to a counselor and get his drinking under control.

A pamphlet from St. Mary's church was tucked between a recipe book and the napkin holder. That got her thinking. Father Fowler had conquered alcoholism four years ago, though he wouldn't reveal the event that served as his wake-up call. Now he counseled anyone who wanted to kick drug or alcohol addiction. She slipped the pamphlet out of hiding and spread it open on the table, noting Fowler's help line. If only Garrick would call.

If he refused to get help, she'd intervene.

Suzanne dialed the number and listened as the phone rang. Three times, four. Her free hand knotted into a fist as she considered the implications. Once she opened this door, there was no closing it. Garrick would be furious. Suzanne accepted the risk, though she feared his wrath. The phone kept ringing. She expected Father Fowler's message to play. Instead, a woman answered. Suzanne recognized the voice as Thea Barlow's.

"I'm trying to reach Father Fowler, Ms. Barlow."

"Father Fowler is in the confession booth. Is everything all right, Mrs. Tillery? You sound upset."

Suzanne bit off a sob and wiped what remained of the napkin across her nose.

"It's my husband. Garrick. I can't take his drinking anymore, and I don't know how to save our marriage."

"Calm down, Mrs. Tillery. Father Fowler has seen this before, and no mountain is insurmountable. Would you like Father to sit down with Garrick, or do you prefer group counseling?"

Suzanne pictured Garrick's reaction once Father Fowler cornered them in a locked room. She imagined the heat of her husband's glare, the anger rolling off his body. Garrick needed help, but Suzanne understood how important it was to support her husband through the process.

"I should be there with Garrick."

"Very good." Barlow ripped a sheet of paper out of her notebook. "Father has openings in the middle of next week, if you'd like to make an appointment."

"There's nothing sooner?"

"I'm afraid not. But if you give me Mr. Tillery's number, Father will call him tomorrow. Sometimes a phone conversation is all it takes to awaken a man from an alcohol-fueled haze."

Suzanne wondered how much Barlow knew about Father Fowler's addiction. Inside the church, the rumor mill never stopped. One theory suggested Fowler got away with manslaughter four years ago after he ran Sheriff Gray's wife off an icy road. That was a far-fetched rumor Suzanne didn't believe.

"I would appreciate it if Father called Garrick."

"What are your husband's work hours?"

Picking the lint off her shirt, Suzanne dropped her voice.

"Garrick lost his job in May."

"I'm sorry."

"His shift supervisor smelled alcohol on his breath, though I don't believe he drank on the job. Garrick had been at Hattie's until midnight and woke up late for work. He rushed in without showering or brushing his teeth."

"Don't make excuses for your husband, Mrs. Tillery. You'll only enable his behavior."

"You're right. Are you sure Father can't fit us into his schedule this week? I'll feel better after Father sits down with Garrick."

"There is one possibility. You're not required to answer, but I must ask if you entered Garrick's name into the prayer jar."

The prayer jar sat on a polished table in the vestibule. People slipped prayer requests into the jar when loved ones fell ill and only God could save them. She hadn't considered putting Garrick's name in the prayer jar to help him kick his alcohol addiction.

"Father will pray for anyone in need," Barlow continued. "If you will allow, I'll place Garrick's name in the jar and save you a trip to the church."

"That's very kind of you."

"Think nothing of it." Another phone rang in the background. "I'd better answer that. Stay strong, Mrs. Tillery. Father Fowler will call Garrick tomorrow."

The tension rolled off Suzanne's shoulders after she hung up the phone. A moment later, headlights swept across the windows and lit the house. Night had crept up on her, and when the lights shut off, the house plunged into darkness. She slipped the phone into her pocket, as if she needed to hide it from Garrick. A truck door slammed. Footsteps dragged across the driveway.

She caught the booze stench the second he stumbled inside. Pink tinged his eyes. She caught her breath when she spied blood splashed across his shirt.

"What happened to you?"

He wiped his hand across his mouth and glared at her through the tops of his eyes.

"The hell you talking about?"

"All that blood." Her eyes followed the trail to his hand. A deep gash burrowed through his flesh. "How did you cut your hand?"

"Fishing," he said, muscling past.

How did he hurt himself fishing? He staggered into the kitchen. The refrigerator door whipped open with a sucking sound. Bottles rattled, then the crack of a beer can opening. Mustering up what little courage she had left, she set her hands on her hips and blocked the entryway to the kitchen.

"You don't need another, Garrick."

"Fuck off."

"What did you say?"

"You heard me. I'll drink as much as I want. I didn't marry you to replace my mother."

He guzzled half the beer, belched, and slammed the can on the counter. Foam drizzled down the sides.

"Tell me where you went today."

"Fishing. Is that a crime?"

"You didn't go to Hattie's?"

Garrick wobbled on his feet.

"I may have stopped by. Just for a few hours."

"And your hand. How did you cut yourself fishing?"

"Got the hook stuck in my skin and pulled it out too fast."

She eyed the laceration. That didn't look like a fishing accident. It appeared as if something with sharp teeth had taken a chunk out of his hand.

"You're lying to me."

"You're lying to me," he mocked in slurred falsetto.

Garrick snatched his beer off the counter and climbed the stairs.

"Now where are you going?"

"Upstairs, you nagging bitch. Leave me alone."

The bedroom door slammed. Suzanne quivered in the entry-way, frozen to the floor. It took a minute for the shock of his words to wear off. Then she raced up the stairs after him and threw the door open. She found him hunched over at the window. He spilled the beer and hid the binoculars.

"What are you up to?"

She stomped to the window as he fumbled with the blinds. Forcing herself in front of him, she peered across the street. Ambrose Jorgensen, Kay Ramsey's daughter, bent over and hefted a grocery bag out of her car. The woman showed plenty of leg.

"I knew it. You're cheating on me."

He looked at her cross-eyed.

"Huh?"

"You were staring at her with the binoculars. Is that what you want, Garrick? Do you crave a younger woman? Let her be. For God's sake, her father just died."

He grumbled, waving away her argument.

For years, she'd convinced herself he hadn't raped that teenager. The girl must have lied about her age and talked him into bed, as Garrick claimed. He'd been drunk then too, and she'd accepted his story to save their failed and flailing marriage. Now she reached beneath the chair and grabbed the binoculars, shifting them behind her back when he lunged for them.

"The insanity stops now. I may not be the woman you once desired. But I'm still your wife, and you won't treat me this way. Father Fowler is calling you tomorrow."

Garrick swung his head around.

"Why would you contact Fowler?"

"You need help. You can hate me for making you go to coun-seling. But I won't watch you throw away our marriage."

He stood. Despite his wobbling legs, she could see the searing fury burning through his body. In that moment, she was sure he'd strike her. Knock the taste out of her mouth and leave her bloodied and sobbing.

Or worse.

Instead, he shoved her aside and rushed down the stairs.

"Now where are you going?"

The door closed, and his truck motor rumbled. That was the last she saw of Garrick Tillery until morning.

13

The plastic containers strewn across the passenger seat of Raven's Nissan Rogue held sliced vegetables and fruit—green peppers, sugar snap peas, cherry tomatoes, strawberries, grapes. During yesterday's stakeout, her stomach performed somersaults after her fast food binge, and today she determined to eat right, no matter how boring the surveillance became.

She parked in a municipal lot across the street from the trading firm where Damian Ramos worked. At nine this morning, he'd driven past the building and into the parking garage a half-block from the firm. She'd squeezed the Rogue between a sporty compact and a black Ford Escalade, before Damian strutted down the sidewalk in a vested, dark-blue pinstripe suit and polished shoes. His black hair was slicked back, making him seem like a character out of a Scorcese film. She snapped several photographs before he vanished inside the building.

She hadn't left the Rogue since, and her legs had cramped up on her. Windows lined the trading firm, and she couldn't shake the creeping sensation that someone stared at her behind the glass. The day was too bright to see inside, though she caught shadows moving past the windows every few minutes. She fiddled with the radio and crunched on a pepper, wishing for an oversize bag of potato chips. Or Doritos. Something salty and cheesy she'd regret.

At eleven, the front door swung open. Damian stepped into the summer heat and slipped black sunglasses over his eyes. Raven lifted the camera, but Damian was already moving. He took off down the sidewalk and turned the corner as she debated driving after him or stepping out of the Rogue. A parade of vehicles stopped at the red light and blocked the entrance to the parking lot. She slid the camera beneath the seat and grabbed her phone. The iPhone took decent pictures, not as crisp as the Canon. But she needed to appear inconspicuous.

Raven located sunglasses in her glove compartment and slid them on. Unable to locate a baseball cap in the trunk, she settled on a beanie hat. A blue city bus with a musical advertised across the side coughed a black plume of exhaust while she waited at the curb. She ducked her face into the crook of her arm and crossed after the light changed. Damian turned left at the end of the block. She jogged to catch up.

When Raven reached the corner, she pulled up and turned around. Damian stood ten feet from her at a food truck, searching for his wallet as a man with a gray beard handed him something covered in chili. The food scents made Raven's stomach growl. She feigned studying her phone as he took his time, counting out exact change. The man inside the food truck grumbled and accepted the money, shooting a pointed look at the tip jar. Damian didn't notice or didn't care. Raven ground her teeth. The market analyst acted like a big shot in front of the blonde girl at the gym. He was just a typical cheapskate, stealing every penny from the world. But she had to admit, he pulled her eyes in his tight slacks. He slung his jacket over his shoulder.

"Hi there."

She jumped at his voice. Damian stood a step away, almost on top of her, his shadow swallowing hers on the pavement.

"Do we know each other?" she asked, slipping the phone into her pocket.

"Not by name. I've seen you at the gym. Benson's Barbells in Kane Grove."

"Uh, I haven't worked out there in over a year."

"But I saw you there yesterday. In the parking lot around five o'clock?"

He saw her through the window?

"Oh, right. I was considering buying a membership."

"Did you?"

"I..." She swallowed when he removed his sunglasses. The blues of his eyes reminded her of the Caribbean on a calm day. "I got a phone call and had to run."

He crossed his arms over his chest.

"That's a shame. You'd make a helluva training partner. You're in fine shape. You must do something to burn the calories outside of gym time."

"I work out in my basement and run hill sprints when the weather allows."

"I can teach you my favorite aerobic activities if you're game."

Did he just wink at her? And why were her palms sweaty?

"So, do you work in Syracuse?" he asked.

"No, I'm visiting a friend. Meeting her for coffee, actually."

"Meeting *her*. That's good to know. Does she have a smoking hot body like yours?"

He ran his eyes from her chest to her legs. She stood speechless as the wind played through her braids.

"Anyhow, my name is Damian. Damian Ramos."

Damn. This was the part where he expected her name.

"Oh, I'm Gwen. Gwen Stephani." He arched his eyebrow.

"Stephani with a *ph*. Yeah, everyone laughs when I tell them my name."

"The famous Gwen doesn't hold a candle to you." Oh, please. He brushed his hair back, though it held solid against the breeze. "I'd better get back to work. My office is right around the corner. Maybe I'll see you at the gym sometime."

"Possibly. I'm weighing my options."

"Well," he said, pulling a business card from his wallet. "Here's my card. The number on top is my office line, the number on the bottom is my cell. Call either, but I prefer the bottom."

Raven clamped her teeth down on her tongue.

"Yeah, sure."

She prayed he wouldn't ask for her number.

"We should train together sometime. Burn some serious calories, yeah?"

"That's me. I'm all about burning those calories."

"Cool, Gwen. I look forward to your call."

He strutted away and headed up the block. Raven didn't know how to react. She watched him until he vanished. Then she took a side street lined with small businesses, figuring he might spot her climbing into her Rogue across the street from the firm. He conducted himself like a frat boy. But she wasn't buying it. Not completely. The guy was a creep, but he laid it on too thick.

Was Damian on to her?

14

A copy of the missing person's report had been on his desk when Thomas arrived for work Wednesday morning. Duncan Bond phoned the county sheriff's office at sunset after his wife, Cecilia, who'd gone for a walk around four o'clock, hadn't returned home from the village park.

Twenty minutes ago, a jogger reported a body in the river, caught in a bend amid broken branches and waterlogged leaves. Now Thomas drove the cruiser into the village park with the dreaded certainty the jogger had found their missing person.

The terrain allowed Thomas to navigate the cruiser through the grass. He stopped at the ridge overlooking the water. Sheriff Gray pulled beside him and glanced over at Thomas. Thomas saw the worry pouring out of Gray's eyes.

"You bring gloves?" Thomas asked as he searched through his kit.

"In the trunk."

After they gloved up, they descended the terrain to the dirt trail running along the river. A man in shorts and a tank top waved his arms over his head to get their attention. As they approached, the man pointed at the body, face down in the river and bobbing with the current. Already Thomas determined it was a woman. Her gray-blonde hair floated atop the water and fanned out like a peacock spreading its feathers. The man backed away from the water when Thomas and Gray waded in. A dozen onlookers watched from the ridge. One woman held a child in her arms. The icy water made Thomas catch his breath.

"I'm too old for this shit," Gray said, grabbing hold of a tree branch overhanging the water so the current didn't knock him over.

"One foot in front of the other," said Thomas.

His toes numbed inside his boots. Along the ridge, a horn scattered the looky-loos as another vehicle jounced to a stop. Virgil Harbough, the county medical examiner, had arrived. Thomas reached out and snagged the woman's ankle. He spotted the pulpy laceration on the back of her head as he dragged her toward the shore. A wave smashed Thomas from behind and soaked him from head to toe as Gray helped Thomas lift the woman. Fighting the current, they carried her up the bank and laid her out on the grass. With the woman facing skyward, Gray knelt and performed the sign of the cross.

"That's Cecilia Bond," said Gray, wiping the water off his face.

"You know her?"

"She moved to Wolf Lake a decade ago. Kind woman. I used to see her at the Broken Yolk when I grab coffee in the morning."

"Used to?"

Gray shrugged.

"I haven't run into her in a year or two. I wonder if she fell ill. From the looks of her, she lost a lot of weight. Her cheekbones were never that drawn."

Virgil eased down the bank. Two members from the county forensics team accompanied Virgil. Slight of build, the gray-haired sixty-year-old ME took slow, careful steps down to the trail.

"What do you have?" Virgil asked.

"A jogger spotted a woman in the river," Gray said. "That's Cecilia Bond. Her husband reported her missing last evening around eight o'clock."

Thomas parted Cecilia's matted hair and said, "Another laceration and more bruising along her temple."

Gray pointed up the ridge to the overlook.

"It's possible she fell off the platform and smashed her head on the rocks."

Several large, jagged rocks jutted out of the river below the bank. Thomas searched for a blood smear, knowing the water would have washed it away.

"Or someone hit her."

"That would turn this into a homicide. If she was sick, it's not beyond reason she slipped off the platform and struck her head."

Thomas rubbed his chin.

"She has another laceration on the back of her head. How could the back of her head and temple strike the rocks simultaneously?"

Gray pulled his lips tight. Wolf Lake had dealt with a serial killer three months ago. The sheriff didn't want to accept another murderer was loose in the upscale village.

A confusion of shoe prints covered the trail. Thomas photographed the prints while a female forensics technician assessed whether she could take casts. With the number of joggers and hikers crossing the river trail, it seemed impossible they could pick out Cecilia's assailant. Then again, perhaps Gray was right about Cecilia falling off the overlook. Given the distance from the platform to the river, a fall would have left bruising and lacerations, and could have broken the woman's neck.

Thomas gave Virgil and his team room to work. While the ME examined the body, Gray supervised, and Thomas cleared away the onlookers. A half-hour later, the forensics team lifted Cecilia onto a stretcher and hauled the dead body up the ridge.

Thomas turned to Gray.

"What do we know about the husband, Duncan Bond?"

Gray stroked his mustache, still beaded with water droplets.

"He's an eccentric."

"How so?"

"He keeps to himself, and he spends too much time at St. Mary's. The guy found religion," Gray said, making air quotes around religion. "He committed his life to the church."

"Isn't that Father Josiah Fowler's church?"

"Yep," Gray said.

Thomas spotted the heat in Gray's eyes when he mentioned Fowler.

"Do you believe Duncan Bond is capable of murder?"

"He's weird, not a murderer. But I always suspect the spouse first."

Thomas set his hands on his hips and strode to the riverbank. An orange kayak caught his attention. A mustached man paddled with the current, arrowing toward the bank. Waving at the man, Thomas shouted, "Bring the kayak to the bank!"

"What?"

It was difficult to hear over the roar of the river.

"Your kayak. Bring it ashore and get out of the water."

The man nodded and stroked the water until the kayak angled toward them. Drenched from the thighs down, Thomas stepped into the current and helped the man.

"How often do you kayak on this river?"

The man slung the water off his face and climbed out. Gray lent his hand and led him out of the water.

"Two or three times a week. The rest of the time, I'm on Wolf Lake."

The man seemed familiar to Thomas. He must have seen him on the lake.

"I'm Deputy Shepherd, and this is Sheriff Gray."

"Jasper May," the man said, shaking their hands.

"Were you on the river yesterday between the hours of three and eight o'clock?"

Jasper bobbed his head up and down.

"Six-thirty. Work ran late, so I didn't get to the river until after dinner."

"Did you see a woman in her early sixties walking along the river?"

Jasper crinkled his eyes in thought.

"Yeah. Light-haired woman. I suppose she was around that age. But I didn't stop to talk."

"Did she climb to the platform or walk along the ridge?"

"Not that I noticed. She walked the dirt trail along the water. The one we're standing on."

Thomas glanced at the sheriff. That punched a hole in Gray's theory.

"Was anyone else on the trail when you rode past?"

"Two joggers."

"Did you recognize them?" Gray asked.

"No. A couple women in their thirties or forties."

"Any men on the trail?"

Jasper pondered the question.

"Not that I recall." After a pause, Jasper snapped his fingers. "You know, there was a guy. He wasn't on the trail, though. A fisher sitting on the bank. I remember because he'd cast his line so far into the water, I almost rode through it. The guy cursed at me, but I kept going."

"Any idea who the fisher was?"

"Sure," Jasper said. His mouth twisted. "He hangs out at Hattie's and gets sloppy drunk. I think his name is Garrick."

"Garrick Tillery?" asked Gray, straightening his shoulders.

"Yeah, that's the guy."

15

Scents of toast and bacon rolled past the screen door as Deputy Aguilar approached Garrick Tillery's residence. Lambert eyed the windows.

"Weren't we just here?" Aguilar asked, glancing down the road at Kay Ramsey's house.

"Trouble seems to be everywhere on this street."

The Wolf Lake residential neighborhood appeared like any other in the village—single-family homes with a couple vehicles in the driveways, kids riding bicycles and running from one yard to the next. But Aguilar's skin tingled as they climbed the stoop to the Tillery house. Potted flowers greeted them outside the white two-story. Aguilar heard grease crackling on the stove, the clink of silverware.

"So this guy raped a minor. But the wife stayed with him."

Lambert rapped his knuckles on the door.

"Hopefully, she'll see the light after we're through here."

Someone set a spatula down on the stove. Footfalls crossed the downstairs. Suzanne Tillery's eyes widened at the sight of the two deputies standing on the stoop.

"Yes?"

"Is your husband home, Mrs. Tillery?" Aguilar asked, peering around the woman.

It was too dark to see past the entryway. Suzanne covered her mouth.

"Oh, God. What did he do?"

"Is he inside the house?"

Without answering, Suzanne spun on her heels and stomped up the stairs. Her voice carried back to the deputies.

"What have you done this time, Garrick? You'd better drag yourself out of bed."

A grunt came from the second floor.

"Will you stop yelling? I've got a goddamn headache, and you're making it worse."

"The sheriff's department is here. Put something on."

"The sheriff's department? What do they want?"

"Probably to arrest you for whatever fool thing you did last night."

Suzanne rushed down the stairs.

"He's on his way," she said, leaning in the doorway.

"May we come inside?" Aguilar asked, her hand close to her gun, just in case Garrick owned a weapon.

Suzanne shot an uncertain glance over her shoulder. Her mouth quivered as she turned back to the deputies.

"I guess so. You won't arrest him, will you?"

Aguilar didn't reply as she followed Lambert inside. Dots of spilled paint marred the wooden staircase, and the steps ended at a darkened landing. The television played a talk show in the living room. A popping, splattering sound emanated from the kitchen, and Suzanne hurried away.

"I'm sorry," she said over her shoulder. "If I don't turn the stove off, I'll burn his breakfast."

Lambert took a cautious step into the living room and lifted his chin at Aguilar.

"Kinda late to eat breakfast."

"That's what you get when you spend the night at Hattie's."

The steps groaned. Garrick Tillery's shadow touched the wall before he appeared. Aguilar steadied herself. Something about Garrick Tillery threw her off. When the hungover man stepped into the entryway, Aguilar met Lambert's gaze. Garrick's shirt was a smock of blood. It looked as if someone had splashed him with scarlet-red paint. The liquor stench made Aguilar's eyes water.

Suzanne, who'd returned from the kitchen, dropped her mouth open.

"When I told you to put something on, I meant something presentable."

Tillery scratched his head. His eyes drifted to his shirt, as though seeing it for the first time. As the rotund man shifted his feet, Aguilar spied the laceration across Garrick's hand.

"What happened to your hand, Mr. Tillery?"

He lifted his injured hand and stared in confusion. With his free hand, he rubbed the sleep from his eyes.

"Oh, that. I did it fishing."

"What about the blood on your shirt? That happen fishing, as well?"

"I...I don't remember."

"Must have been one helluva fish."

"Didn't I tell you to throw your shirt in the garbage?" Suzanne asked. "It's ruined. Why would you wear it again?"

"Mr. Tillery," Lambert interjected. "Were you at the river at six-thirty last night?"

Tillery wobbled on his heels. His pallid face took on a green tinge, and for a second, Aguilar worried Garrick would vomit on them.

"Yeah, I was there."

"And was Cecilia Bond at the river?"

Suzanne swung her glare to Garrick and said, "I knew it. You're cheating on me. But why Cecilia Bond? Don't you know the poor woman is ill?"

Garrick's eyes narrowed in confusion.

"What? Cecilia? I'm not cheating on you. And if I was, I wouldn't with a seventy-year-old."

"She's not seventy."

"Mrs. Tillery, please," Aguilar said, shutting Suzanne out of the conversation. "Mr. Tillery, answer the question."

"What question?"

"Did you see Cecilia Bond at the river?"

"Uh...I might have."

"Yes or no."

"Yeah...yeah, she was there."

"Explain how you hurt your hand fishing."

"The hook. I was drunk, and I got the hook caught in my hand."

Aguilar shared a look with Lambert. Her partner wasn't buying the explanation.

"Garrick, I need you to come with us to the station."

Garrick ruffled his hair. He still appeared half-asleep.

"Now?"

"Yes, right now."

"I should change first."

"No, sir. You're fine dressed as you are."

A grave expression fell over Suzanne's face.

"Why did you ask Garrick about the blood? Did he hurt Cecilia? Oh, God."

STANDING beside Sheriff Gray outside the interview room, Thomas peeked through the window as Aguilar and Lambert questioned Garrick Tillery. The drunk slumped against the table, wrists cuffed behind his back, straggly hair hanging over his eyes. Aguilar had taken his shirt, and Tillery sat bare-chested during the interview.

"What are you going to do?" Thomas asked.

Gray blew out a breath.

"Unless Aguilar gets something out of him, I'll have to let him go. I don't have anything on the guy, except a local on a kayak noticed Tillery fishing while Cecilia Bond walked along the river. Hell, I can't definitively say she didn't tumble off the platform on her own."

"So you're letting him walk?"

Gray played with his mustache.

"I'll keep him overnight. Give him time to work off his bender. But I can't justify holding Tillery unless we find evidence implicating him."

"You're testing the shirt for Cecilia Bond's blood, right?"

"Hell, yes. But it will be days before we get the results back."

Inside the interview room, Garrick shook his head, swinging his hair back and forth as Aguilar pressed him with questions.

"He lives five doors from the Ramsey house."

Gray swung around to Thomas and gestured at Garrick with his thumb.

"You think that idiot murdered Lincoln Ramsey?"

"The daughter swears someone was inside the house when Lincoln died."

"Yeah, and none of you found a shred of evidence supporting her claim. Look, I see where you're going with this. Don't jump to conclusions. Garrick Tillery might be a lot of things. But a serial killer?"

"Serial killers are chameleons, Sheriff."

"That guy is too stupid to hide a crime." Gray's phone rang.

Virgil Harbough's name appeared on the screen. "That's the medical examiner. I'll take this in my office."

While Gray spoke to Virgil, Thomas watched his fellow deputies interrogate Garrick Tillery. Tears streaked the man's face, and snot crusted his nose. A minute later, Gray strode back to the window.

"Virgil has Cecilia on the table. I need to be here when Aguilar and Lambert finish with Tillery. Can you sit in while he goes over the autopsy findings?"

"Sure."

"Then get over there. Virgil gets impatient when we keep him waiting."

16

A car accident at the edge of the village slowed Thomas from reaching the medical examiner's building. One hundred yards up Route 15, ambulance lights revolved as a train of cars waited for traffic to clear. The phone rang and switched over to the cruiser's speakers.

"Thomas?"

His chest tightened upon hearing his mother's voice. She'd refused to return his calls for months and wouldn't have phoned him unless something happened to his father.

"What's wrong? Is—"

"Nothing has changed with your father."

He released a breath.

"I'm happy to hear that."

There was a pause on the other end of the line. He pictured his mother pacing the kitchen with the phone pressed to her ear, searching for the right words.

"Your father and I had a long talk after your visit."

"And?"

"And we'd like you to come for dinner again."

"I appreciate the invitation. But I'm not giving up my career to run Shepherd Systems no matter how much you argue."

"If we spend a few hours together, I'm certain we can formulate a solution. Let's speak as adults."

An emergency worker in reflective yellow and orange waved traffic through. The glut finally cleared.

"I'd like that, Mother. But I'm driving now."

"There's a Thursday evening mass at St Mary's tomorrow. It will mean a lot if you accompany me to mass."

"I didn't realize they had mass on weeknights."

For that matter, he didn't know his mother went to church. Jogging his memory, he recalled fidgeting in the pew under his mother's severe eyes when he was in preschool. Attending church was a rarity in those days, and they stopped going a few years after.

"What time? I have dinner plans at five o'clock."

"Seven-thirty. You'll meet me at the steps, Thomas."

Once Lindsey Shepherd decided, there was no arguing the matter.

"I'll see you then."

The Nightshade County Medical Examiner's office was a three-story, red brick edifice with glass frontage reflecting a dozen doppelgangers of the sun. Autopsies took place on the first floor at the end of a long corridor lit by florescent strip lighting. Thomas peered at Cecilia Bond's corpse as Virgil Harbough stood on tiptoe and directed the spotlight over the dead woman.

"Almost forgot," Virgil said, reaching inside his lab coat. He removed a jar of Vick's and held it out for Thomas. "This well help."

"None for me."

Thomas fought the nausea rolling through his stomach. When he first attended an autopsy in Los Angeles, he placed Vick's under his nose to mask the death scents. While his colleagues refused to enter an autopsy room without Vick's, Thomas discovered it opened his sinuses too wide, amplifying the stench.

"You sure? The smell puts people off."

"I'm fine."

Virgil let out a sigh and set the jar on a metal cart.

"This one hits where it hurts. I've seen Cecilia Bond around town. Such a kind woman."

"So you knew her."

"Yes."

"How did Mrs. Bond die? We found her face-down in the river and fully clothed, so it didn't look like a rape. The sheriff believes she fell in and drowned."

Virgil glanced at Thomas through the tops of his eyes and shook his head.

"Cecilia Bond did not drown. When someone drowns, we expect to find froth in the trachea and bronchial tubes. The lungs hyper-expand. And if the victim panics and opens her mouth, there's a good chance her stomach will contain water."

"And that's not present with Cecilia Bond's body?"

"Not at all."

"Then what killed her?"

Gesturing at the bruising on Cecilia Bond's temple, Virgil said, "She has a nasty contusion. It's conceivable she fell into the river and smacked her head against the rocks. Then the current dragged her downstream. She would have been dead before the water pulled her under."

"That doesn't explain the contusion behind her head."

"Not unless she tumbled and hit her head twice."

"So you believe someone attacked Cecilia and tossed her into the river, making it look like a drowning."

"No, I'm not saying that. Cecilia Bond was a very sick

woman. In her condition, her balance would be compromised. She could have fainted."

"How do you know she was sick?"

"I found lesions on her kidneys. My guess? Diabetic nephropathy."

"That might indicate advanced kidney disease."

"Very good, Deputy Shepherd," Virgil said with a wink. "Our Cecilia wouldn't have lived much longer. Even if she found a donor, it would have been an uphill battle to reverse her deterioration."

Diabetic nephropathy and COPD. Cecilia Bond and Lincoln Ramsey were on their proverbial death beds.

"She's covered in scratches," said Thomas, directing the spotlight. Several thin, shallow cuts marred her arms and face.

"It could have happened after the water dragged her under."

"Doubtful. The scratches aren't coincident with bruising, and those river rocks would do a lot more than take a thin slice of surface tissue."

"What are you saying?"

"She ran from someone. These are the marks she'd pick up fleeing through the woods. The river trail runs through the forest about a half-mile from where we found the body, correct?"

"Yes, and it empties onto a second river trail after a five-minute walk."

Thomas bent over and examined the dead woman's hand.

"The nail on her right index finger snapped off."

"I scraped underneath. If someone attacked Cecilia Bond, and she broke a nail fighting him off, the lab should find DNA."

Thomas stood back and shifted his jaw.

"Virgil, did you find anything interesting when you autopsied Lincoln Ramsey?"

The medical examiner scrunched his face.

"Lincoln Ramsey didn't require an autopsy."

"Why?"

"His death wasn't suspicious, young man. He'd been sick for a long time. I'm amazed Lincoln Ramsey lived to see summer."

"Has Ramsey's body gone to the funeral home yet?"

"Well, no. He leaves Friday, and the funeral is Saturday morning."

"You need to autopsy Lincoln Ramsey."

"Until your department tells me Ramsey's death requires an autopsy, my hands are tied. I plan to send the body to the funeral home on schedule."

Thomas moved his eyes over Cecilia Bond's swollen body. If he didn't convince Gray to change the report, they'd lose their only chance to prove someone murdered Lincoln Ramsey.

17

R aven tapped her nails on the steering wheel and blew out a flustered breath. The interior of the Rogue had to be ninety degrees, even though she'd opened the windows.

Where the hell was Damian Ramos? The boy toy finished work at four, but he never exited the building with his workmates. After running into Damian at the food truck, Raven had located a second-hand clothing shop down the road from the trading firm. While Damian traded, or whatever market analysts did all day, Raven purchased a baseball cap, a mauve v-neck t-shirt, and a skort. Then she drove into a grocery store parking lot and changed her clothes. If Damian spotted Raven again, he wouldn't recognize her after the outfit change.

Her legs drummed with anxiousness. As she stuck the keys into the ignition, about to give up for the day, Damian pushed through the glass doors and strode down the sidewalk. Raven fired the engine and swung the Rogue into traffic, drawing an angry horn. She stomped the gas and trailed him to the parking garage. When he pulled open the steel door and climbed the concrete stairs, she muscled the Rogue between two curbside hatchbacks and crossed the road.

Raven kept one eye glued to Damian, Sadie's fiancé visible behind the windows as he climbed to the top floor. A second door rested on the opposite end of the parking garage. Raven chose the alternate stairway and sprinted up the steps. She opened the door to the upper level and stepped inside the garage. Half the spaces were unoccupied. A thick oil and gas scent tickled her nose.

Footsteps scuffled across the blacktop. Raven threw herself behind a concrete pillar as water dripped from the roof and wet her shoulder. Leaning her head around the pillar, she spotted Damian a dozen parking spaces away. The black Audi beeped when he unlocked the car. After he tossed his jacket over the seat, he set the briefcase down and paused. He turned his head toward Raven. She swung around the pillar, back pressed against the concrete as the breath flew in and out of her chest.

The parking lot went silent. Just the drip, drip, drip off the ceiling. Horns honked on the street below.

More footsteps. Raven prayed Damian hadn't seen her. She concocted stories in her head, excuses for why she'd followed him into the parking garage. None held water. Unless she pretended she was interested in him. Yeah, a conceited creep like Damian would believe that story.

Damian paced the parking garage, as if canvassing the area. He stopped behind the Audi and popped the trunk as Raven crept out of hiding. She knelt behind a Subaru Outback and peered around the bumper. Silent as a windless night, Damian glanced up and down the garage. Then he lifted the briefcase and set it inside the trunk.

Moving on cat's paws, Raven removed her camera and photographed Damian. Her eyes widened. Two spools of rope and a roll of duct tape lay in the trunk. Nothing else beside the briefcase. What was a market analyst doing with rope and duct tape? She couldn't think of a home project which required both. Except kidnapping.

Raven leaped behind the Outback when Damian slammed the trunk.

18

Thomas set the tray of eggs, toast, and bacon inside Garrick Tillery's cell. The groggy drunk barely flinched when Thomas stepped through the cage. As Thomas set the utensils on the tray, Garrick groaned and placed a hand over his eyes, shying from the light like a dying vampire. The Broken Yolk provided breakfast to prisoners, not that the Nightshade County jail saw many visitors. Sheriff Gray supported Ruth's business. It wasn't a secret the Broken Yolk was close to going under, the younger crowd favoring vegetarian and vegan options available in the village center, the older, loyal customers dying off or moving.

Garrick swung his legs off the cot and stared hazy-eyed at the tray. Next, he gazed around the cell as though seeing it for the first time. He hadn't requested a lawyer, hadn't pounded his fists against the bars and demanded release. He seemed content to stay as long as Gray gave him a free room. That might suggest innocence, except Thomas had witnessed murderers shutting down and giving up, overcome with guilt.

"Eat your breakfast before it turns cold."

Garrick scrubbed his face. For the first time, Thomas noted

the scratches on the prisoner's arms. They were mirror images of the cuts covering Cecilia Bond's arms and face—shallow and angry, not deep enough to draw blood.

"How did you get those scratches, Mr. Tillery?"

Garrick shuffled to the tray and carried it back to the cot. He set the tray in his lap, lathered the scrambled eggs in ketchup, and spooned a heap into his mouth. He chewed with his mouth open, the eggs tinged red by the bloody ketchup.

"Mr. Tillery? The scratches?"

He set the spoon down and raised each arm, studying the pink and red markings.

"Got 'em trimming Suzanne's rose bushes. The bitch grows them all over the yard, and the village won't take the cuttings. I gotta cut them every few weeks and burn the trimmings in the fire pit. Otherwise, I'll be up to my ass in prickers."

"You spend much time in the woods?"

"The woods?"

"Hiking, hunting, taking a walk to clear your head."

"What the fuck are you talking about?"

"Were you in the woods Tuesday evening?"

Garrick swiveled his head toward Thomas, the first signs of intelligence glimmering in the drunk's eyes.

"You can't fish in the woods, genius. Let me eat in peace. When do I get out of here? You can't hold me forever."

"Take it up with the sheriff. That's not my decision to make."

Garrick cursed under his breath and shoveled another scoop of eggs into his mouth as Thomas locked the cage behind him. Gray emerged from his office when Thomas passed by.

"Duncan Bond will arrive in fifteen minutes. I'd like you to sit in on the interview. You give Garrick his food?"

"Yeah, he's halfway through breakfast. He wants to know when you're releasing him."

Gray removed his hat and ran a hand through his hair, then set the hat down.

"Like I told you, I can't hold him without evidence."

"The scratches on his arms match Cecilia Bond's."

"What did Virgil say?"

"For one, she was dying from kidney disease. Cecilia Bond died before she hit the water. It wasn't a drowning. She also broke a nail. Virgil sent the scrapings to the lab for DNA analysis."

"Are Garrick Tillery's cuts deep enough to suggest Cecilia took a chunk of his skin?"

"Possibly. We'll find out when the results come back. But by then, Garrick will be a free man."

Maggie's voice carried from the greeting area. Duncan Bond had arrived. Gray glanced at Thomas.

"Ready?"

"Let's see what Duncan Bond has to say."

The interview room felt like a sweat tent under a Death Valley sun. Thomas smiled inside. Gray had turned up the heat, an old trick to make suspects uncomfortable. The problem was, Thomas would sweat bullets if the interview ran long.

Duncan Bond sat across from Sheriff Gray and Thomas, the man's forearms flat on the table. The thinning hair atop his head, somewhere between sandy-brown and gray, left plenty of real estate uncovered. He wore oval, oversize glasses that amplified his eyeballs, and the drawn face and dark splotches beneath his eyes suggested Duncan Bond hadn't slept since they found his wife floating in the river. A bandage covered Duncan's cheek.

"What happened to your face?" Gray asked.

Duncan lowered his head and rubbed his temple.

"I cut myself shaving this morning."

Before Duncan raised his eyes, Gray gave Thomas a pointed look.

"First off, we're very sorry for your loss, Mr. Bond. Cecilia was a kind woman, a staple of the Wolf Lake community."

"Did you know my wife, Sheriff?"

"In passing. But everyone spoke highly of her. She'll be missed."

A hurt sound came from the man's throat.

"Why am I here?"

Thomas tapped a pen against his notepad and said, "Cecilia was dying."

"Yes. She had kidney disease, and we hadn't found a donor. There was still time, though."

"So she was in the National Kidney Registry."

"For over a year. Every day, I prayed for a match. This will sound crazy unless you have faith. But I believe we were close to having our prayers answered. Cecilia wouldn't do her part. She took stupid risks when she should have prayed alongside me and made sure God heard us."

"What sorts of risks?"

Duncan fell back in his chair, defeated.

"She wouldn't listen to anyone. Not to her doctor, not to me. Cecilia insisted on going for walks alone."

"You didn't walk with her?"

"What difference would it make? I did everything I could to make her healthy—I prayed all day and night."

"So you allowed your wife, who was suffering from advanced kidney disease, to hike along the river by herself?"

A flash of anger moved through Duncan's eyes.

"I never allowed it. Cecilia set her own rules, and she was too stubborn. Nobody talked sense into her."

Gray cleared his throat.

"Mr. Bond, where were you between the hours of six and eight o'clock Tuesday evening?"

Duncan gave the sheriff a blank, glassy-eyed stare that reminded Thomas of Garrick Tillery waking up.

"Tuesday evening?"

"While your wife went to the park."

"Oh." He lowered his face into his hands and breathed between his fingers. "At the church, praying for my wife."

"Which church?"

"St. Mary's."

"Can anyone corroborate your whereabouts?" Thomas asked.

Duncan gave the question extended consideration.

"I was there alone. Anyone is free to pray inside the church before nine. That's when they lock the doors."

"So nobody saw you there."

Duncan wiped the sweat off his forehead.

"It's hot in here."

"Our apologies," Gray said. "We're having difficulty with the heating and cooling system. The county budget isn't what it used to be. Can I get you anything to drink? Soda, water?"

"Um, sure. Water would be fine."

Gray nodded to Thomas, who rose from his seat and retrieved a bottled water and glass from the kitchen. The temperature outside the interview room felt wintry as Thomas's body adjusted. He knew what Gray was up to. Duncan would leave DNA on the glass.

Inside the interview room, Thomas poured the water into the glass and slid it across the table to Duncan.

"Thank you," Duncan said, raising the glass in a half-hearted salute.

Gray eyed the lip marks after Duncan set the glass down.

"Better?"

"Yes." Duncan swiped his sleeve across his forehead. "Now

that you asked, someone saw me inside the church Tuesday evening."

Gray leaned forward.

"Who?"

"Father Josiah Fowler."

The sheriff pressed his lips together.

"So if we call Father Fowler," said Thomas, scribbling a note. "He'll remember you."

"He should, yes. Father Fowler said hello on his way into the church. I was leaving."

"So he wasn't there when you arrived." That weakened Duncan's alibi, if nobody knew how long he'd spent inside the church. What if he murdered his wife, then drove to the church to pray for forgiveness? "Any idea where Father Fowler had been?"

"No, but he was in a rush. He barely said a word to me, and that's unlike Father. Boy, it's hot in here. You need to get the cooling fixed."

Duncan guzzled the last of the water.

"Let me get that out of your way," Gray said, plucking the glass by the bottom and setting it beside him.

"Mr. Bond," Thomas said, holding the suspect's eyes. "Earlier, you told us you were frustrated with Cecilia. Did you fight often?"

"We argued, if that's what you mean."

"Did the fights turn physical?"

"I'd never harm my wife, and I don't appreciate the implication."

"We found bruises on Cecilia's body."

"She was always falling. It was the kidney disease and her medication. Cecilia never should have left the house."

"Yet you allowed her to drive a car to the park and walk along the river without supervision."

"I couldn't talk her out of it. Once she makes her mind up, there's no changing it."

The questioning continued for another ten minutes. By then, even Gray couldn't take the heat any longer.

"We'll contact you if we have more questions," Gray said, holding the door open for Duncan.

After the man crossed the parking lot to his vehicle, Gray sat on the edge of his desk.

"What do you make of Duncan Bond?"

"He's arrogant and domineering," Thomas said. "I can picture Duncan losing control."

"And striking his wife?"

"I wouldn't put it past him. That bandage on his cheek. Pretty convenient he cut himself shaving after his wife ended up dead in a river."

"Hours after they argued," Gray added. "Perhaps Cecilia fought back when he attacked her."

"He doesn't have an alibi. Fowler didn't see Duncan arrive."

Gray narrowed his eyes.

"Speaking of Father Fowler, what's his alibi?"

Thomas stared at Gray. No one could convince the sheriff Fowler hadn't run Lana off the road. But accusing the man of murder seemed far-fetched.

"You're not suggesting Fowler killed Cecilia Bond. Where's the evidence?"

"Father Fowler was close with the Ramsey family, and Lincoln ended up dead. Duncan Bond prayed for Cecilia beside Fowler, and she's dead too. Maybe Father Fowler enjoys playing God."

"You'll ruin our appetites," Raven said, setting her feet upon her desk.

Inside Wolf Lake Consulting, the wall-mounted television played a talk show while Chelsey puttered around in the kitchen. The converted house felt more like a home every day. They'd stocked the refrigerator, the cupboards held enough snacks for them to survive the zombie apocalypse, and potted plants sat in every corner. Even the bedroom at the end of the hall, formerly a storage room, contained a twin bed with blackout curtains over the windows. If work kept Chelsey or Raven late, they had a place to crash.

Raven grabbed the remote and flipped the channel, scanned the sports scores, the news, the movie channels, then gave up. Two hundred channels and nothing worth her time. Chelsey carried a bowl of chips into the office and set the food on an empty desk. The desk was ostensibly for the next investigator, if Chelsey got around to hiring help. Chelsey ran back to the kitchen and returned with a jar of salsa.

"Dig in," Chelsey said, munching on a chip.

Raven resisted at first. She couldn't stomach junk food after the greasy binge outside Benson's Barbells. But chips and salsa almost qualified as healthy, right? Raven spooned the salsa with a chip and popped it into her mouth. Spicy. After she swallowed, she dunked another chip and glanced at Chelsey.

"What did Sadie Moreno have to say?"

Sadie had phoned Chelsey a half-hour ago while Raven researched Damian Ramos, searching for a crack in his armor.

"She asked for an update on the investigation."

Raven crunched a chip and brushed the crumbs off her hands.

"What did you tell her?"

"That Damian made a pass at you yesterday."

"Oh, wonderful. That won't be the least bit uncomfortable when she stops by."

"She deserves the truth, and she's aware Damian flirts behind her back. Hopefully that will be enough for Sadie to call off the engagement."

"Did you tell her about the blonde girl at the gym?"

"Not yet. We can't prove Damian is having an affair. And since you were outside, shooting through the windows, we don't know what they were talking about. Based on what you told me, it's a safe bet Damian flirted with the girl. But I can't jump to conclusions."

"I'll drive over to the gym this afternoon and..." Raven palmed her face. "Oh, snap."

"What?"

"The cookout. I completely forgot it's at five o'clock. What do you want me to do? If I drive to Kane Grove, would you do me a solid and pick up LeVar? I'm sure Darren and Deputy Shepherd wouldn't mind if you took my place at the cookout."

"Oh, no. I'll drive to Benson's. Go to the party and have a good time. And I see what you're trying to do."

Raven swept her braids over her shoulder.

"What's that?"

"You want me to attend this cookout and hit it off with Deputy Shepherd. I'm on to your trickery, girlfriend."

"It wouldn't hurt for you to get out of the house. The Mourning family will be there." Chelsey bit her lip. "What's that look about?"

"What?"

"I mentioned Deputy Shepherd's neighbors, and you turned ice cold."

"I didn't."

"You're worried Thomas will hook up with Naomi Mourning. That's what's bugging you."

"What gave you that idea? Deputy Shepherd and I are ancient history. I moved on. And you should drop the conspiracy theories. This isn't a cheesy sitcom where two long-lost lovers reunite."

"You're impossible."

"Tell me again about the contents of Damian's trunk."

Raven shook her head as Chelsey dodged the issue. Grabbing her phone, she paged through the images. The picture she'd snapped when Damian opened the trunk came out blurry. Also, Damian had shifted his body and blocked her view.

"The trunk was spotless, except for ropes and duct tape. And his briefcase."

"That's not proof he's a kidnapper."

"No, but if he's after Sadie's money, Plan B might be abduction."

"So Sadie calls off the marriage, and he kidnaps her and holds her for ransom."

"Not much of a theory, is it?"

Chelsey sat in a rolling chair with a handful of chips, dunking one at a time as she spoke.

"There's one issue I can't wrap my head around."

"What's that?"

"Why is Damian going after Sadie Moreno's money? He's a market analyst for a successful trading firm, and from your pictures, I can see he dresses for success. Those aren't bargain rack suits. The man has money."

"It makes no sense to me, either," Raven said, pushing the bowl aside so she didn't gorge herself before lunch.

"Unless he's greedy. The world is full of wealthy people who got into trouble after seeking more. Some people are never satisfied until they own everything." Chelsey's eyes smiled at Raven. "So the boy toy made a pass at you. I want the deets."

"I'd rather not talk about it."

"Did you bat your eyelashes and show a little leg?"

"Oh, here we go."

"Seriously, what happened?"

Raven set an elbow on the desk and rested her head on her palm.

"I followed him to a food truck a block from the trading firm. He noticed me on the corner."

"I can't believe he recognized you from the gym."

"I can't, either. When I went through the pictures, I couldn't find him staring at my camera. How did he see me inside my vehicle?"

"Guess he's always searching for a pretty face."

"Shut it. Anyhow, he suggested we burn some calories together."

"Subtle, isn't he?"

"What a leech."

"Did he ask for your number?"

"No, thank goodness."

Chelsey popped another chip in her mouth.

"He didn't even get your name?"

"Well..."

"Raven?" Chelsey asked, drawing out her friend's name. "What did you tell him?"

"I didn't give him my real name. I told him my name was... Gwen Stephani, with a *ph*."

Chelsey laughed and choked on her food, almost tumbling out of her chair. It took a long time before she composed herself, and even then, her eyes glassed over with humor. Hitches of laughter kept leaping out of her chest.

"Tell me you didn't."

"I panicked, okay?"

"Gwen Stephani. That is, no doubt, the funniest fake name I've ever heard."

"You're quite the comedian, Chelsey."

"Did he buy the name?"

"He seemed to. I'm supposed to call him so we can *train* together. And I told him I'd gone to Benson's, inquiring about a membership."

"That's not a bad idea," Chelsey said, leaning back as she crossed her legs at the ankles. "If you work out at Benson's, you can monitor Sadie's boy toy. Who knows? Maybe he'll ask the beautiful Gwen Stephani for a date."

"Stop."

"I can picture it now. He'll be like, 'hey baby, hey baby, hey.' And you'll tell him you're up for a *hella good* time."

"Enough with the jokes, or you and I are gonna tussle."

"Ooooh, I'm so scared. I'm sorry, Raven. I'm *just a girl*."

Raven tried to hold her death stare. But Chelsey's smirk got the best of her, and she burst out laughing.

"I wonder how many years it will take before I live that down."

"Tell me your retirement date, and I'll give you an answer."

Raven pushed the chair away from the desk, craving tea. As

she stood, the face on the television pulled her eyes to the screen.

"Oh, my God."

Chelsey followed Raven's gaze.

"What's wrong?"

"The blonde girl on the television. That's the girl Damian flirted with at the gym."

Chelsey snatched the remote and boosted the volume. The news anchor's voice spoke as the woman's photo covered the television. The phone number for the Kane Grove Police Department scrolled along the bottom.

"Twenty-four-year-old Ellie Fisher of Kane Grove has been missing since Tuesday evening around six o'clock. She was last seen at Benson's Barbells gymnasium in Kane Grove. Anyone with information about Ms. Fisher is urged to call the Kane Grove Police Department at..."

"Show me your pictures again." Chelsey said, lowering the volume as the reporter repeated the message. Her eyes kept darting to the television as Raven clicked through her computer files.

Raven loaded a photograph of Damian and the blonde girl beside the Smith Machine. Damian had slung a towel over his shoulder. He leaned over the girl, as if he wanted to kiss her. Drawing a square around the girl's head, Raven zoomed in and pulled out the details.

"That's her," Raven said. "Ellie Fisher."

Chelsey nodded, jotting down Fisher's address.

"That's a tad suspicious. Damian was all over Ellie at the gym, and she never made it home."

"And Damian had ropes and duct tape in his trunk."

"Why kidnap Ellie? What's his motive?"

"It's like you said. Some people want it all and are never

satisfied. Or he's a psycho. What do we do now? Should we call the sheriff's department?"

"All we have on Damian is he spoke to Ellie Fisher at the gym. The contents of his trunk don't prove he kidnapped Ellie Fisher."

"Or that he murdered her."

"I'll phone the sheriff's department and the Kane Grove PD to fill them in. Until then, we have Ellie Fisher's address. I'll find out what I can about this girl. Don't let Damian Ramos out of your sight."

The neighbors across the street were hosting a garage sale in front of a pale-blue Cape Cod when Thomas and Aguilar pulled their cruisers to the curb outside Kay Ramsey's house. Another vehicle sat in the Ramsey's driveway, and Thomas recognized it as Ambrose Jorgensen's. The daughter opened the door before Thomas knocked.

"Let me guess. You have evidence on my father's case."

"Is your mother home?" Thomas asked.

"She's napping in the guest room." Ambrose wrung her hands together. "Mom can't bring herself to sleep in her own bed. Not since…"

"We understand. Deputy Aguilar and I wish to speak to you about the events leading up to your father's death Sunday night."

"I'll wake my mother. Come in, please."

Ambrose held the door open. The downstairs looked military-clean, not a pillow out of place on the couch, the bills neatly stacked on a table beside the door. The house smelled of lemon cleaning spray. While Ambrose climbed the stairs, Aguilar nudged Thomas.

"You think Garrick Tillery had something to do with Lincoln Ramsey's death?"

"He's on my radar. Don't mention his name unless they bring him up first. I don't want them assuming their neighbor murdered Lincoln until we have evidence he's involved."

Muffled voices followed from upstairs. Then the squeak of bed springs before footfalls moved across the upper landing. Ambrose linked her elbow with Kay's, the daughter nursing her mother down each stair. Aguilar glanced at Thomas. She'd noticed the same thing—Kay Ramsey had aged twenty years since Sunday night.

"Careful, Mom. Hold the rail."

"I've got it. You don't need to help."

Kay's eyes were red and sloughed, sliding down her face. Her hair appeared recently brushed. But her face still held a pink imprint from sleeping on the corner of her pillow.

"Good morning, deputies," Kay said, standing at the bottom of the landing. She grasped the banister until she found her sea legs. "Did my daughter put ideas into your head again? The COPD killed my Lincoln. Nobody murdered him."

"Come sit, Mom," Ambrose said, leading her mother toward the sofa.

Kay pulled her elbow free.

"I can walk." As she dropped into a recliner, she gestured at the couch. "Sit, deputies. May I get you anything to eat or drink?"

"No, ma'am," Thomas said. "We'd like to ask you a few questions and have a look around the house. Then we'll get out of your way."

"No rush." Kay waved a hand through the air. "I don't get visitors these days." She tugged the curtain. Ambrose, standing beside the recliner, helped her mother open the drapes. As Kay craned her neck to look outside, she said, "That nice Mrs. Tillery used to visit. Haven't heard a peep from her since Lincoln passed. Everyone else brought casseroles and pies and soups and...you get the picture. I appreciate their kindness. But what will I do with all that food?"

"Mrs. Ramsey, the night your husband died, you mentioned a shadow moving through your neighbor's yard."

"That's right, Mom," Ambrose said, setting a hand on her mother's.

"That could have been anyone. The kids run amok after dark, playing hide-and-go-seek, racing around on their bicycles. None of them have lights. I worry someone will speed through the neighborhood and hit them."

"Did you hear the kids in the yard?" Aguilar asked.

"No. But if they were playing their game, they'd have kept quiet, right?"

"Over the last few months, did you receive threatening phone calls or notice strange vehicles in the neighborhood?"

"Nobody ever calls. Our family moved away or passed on. Only Ambrose stayed."

Ambrose patted her mother's hand and smiled down at her.

"Mom, what about the brick?"

Kay scoffed.

"That was two winters ago. A deputy took pictures and asked us questions. But we never found out who did it. We replaced the window and installed a security system. Problem solved."

Thomas sat forward.

"What's this about a brick?"

Ambrose leveled Thomas with a glare.

"Someone threw a brick through the living room window. For some reason, my mother doesn't consider it a big deal. While my father had friends in Wolf Lake, he made a few enemies over the years."

"Enemies. Anyone in particular?"

Thomas turned his attention to Kay. She pressed her lips together and glanced outside. Across the street, a young couple lifted an antique dresser on to their pickup. Ambrose touched her mother's shoulder.

"Mom?"

"Lincoln had an issue with some man at the bank," said Kay, wiping a tear off her eyelid.

Thomas clicked his pen.

"An employee?"

"No, a customer. Something about a loan. I don't know the specifics because Lincoln never spoke about work. When the clock struck five, his workday ended. The rest of the day belonged to his family."

"Did this customer threaten your husband?"

Kay shrugged.

"If he did, Lincoln didn't say."

"The incident with the brick," Aguilar said. "This occurred two years ago this February?"

"That's correct."

"What about the problem at the bank?"

"Maybe a year earlier. It happened too long ago to say for certain."

Thomas noted the approximate dates. He set down the pad and asked, "Is there anyone at the bank who would remember the argument?"

Kay glanced up at her daughter, then back to Thomas and Aguilar.

"Lincoln was close with Earl Horton. Earl joined the First National Bank of Harmon a few years after Lincoln arrived. They were tellers when they started, and both shot up the ranks. Earl handled small business loans."

"Mark my words," Ambrose said. "The man who caused trouble at the bank is the same man who broke the window. And if he was crazy enough to throw a brick through a window in broad daylight..."

Thomas tucked the pad into his pocket.

"Is there anything else you can think of? Anything strange that happened in the neighborhood in recent weeks?"

Kay crossed one leg over the other and shook her head.

"It's so quiet here, it's almost boring. Our neighbors are good people, Deputy. Nobody here would harm Lincoln."

But Thomas caught trouble in Kay's eyes when she glanced down the road.

"You mentioned a security system," Aguilar said. "Do you keep it armed when you're home."

"If I didn't," Kay said, glaring at Ambrose. "My daughter would have my hide. Two years we've paid a monthly fee for this service, and we haven't needed it once."

After Ambrose repeated her version of what happened Sunday night, the daughter insistent someone broke into the house, the deputies wrapped up the interview. Kay Ramsey begged Thomas and Aguilar to take an apple pie or a fruit cake. They refused, but somehow Aguilar ended up with a mason jar of chicken soup.

"What?" Aguilar asked as Thomas laughed at her with his eyes. "She wouldn't take no for an answer." After Aguilar set the soup inside the cruiser, she stood beside Thomas on the sidewalk, one hand on her hip, the other rubbing her chin. "Did you notice Mrs. Ramsey staring at Garrick Tillery's house after she claimed no one would hurt her husband?"

"Sure did."

"The guy got a drunk and disorderly over the winter, and he has a sexual assault on his record."

"And an eyewitness put him inside the park moments before Cecilia Bond ended up dead in the river."

Aguilar strolled through the grass.

"So Kay and Lincoln Ramsey have a security system, and Ambrose claims someone sneaked into the house and murdered her father. Yet the alarm never went off."

Thomas pointed at the master bedroom window along the side of the house. A porch roof hung below the window, shielding a side entrance.

"Security companies don't connect second-floor windows unless they're over a roofed porch. And the cheaper companies skip the second-floor, even if a lower roof exists. Do we know which company they hired?"

"Lake Tech," Aguilar said, twisting her mouth.

"That bad?"

"They're the worst. A child with a slingshot could rob a family without triggering a Lake Tech alarm."

They stopped below the master bedroom and glanced up.

"Lambert couldn't find a print on the window. But he noted the screen was out of its tracks."

"So Garrick Tillery scaled the porch, stood on the roof, and jostled the screen open," said Thomas, the doubt reflected in his voice.

"You saw this guy. Is he capable of climbing up to the roof and breaking through a window? I wouldn't describe Tillery as agile. Given his constant level of inebriation, he'd tumble off the roof before he hurt anyone."

"He's a violent offender. That puts him at the top of my suspect list."

Aguilar's radio squawked. The sheriff's department got a lead on the Ellie Fisher missing persons investigation. Fisher's roommate had reported the girl missing. No one had seen Fisher since she left a gymnasium in Kane Grove Tuesday night.

"Never a dull moment," Thomas said, climbing into his cruiser. "Find out what you can about this argument at the First

National bank. I'll check out Fisher's apartment and meet you back at the station."

He cranked the engine. Two people dead, and a girl missing. Was the Ellie Fisher disappearance related to the Cecilia Bond and Lincoln Ramsey cases?

21

THURSDAY, JULY 16TH, 12:20 P.M.

Chelsey parked her green Honda Civic outside Ellie Fisher's apartment. The brick, two-story complex resided inside the village center, an easy walk from shopping and restaurants. Though the apartments appeared tiny from the outside, each featured a walk-out balcony, pre-finished silver hardwood flooring, and white walls embellished with black-and-white photography of Wolf Lake. The complex catered to young, upwardly mobile professionals, fresh out of college and eager to save money while hanging on to a modicum of luxury.

She checked her notes before climbing out of the car. Ellie Fisher's roommate was Lizzie Todd, a twenty-three-year-old, self-employed interior designer with an art degree from the Rhode Island School of Design. Chelsey waited for traffic, then crossed the road and climbed the concrete steps. A locked door barred entry unless someone let her inside. Running her finger over the buzzers, she located the second-floor apartment for Fisher and Todd and pressed the button. After receiving no response, she pressed it again, wondering if the buzzer was out of order.

"Who is it?"

The annoyed voice booming from the speaker caught Chelsey by surprise.

"Ms. Todd?"

"Yes?"

"My name is Chelsey Byrd. I'm investigating Ellie Fisher's disappearance and would like to ask you a few questions."

Todd waited several beats before unlocking the door. Chelsey stepped into the entryway and found the stairs. Fisher and Todd lived on the second floor in apartment seven. A Middle Eastern girl carrying a backpack passed her in the hall as Chelsey scanned the numbers. Lizzie Todd answered on the first knock, as though she'd waited beside the door. She kept the chain hooked and studied Chelsey through the thin opening.

"Show me identification."

Chelsey removed the driver's license from her wallet.

"That's not a police badge."

"Because I'm not a cop." Lizzie pressed the door closed, but Chelsey blocked it with her foot. "Please, I'm a private investigator."

She handed Lizzie a business card for Wolf Lake Consulting. The girl divided her glare between the card and Chelsey.

"All right," Lizzie said, removing the chain.

The apartment interior appeared immaculate despite its microscopic dimensions. A potted palm sprouted in the living room, and the glass tables made the inside appear more spacious than it was.

"When is the last time you spoke to Ellie?"

Lizzie, barefoot in sweatpants and a yellow t-shirt with *Providence* written across the front, slid her hands into her pocket and leaned against the kitchen granite. Green eyes and a button nose highlighted the girl's face. Sandy hair perched atop her head in a bun.

"Tuesday morning before we left for work. We were supposed to go to dinner Wednesday evening."

"Did Lizzie complain of a guy following her?"

"No. Should she have?"

Chelsey removed her phone and called up an image of Damian Ramos talking with Ellie Fisher at the gym.

"Do you recognize the man in the photograph?"

Lizzie shook her head.

"I've never seen him before."

"He seemed interested in Ellie."

"Trust me. She wasn't interested in him." She tugged on the refrigerator door and slid the coconut milk aside. "I made a green smoothie. You want half before it goes to waste?"

The smoothie looked like someone blended a frog.

"Um, sure," Chelsey said, not wanting to be rude. "What's in it?"

"Lots of stuff. Kale, beet greens, collard greens, swiss chard." When Chelsey screwed up her face, Lizzie added, "Plus one banana and mixed berries."

As she poured the concoction into a glass, Chelsey glanced out the kitchen window. She could see all of downtown, the shopping district laid out in neat rectangles. The lake shimmered in the distance.

"You claim Ellie wasn't interested in the man in the picture. How can you be sure?"

Lizzie cocked an eyebrow.

"You don't know?"

"What am I missing?"

"Ellie and I aren't just roommates, Ms. Byrd. We're dating."

Lizzie handed Chelsey the glass. Chelsey brought the smoothie to her lips, tempted to plug her nose before she took a sip. Cold, but tastier than she'd expected.

"It's good."

"You like?"

"I do. So Ellie is a..."

"Lesbian, yes. It's okay, Ms. Byrd. It's not a four-letter word." Lizzie sighed. "But she's also a flirt. And Ellie will bat her eyelashes at anyone—man, woman, it doesn't matter."

"Does the flirting ever lead to more?"

"Not Ellie. She's a show off at heart. But she's loyal, and that's why I don't mind." Lizzie tilted Chelsey's phone and took another look at the photo. "He's a hunk, if you're into that sort of thing. I suppose if I was attracted to guys, I might be interested. Who is he?"

Chelsey wasn't sure she should give Lizzie Damian's name. Lizzie played it cool now. But what if she went after Damian?

"His name is Damian Ramos. He works out with Ellie at Benson's Barbells in Kane Grove."

Lizzie scoffed.

"That meat market? Not surprised she met a guy like that at Benson's. What's your interest in this Damian Ramos guy?"

She couldn't tell Lizzie about Sadie Moreno.

"His name came up in another case. We're monitoring him."

"Is he dangerous?"

Chelsey hesitated. Yes, she trusted Raven's opinion and believed Damian was dangerous.

"He's a market analyst."

"That doesn't sound dangerous, unless he loses your money."

Chelsey sipped her drink and set the glass on the counter.

"Don't take this the wrong way. But you don't seem concerned your girlfriend is missing."

"Ellie is the type to take off without telling you. Last autumn, she called out sick and drove to Vermont to sightsee and enjoy the autumn colors. I didn't know she'd left town until she checked into her hotel room and called. She's in Cape May or Virginia Beach, lying in the sun."

"So she disappears frequently?"

Lizzie shrugged.

"She had a rough childhood. Her mother walked out on them, and the father was an alcoholic. Ellie preferred being alone. She doesn't speak with her father anymore. But her grandmother left an inheritance. Ellie could retire today and live comfortably."

"May I ask how much the grandmother left her?"

"Ellie doesn't talk about it. But I've seen her bank statements on the counter. She's worth close to a million dollars."

"I have to ask you this, Ms. Todd. You say Ellie is faithful. But is there any chance she hooked up with Damian Ramos? Maybe Ellie likes guys more than she lets on."

Lizzie's eyes swiveled to the window. She lost herself in thought before she shook her head.

"I'd know if Ellie cheated on me. And you can't fake what we have. Ellie and I connect."

Chelsey nodded.

"Can you recall a man calling the apartment recently?"

"We don't have a land line, only our cells."

"Would you allow me to search through Ellie's belongings?"

"Is that necessary?"

"Just in case she left something behind that will tell us where she vanished to."

Lizzie mulled over her decision.

"I guess that's okay."

The bedroom barely contained the queen-size bed and dresser. The bedroom opened to a bathroom, and Chelsey checked there first. Lizzie leaned in the doorway while Chelsey opened the cabinets. No unusual medications.

"What is it you're looking for?"

Without answering, Chelsey sifted through the bedroom, pulling open the dresser drawers. Folded skirts and tees, nothing hidden and tucked beneath the clothes. She could feel Lizzie's impatience building before the buzzer sounded. Lizzie threw her hands up.

"I need to get that. Are you almost finished?"

"One more minute, and I'll get out of your way."

Lizzie hesitated in the doorway as Chelsey ducked her head beneath the bed. A lost sock and spare change. Nothing else. Lizzie's voice carried from the kitchen.

"Who is it?"

"Deputy Shepherd with the Nightshade County Sheriff's Department."

Chelsey leaped to her feet. Thomas was the last person she expected to run into. But it made sense Sheriff Gray sent a former LAPD detective to investigate Ellie Fisher's disappearance.

She caught her reflection in the mirror and scowled. Her hair stuck out in multiple directions, tossed about by the relentless lake breeze. She pulled it back and retrieved a headband from her bag. There. She wasn't hideous anymore.

As Chelsey turned out of the bedroom, Lizzie said, "Wait. You look different now. Did you do something to your hair?"

"I need to get back to the office. If you hear from Ellie, call me."

"Okay." Chelsey rushed to the door. Lizzie grabbed her arm. Her eyes glistened, and her lips quivered with sudden terror. "Ms. Byrd, please tell me Ellie is alive. The sheriff's department is involved, so it must be serious."

"I'll do everything I can to find her and bring her home."

Thomas's footsteps echoed as he climbed the stairs.

"If anything happened to Ellie..." Lizzie's stoic facade shattered before Chelsey. She'd blocked her fears for too long, and the dam burst. "I'll help any way I can."

"We'll find Ellie. I promise." Chelsey opened the door and checked the stairwell. The deputy's shadow crept up the stairs. "Is there another way out of here?"

"There's a second set of stairs through that door," she said, pointing toward a closed door at the opposite end of the hall. "But it leads to the back parking lot."

"That's fine. I'll contact you as soon as I hear anything."

When the door closed, Chelsey bolted for the exit.

"Chelsey?"

Too late.

She swiveled on her heels. Thomas stopped beside apartment seven, his aqua-colored eyes childlike and inquisitive.

"Hey, Thomas."

"Why are you...did you interview Ellie Fisher's roommate?"

"Yeah, I did."

He straightened his shoulders.

"We can't have a repeat of the LeVar Hopkins investigation." During the spring, Chelsey pursued LeVar when she suspected he'd murdered Erika Windrow. "If you have information about Ellie Fisher's disappearance, share it with me."

"I have nothing to share yet."

"Then why are you here?"

Chelsey adjusted her bag over her shoulder.

"Raven and I are looking into another case. A woman hired us to follow Damian Ramos."

"Who is Damian Ramos?"

"The woman's fiance. She suspected he was cheating on her and wanted her money." Thomas glared at Chelsey. "The woman is wealthy, and her first husband swindled her."

"All right, but what does this have to do with Ellie Fisher?"

"Raven caught Damian chatting up a girl at Benson's Barbells in Kane Grove. That girl turned out to be Ellie Fisher."

He widened his eyes.

"You're just telling us this now?"

"I phoned your office."

"But you didn't mention Damian."

Chelsey bit the corner of her mouth.

"I should go, Thomas."

As she turned down the hallway, his words followed her to the door.

"Don't hold back on me, Chelsey."

22

THURSDAY, JULY 16TH, 5:00 P.M.

Nothing overcame a stressful day like barbecue and good friends.

Thomas set the hamburgers and hot dogs beside the grill and watched Darren flip steaks.

"I told you I got a Porterhouse," Darren said, setting the tongs down to shake hands with Thomas.

"It's not a summer cookout without burgers and dogs."

"No arguments there, Deputy." Darren lifted his chin at Jack. The Siberian Husky pup sniffed around the picnic table and accepted pets from Naomi and Scout. "Won't he run away without a leash?"

"Jack is family now. He knows where home is."

"If you say so."

Thomas met Naomi's eyes across the table. Dressed in a black sundress with floral print, her hair tied back and showing off her natural, flawless complexion, she drew Thomas's attention. He glanced away and feigned interest in the Porterhouse.

"I caught that," said Darren. "There's something between you two. Go on, man. Talk to her. I'll handle the grilling."

"She's just my neighbor."

"Right."

Raven's Nissan Rogue pulled in front of the cabin with Serena in the passenger seat, the mother bright-eyed and looking ten years younger than she'd appeared when Thomas found her dying in her apartment after a heroin overdose. Serena's frail body had filled out. Her braided hair, which she wore like Raven, glowed with health. It had fallen out in clumps while she lay in the hospital bed. Darren's eyes narrowed when LeVar climbed out of the backseat. Thomas clamped his mouth shut. Until Darren gave LeVar a chance, he'd never trust the teenager.

Jack bounded to LeVar and stood on his hind legs, licking the teenager's face as Serena kept a healthy distance.

"It's cool, Ma," LeVar said. "He's friendly."

Serena set a sweet potato pie on the picnic table as Raven made introductions. Raven's sapphire nails matched the lake, and her jean miniskirt ended an inch above her knees. Whenever Raven moved, Darren followed the private investigator with his eyes. Thomas stifled a grin and made his way to the gathering, where he accepted a hug from Raven.

"Thank you so much for inviting my mother."

"I wouldn't have it any other way. Where's your partner in crime?"

Raven rolled her eyes.

"Chelsey couldn't come."

"Couldn't, or wouldn't?"

"Something tells me you already know the answer."

Thomas pulled Raven aside.

"I ran into Chelsey at Lizzie Todd's apartment this afternoon."

"Ellie Fisher's roommate?"

"Chelsey mentioned Damian Ramos. If this guy had anything to do with Ellie Fisher's disappearance, Wolf Lake Consulting needs to keep us in the loop."

"One hand washes the other, right?"

"I can't promise Sheriff Gray will extend you the same courtesy. But you can count on me."

Raven met his eyes and nodded.

"You have a deal, Deputy Shepherd."

When LeVar slapped Thomas on the back, Raven strode to the picnic area and joined the others.

"Speaking of dawgs, it's my man, Deputy Dog."

"How are you, LeVar? I haven't seen you in..." Thomas closed his eyes in mock concentration. "Almost twenty minutes."

"Miss me that much?"

"Right. Hey, I have a cooler full of drinks in the trunk. Help me carry it to the picnic table."

"I got you."

Ice, already melting in the July heat, sloshed inside the cooler as they set it beneath a leafy maple tree. From the corner of his eye, Thomas noticed Darren's wariness when he glanced at the former gang member.

"Thanks, LeVar. Tell me something. Is your sister seeing anyone?"

"You interested, playa'? Be careful with her. She's the killer in the family."

"Do me a favor."

"Sure thing."

"My buddy, Darren—he's the one flipping burgers and steaks. Introduce him to your sister."

"Don't they already know each other?"

"Not well. Your mission, should you choose to accept it, is to break the ice."

"You mean set them up."

"Just get them talking. Work your magic."

"*Aight.*"

When LeVar's eyes traveled to the state park ranger, Darren dropped his attention to the grill.

"He don't seem like he wants anything to do with me."

"He's standoffish until he meets people. Come on, LeVar. Play matchmaker."

"All right, Deputy Dog. If you say so." LeVar whistled at Raven, who shot him a *don't-mess-with-me* glare. "Raven, we got business to discuss."

Thomas sat across from Serena while Naomi set paper plates on the picnic table, weighting them down with utensils. Jack had made a new friend and wouldn't leave Serena's side.

"I'm Thomas," he said, reaching his hand across the table.

Serena took it.

"I remember you from the hospital, Deputy. You saved my life."

"The paramedics saved your life. I just made a phone call."

She laid a hand atop his.

"That's not how my son tells the story. Thank you for everything. Especially for giving LeVar a fresh start and a roof over his head."

"Your son is a special man. You should be proud."

"He'll have his GED before summer ends." Serena's eyes glassed over. "I'm the one who held him back all these years." She set her hands on the table and lifted her chin. "But I'm better every day, and I have my children to thank for it. And you, Deputy Shepherd."

"Call me Thomas, please. How are you feeling?"

She blew air out of her bottom lip.

"Some days, like a million bucks. Others, I'm wound tighter than a two-dollar watch. My daughter keeps me grounded, and I found Narcotics Anonymous meetings in Kane Grove."

At the grill, LeVar, Darren, and Raven chatted and laughed.

Now that Darren and Raven were talking, the state park ranger's stance on LeVar thawed.

"My boy grows every day," Serena said. "We just needed to get away from Harmon. Look at him. Three months ago, he ran the streets with Rev. Now, he's hanging out with law enforcement and talking about college classes."

Scout, who'd wheeled herself beside the trees to watch the boats float across the lake, returned to the table.

"You've met my neighbor, Scout?" Thomas asked Serena.

"Briefly," Serena said.

"Scout's a budding detective. Maybe even an FBI profiler. Tell Mrs. Hopkins how you catch criminals on the internet."

As Scout and Serena struck up a conversation, Darren and LeVar carried the steak, hamburgers, and hot dogs to the table. Raven slid beside her mother. Then Darren, wearing a permanent grin, sat next to Raven. They passed fruit salad, rolls, and meat around the table, the easy conversation flowing like fine wine. Moments like this made life worth living, Thomas thought, as he broke a piece of hot dog and tossed it to Jack.

"So," Darren said, giving LeVar an amused grin. "Tell us what it's really like living with Thomas."

LeVar set down his hamburger, finished chewing, and swallowed.

"He's not so bad for a cop. Though Scout and I need to teach him about hip-hop. He still thinks Kid 'n Play are a thing."

"That's not true," Thomas said, pointing his fork at LeVar. "Besides, there's no way I could rock a high-top fade with this hair."

Laughter rolled around the table.

"But seriously, I owe him more than I could ever repay. I've never been happier." For a moment, Thomas spotted a tear in LeVar's eye. The teenager wiped his forehead to conceal his emotion. "Dude even got me a job at the Broken Yolk."

Naomi sipped her Coke and said, "We love that place. Best coffee and donuts in the state."

"I didn't get you the job," Thomas said, giving LeVar a pointed look. "That was all you."

"Yeah, but you introduced me to Ruth. No way Mrs. Sims would have hired me, if you hadn't talked me up like I was running for mayor."

"How do you like working at the Broken Yolk?" Darren asked.

"I love it. But I won't be there much longer."

"Why is that?"

They all stared at LeVar now.

"You haven't heard? Ruth is closing shop. I didn't want to say anything. But that place is bleeding money."

Serena touched her mouth.

"I had no idea. That would be a travesty if the Broken Yolk went under."

"Some think gentrification doesn't occur in wealthy villages like Wolf Lake," Raven said, glancing around the table. "But that's what's happening to Ruth Sims. Young, wealthy businesses are running the Ma and Pa shops out of town."

"Many are chains," Darren said, drawing a nod from Raven. "They lower prices to steal customers from established businesses. Then, after the older restaurants close, they jack the prices up. Pretty soon only the rich, mobile types can afford to eat in the village."

Naomi glanced at LeVar and said, "There must be something we can do to help."

"Y'all know Ruth. She don't want nobody's help. Thinks she can do it all on her own."

"I wrote strategic plans for small businesses while I lived in Ithaca. If Ruth would let me help, I'd love to speak with her."

"Good luck. Unless she knows you, she won't open up."

"We'll go together," Thomas said.

Darren winked at Thomas, the corner of his mouth lifting into a grin.

After they finished dinner, Serena cut into the sweet potato pie and passed slices around the table. Though Thomas was stuffed, he couldn't resist the aroma.

Between bites, Darren said, "I heard the sheriff's department is taking a second look at the Lincoln Ramsey case. Is it related to Cecilia Bond?"

Thomas set his fork down. He'd hoped the investigations wouldn't come up over dinner.

"We're not taking anything for granted."

"But Lincoln Ramsey had COPD," Naomi said.

"And Cecilia Bond suffered from advanced kidney disease."

"Why would someone murder Mr. Ramsey? Everyone loved him."

"Not everyone." Thomas wiped his mouth on a napkin. "But I can't speak about the case. We're still investigating."

They nodded, the tone suddenly somber.

"Perhaps someone murdered Mr. Ramsey and Mrs. Bond to put them out of their misery," Scout said as she swiped through her phone.

"What did you say?" Naomi asked, her eyes incredulous.

"Run a Google search for angel of mercy serial killers. There was an article about them on the Virtual Searchers website last month." When her mother glared at her for an explanation, Scout set her phone in her lap. "Some serial killers believe they're saving their victims from a lifetime of suffering. Others claim they're doing God's work. Not that it makes them less guilty. I'm just explaining their motivations."

Thomas set his chin on his fists and studied Scout across the table. The theory made sense. Yes, this girl had a future in law enforcement...if her mother didn't lock Scout's computer inside a safe. Naomi was already scared her daughter would venture down another dark path, as she had during the Jeremy Hyde case.

"On that happy note," Raven said, cutting through the sweet potato pie. "Who wants more dessert?"

23

Sweat trickled down Thomas's forehead. Half the village packed St. Mary's church. His hand kept migrating to his collar to loosen his tie. Beside him, his mother knelt upon the hassock, her chin lifted in a stately manner, as if she prepared to address the congregation. Last light arrowed through the stained glass and reflected on her skin. A line extended from the rear of the church to the altar where Father Fowler gave communion.

"You don't believe any of this, do you?" Lindsey Shepherd uttered from the corner of her mouth.

Thomas blinked and adjusted his knees on the hassock, his legs cramping.

"What?"

"God, the devil, eternal life in heaven. You never believed."

Thomas lowered his gaze to the pew's woodgrain.

"I have my doubts." When she pursed her lips, he went silent for a moment. "What about you? Do you believe there's a god above us, watching over and protecting us?"

"The things you've seen, I wouldn't blame you for losing faith."

Her words left him speechless. He turned to her. She faced forward, her eyes locked on the elderly sisters taking communion.

"Their faith is strong," Lindsey said, nodding at the sisters.

"Why are we here, Mother?"

She didn't answer.

A crowd blocked the exit when mass concluded. Lindsey slipped the pamphlet into her purse, then checked her lipstick in a mirror.

"Sit and be patient," she said. "You were always so fidgety."

Thomas lowered himself to the pew and clasped his hands in his lap. Now that the crowd had thinned, he could breathe again. Had the crowd stolen his breath, or was he claustrophobic?

"How was your *cookout*?" she asked, twisting her mouth as though the word tasted bitter.

"We enjoyed ourselves," he said, trying to picture his parents among his friends, passing burgers and steak around the table, and failing. "You're welcome to join us another time."

"Why? We have food at our house, and I've seen the lake before. I don't understand why people worship a body of water. A glacier melts, and lemmings flock to the shore, as if gathering to witness a divine proclamation."

"Give it a chance. You might enjoy yourself."

She sniffed.

An uncomfortable moment followed in which they had nothing to talk about. A restless child raced among the pews as his father grinned and the mother shot stern looks. Thomas shifted to Lindsey.

"I figured you'd slap the company prospectus on the pew and sell me on Shepherd Systems again."

"Don't make light of our offer, Thomas. Shepherd Systems had its most profitable quarter in company history, and our client list grows by the day. You'd be set for life, and you'd uphold your father's legacy. And last I checked, none of our officers were shot in the back by dissatisfied clients."

Her words stung. They sat in silence as the crowd filtered through the two doors, Thomas wondering why they didn't open the side exits and provide an efficient method for exiting.

"I shouldn't criticize your career choice," she said, surprising him. "We may not show it sometimes. But we're proud of all you've accomplished."

He turned to her. She sat ramrod straight in the pew, her eyes fixed on the empty altar, as though expecting something miraculous to occur.

"Then why go behind my back and coerce Sheriff Gray to cut my position?"

"The company will crumble without a Shepherd at the helm, and I'm too old to take over. This is about the future. The company's and yours."

Most of the crowd had filed past the exit. The church seemed cavernous now, every noise echoing off the ceiling.

"Ready to leave?"

"Just a moment."

It wasn't until then Thomas noticed her lips moving without sound, her eyes clamped shut, brow creased. She was praying. When Lindsey opened her eyes, her body released its perpetual tension.

"Now I'm ready."

Their footfalls sounded like distant bombs as they padded toward the exit. Inside the vestibule, Thomas spotted a glass jar centered on an ornate table. The glass container was a third full with folded notes. Lindsey paused beside the jar and reached inside her purse. Then she shook her head and strode toward the exit. A photocopied announcement lay beside the jar. The church was holding a memorial service for Cecilia Bond this Saturday.

Father Fowler greeted them on the way out the doors. He grasped Lindsey's hand. How many hands had Fowler shook? Thomas searched inside his pocket for hand sanitizer and found none. His heart pounded. He was the next in line, and this amped his anxiety.

"Thank you for coming, Deputy Shepherd," Fowler said, clasping his hands over Thomas's.

In his late-fifties, Fowler's hair remained jet black. Darkness perched below the sharp ridge of his eyes. The man possessed a powerful grip.

"You know my name?"

"I make it a point to learn the name of anyone who comes through these doors." He shook his pointer finger at Thomas. "But in your case, it was easy. You're a celebrity around these parts, Deputy."

"I didn't realize I—"

"You caught that horrible man last April. Were it not for you, the village wouldn't be safe." He narrowed his eyes at Thomas. "Yet I've never seen you inside my church until this evening. You'll come back, yes? It's good to let God into your heart."

A commotion pulled Fowler's attention. Thomas stepped out of line and glanced at the crowd gathered on the sidewalk. A woman shook her head, sobbing, as a couple struggled to console her. Thomas recognized her. Kay Ramsey. His eyes stopped on two faces in the crowd. Garrick Tillery and his wife, Suzanne.

"No, I don't want to live anymore," Kay said, pulling away from the couple.

"Don't say that," the other woman pleaded.

"I can't live without him. Lincoln was my life."

Kay whirled around, almost knocking the woman to the ground. More people rushed to help.

"She shouldn't drive in her condition," someone said. "Don't let her into the car until she calms down."

"Excuse me," Fowler said.

The priest descended the steps, his robes fanning out behind him. He looked almost mythical. When he converged on Kay Ramsey, his frame dwarfed the woman.

Thomas considered following. This morning, he sat inside Kay's living room. He wanted to help the woman. Indecision bonded him to the concrete below his feet. Fowler snapped his fingers, and a tall woman with a sharp nose came to his side to help. Together, they ushered her inside the church.

"Everything is under control," Father Fowler said over his shoulder. "We'll see to Mrs. Ramsey."

"I can't watch this," Lindsey said, turning away.

Before Thomas could react, Lindsey turned on her heels and hurried to the parking lot. Thomas rushed to catch up. When he reached Lindsey outside her Volvo, tears had cut dark streaks through her makeup, and the blood had drained from her face.

"What's wrong, Mother?"

Her hand trembled as she pulled the keys from her purse. Thomas closed his hand over the keys and held her shoulders. Her head fell back, eyes peering up at the coming night as dusk bled across the sky. She'd glimpsed her future in Kay Ramsey, and it was bleak and horrific.

"I must get home to Mason," she said, closing her eyes. "Your father shouldn't be alone. It was a mistake to bring you here, Thomas. I apologize."

"Stay and talk, Mother."

"About what? About lung cancer? Or about the business your father built, shriveling to dust the moment he passes?"

"I want to help."

"We'll figure it out, your father and I."

The door slammed, and the engine rumbled. Thomas watched the Volvo drive into the spreading darkness.

24

D r. Mandal's office smells of incense today. Patchouli with a hint of wood smoke, like a new age cabin on a January morning. She taps her pen against her pad as she studies Thomas, and her vision penetrates deeper than Thomas can dig.

"I had the dream again last night," he says, scratching his arm and watching the sweet smoke curl off the stick and plume toward the ceiling.

She nods and sets the pad in her lap.

"Would you like to talk about it?"

"I'm on an island. Not sure where. Somewhere warm. There's a palm tree in the middle of the island, taller than all the others."

"What do you do?"

"I climb the tree and shimmy up the trunk. Maybe because I'm searching for a way off the island. But I doubt it, because I'm in no rush to leave. The higher I go, the further away the top seems. When I look down, the beach is a hundred yards below and fading fast. The air is thinner here. Helps my sinuses. That's when I spot the tree house at the top of the palm."

Mandal blinks and writes something on her notepad.

"Go on."

Thomas runs a hand over the two-day scruff along his cheeks.

"So I keep climbing, because I want to make it to that tree house, no matter how high I need to go. I'm not afraid to fall, just determined to see what's inside."

"Do you reach the tree house?"

He bobs his head.

"It's the size of a family home when I climb inside. That makes zero sense, right?"

"Tell me about the tree house."

"Windows surround each side. Clouds float past the glass, like translucent pieces of cotton I can touch if I open the windows. I'm too far up to see the island, only the ocean. It's placid, no waves. Running water, electricity. A ceiling fan spills cool air over my face."

"Sounds peaceful."

"It is."

"How does the house make you feel, Thomas?"

His eyes crease in consideration.

"Safe."

"Why do you think you're safe inside the tree house?"

"Because nobody can hurt me there."

Mandal tilts her head.

"Who wants to hurt you, Thomas?"

A vein pulses in his neck.

"People are good to me."

"But inside, a part of you believes people want to hurt you. Like the gangster who shot you in the back. And Jeremy Hyde. You stopped Hyde from harming anyone else, and the LA gangs are on the other side of the country."

"You're right."

"What about the woman you mentioned when you began therapy? Your former girlfriend, the private investigator."

"Chelsey," *he says, and the name rolls off his lips and drifts toward the ceiling with the incense smoke.*

"That was a long time ago, Thomas. Don't blame her for the mistakes she made as a teenager. Major depression is crippling. We should admire her for putting her life together."

"I do admire her."

"But you want more. You want her by your side again."

Thomas shrugs.

"I can't force her to feel the same as I do."

"What about your parents? It must hurt you that they're forcing you to take over Shepherd Systems and lobbying the sheriff to fire you."

Thomas sets his chin on his fist and stares at the carpet.

"Did it ever occur to you they're worried? They're trying to protect their only son, Thomas, not ruin your life."

"Why are you taking their side?"

"I'm not taking sides. You should work in the field of your choice, and I wouldn't want you to live your life for anyone else. But picture things from their perspective. While I consider you strong and independent, you'll always be their child."

"Being on the spectrum doesn't make me helpless."

"If it had, you wouldn't have advanced to detective for the LAPD. Or caught a serial killer and protected your neighbors. But if you ran Shepherd Systems, you'd insulate yourself from the horrors law enforcement officers face every day."

"So you want me to quit my job and run the family business?"

"No, Thomas. That's what your parents want. But what is it you want?"

WHEN THOMAS and Aguilar entered the First National Bank of Harmon Friday morning, customers queued in the lobby to make transactions. The college age female greeter pointed them toward Earl Horton's office at the rear of the bank.

Dressed in a silver-gray suit, Horton shook their hands and gestured at the two chairs in front of his desk.

"I still can't accept Lincoln is gone," Horton said, his eyes wandering to a photograph on his desk. "I look at this picture every day. We hiked the Adirondacks every fall. We were young then. Doubt my knees could hold up these days."

"Mr. Horton, two years ago, a man came into the bank and got into a shouting match with Lincoln Ramsey. Something about a loan."

Horton tossed his pen aside and leaned back in his chair, hands clasped over his belly.

"I'll never forget. Carl Middleton. The bastard runs Middleton Construction. Middleton needed a small business loan. But the bottom lines were all red on Middleton Construction's financial statements. Lincoln came to me and asked if there was anything we could do. He wanted to help Middleton. The man didn't have the assets, and the company wasn't profitable. Had Middleton asked for less, we might have helped. We couldn't justify the risk."

"Middleton Construction still exists," said Aguilar. "I came across their sign during the spring. They replaced a roof in my neighborhood."

"Middleton scrounged enough money to keep his business afloat. Then we had a mini-economic boom in Wolf Lake, and the construction companies benefited from new money flowing into the village."

"Did Carl Middleton threaten Lincoln Ramsey?" asked Thomas.

"He promised he'd make Lincoln's life miserable, that he'd tell everyone Lincoln ruined his business. But you don't have to take my word for it." Horton typed at his terminal and spun his monitor around. "He's all over social media and on chat forums, running down Lincoln and saying the bank cheated him."

Thomas copied the website addresses.

"Are you aware someone broke the Ramsey's window two years ago?"

"I knew," Horton said, sitting back and lowering his eyes. "Lincoln had just begun to deteriorate. Anyone who'd cause trouble in the middle of a health crisis is a monster."

"Did Carl Middleton throw the brick?"

"I'm positive he did."

"Why?"

"Because he's out of control and has no respect for others. A couple weeks after the blowup with the loan, Carl Middleton waited for us in the parking lot. He tried to egg us on, wanted Lincoln to fight him. Middleton is a petulant child in a man's body."

"Did the encounter turn physical?"

"We walked away. I followed Lincoln home, just to be safe. Carl Middleton hated Lincoln with every fiber in his body. The crazy part is, he lucked into an economic upturn and saved thousands in finance fees by not taking a loan. He should thank us, not hold a petty grudge."

"Were there other incidences?"

Horton squinted and glanced toward the ceiling.

"Yes. An incident in the parking lot after church."

"St. Mary's church?"

"That's right. How did you know?"

"Lucky guess," Thomas said, glancing at Aguilar.

"There was a fender bender. Middleton tailgated Lincoln and Kay, probably to intimidate them. Lincoln stopped for traffic, and Middleton ran his pickup into their bumper. The incident ended with a lot of yelling and finger pointing. I don't believe Middleton was ticketed, and I'm certain Lincoln didn't charge him. He just wanted Carl Middleton out of his life."

Aguilar edged her chair forward and asked, "Does Middleton still hold a grudge?"

"I'm certain he does. A man like Carl Middleton never lets go. He's probably dancing on Lincoln's grave now."

Thomas cruised out of the parking lot with Aguilar riding shotgun.

"What's our next move?"

Aguilar lowered the window and released the stored heat.

"We should speak to Carl Middleton. I have a hard time believing he murdered Lincoln Ramsey over a loan. But I lose faith in society every day."

As Thomas took the exit for the highway, his mind wandered back to Horton's words. Carl Middleton attended St. Mary's church, as did Lincoln Ramsey and Cecilia Bond. And that got him thinking about Scout and angel of mercy killers. Had a stressor in Carl Middleton's life pushed him over the edge? Or was Gray right about Father Fowler?

25

FRIDAY, JULY 17TH, 11:15 A.M.

As Thomas motored into Wolf Lake, Aguilar radioed Lambert and had the deputy set up an interview with Carl Middleton. Middleton Construction was on a roofing job in Kane Grove. Carl agreed to come in after lunch.

On their way to the station, they stopped at the Broken Yolk. LeVar worked behind the counter with Ruth Sims in the back, baking a fresh batch of donuts. Thomas scanned the seats. They were the shop's only customers.

"See what I mean?" LeVar asked, keeping his voice low so Ruth wouldn't hear.

"Naomi will talk to her."

"You better hurry. She can't pay her bills if this continues."

Thomas lifted his voice.

"I'll take a blackberry pie, a dozen glazed donuts, and two coffees."

"I'm on it."

Aguilar elbowed Thomas as LeVar bagged the donuts.

"Who do you expect to eat all this junk food?"

"Between Gray, Lambert, and me, the donuts will disappear before four o'clock."

"You're all piggies."

"Ease up, Aguilar. You need to enjoy life now and then."

"I enjoy life. I also enjoy being able to see my feet when I button my pants."

LeVar set the bag and coffees on the counter. After he boxed the pie and rang their order, Thomas held up a hand.

"The pie isn't for me."

"*Aight.* Whatcha want me to do with it?"

"Bring it to your mother. And tell her she's welcome at my house anytime."

"Cool. She loves blackberry pie."

Footsteps shuffled behind the closed door. Thomas didn't want Ruth to know he was keeping her business afloat.

"That's my cue to go. If Ruth asks who bought the donuts, tell her it was..."

"I got it covered."

"Thanks, LeVar. See you at the house."

Gray and Lambert trailed Thomas into the break room like ravenous dogs. No sooner did Thomas open the bag than Lambert snagged a glazed donut and hurried back to his desk.

"Told you the donuts wouldn't last," Thomas said, smirking at Aguilar.

Palming a donut, Gray leaned against the counter.

"Give me the rundown on Carl Middleton."

Thomas repeated Earl Horton's story as Aguilar returned to her desk.

"That's one hell of an escalation," Gray said, brushing glaze off his hands. "Killing someone over a loan from two years ago."

"I don't remember Carl Middleton from school."

"He moved to Wolf Lake from Kane Grove around the time you left for Los Angeles. He's nothing but trouble. I ticketed him for doing fifty in a thirty-five last year. He's a regular at Hattie's."

"Like Garrick Tillery."

"They're friends. Tillery worked for Middleton Construction four, maybe five years ago."

"Something happen that got Tillery fired?"

"Tillery can't hold a job. If he's not hungover at work, he's dreaming of a different job."

Ten minutes after one o'clock, a 4x4 with Middleton Construction emblazoned along the sides pulled into the parking lot. Carl Middleton had a crooked nose that had broken at least twice, auburn curly hair receding up his forehead, and beady, conspiratorial eyes. Middleton's bass-heavy voice rattled the walls.

"Tell the sheriff I don't have all day," he said from the lobby.

Thomas found Middleton leaning over Maggie with his palms set on the desk. He glanced at Thomas.

"Who are you?"

"I'm Deputy Shepherd."

"Where the hell is Gray?"

"I'm conducting the interview with Deputy Aguilar. If you'll follow me."

Maggie glanced at Thomas as if to say, "Thank you for getting that ape off my desk."

Middleton scanned the office as he followed Thomas to the interview room, where Aguilar waited.

"I have a roofing project to complete by the end of next week. You got thirty minutes, then I'm out the door."

"We appreciate you taking time out of your busy day, Mr. Middleton."

"Well, some of us work for a living. Looks like you guys sit around all day with your feet on the desk."

Thomas gestured at the open chair across from Aguilar. Middleton glared at the deputies as he pulled the chair out.

"Can I get you something to drink? Cold water?" Thomas asked, using Gray's playbook.

"Don't waste my time. Whatever you need to ask, get on with it."

Aguilar opened a notepad and said, "Two years ago, the First National Bank in Harmon turned you down for a small business loan. Is that correct?"

"Yeah. Did I come all the way down here so you can rub salt in my wounds?"

"I take it the loan was important to your business."

"I almost lost Middleton Construction. Those two pricks, Lincoln Ramsey and Earl Horton, turned me down over some bullshit excuse. Claimed Middleton Construction was in the red. Does it look like I'm losing money?"

Middleton lifted his arm and displayed the Rolex around his wrist.

"Shortly after the bank turned down your loan, you encountered Mr. Ramsey and Mr. Horton in the parking lot."

"Is that what Horton told you? He's full of shit. I went down there to fight for my loan, and they refused to meet with me. So I followed them to the parking lot and stated my case. Nothing more came of it."

Thomas shuffled his papers.

"You rear-ended Lincoln Ramsey's car in the St. Mary's church parking lot."

Middleton sat back and laughed up at the florescent lights.

"Don't pin that on me. Yeah, we attend the same church, and I was following too close. But I was in a rush and had to remodel a kitchen in Wolf Lake. The jerk waited until traffic cleared, stepped on the gas, then hit his brakes."

"So he wanted you to hit his bumper."

"That's what I'm saying. Lincoln Ramsey set me up and caused the accident."

"Witnesses claim you got into an argument with Lincoln and Kay Ramsey in the parking lot."

Middleton crossed his arms.

"Ramsey started the fight. I tried to walk away. But he kept throwing insults, saying no one would give me a loan, and he hoped my business folded. So I yelled back. Anyone would have done the same. Just because he was a bank manager didn't give him the right to talk down to me." Noticing the flat stares from across the desk, Middleton pounded a fist on the table. "Don't believe me? Ask Father Fowler. He saw the altercation and will tell you Lincoln Ramsey was out of his mind."

"Two winters ago, someone tossed a brick through Lincoln Ramsey's window."

Middleton's grin displayed his teeth.

"I heard about that. Lincoln and his bitch wife got what was coming to them."

"How's that, Mr. Middleton?"

"You think I'm the only person Lincoln Ramsey cheated out of a loan? Half the village wanted that prick dead."

Aguilar's eyes hardened.

"Is that what you wanted, Mr. Middleton? You wanted that prick, as you call him, dead?"

The smile fell from Middleton's face. He pointed at Aguilar.

"Don't put words in my mouth. Lincoln Ramsey and I had our problems. But I moved on. If he burned more bridges, and the smoke blew back in his face, that was his fault."

"Where were you Sunday night between the hours of eight and ten o'clock?"

"Why?"

"Answer the question, Mr. Middleton."

He narrowed his eyes. After a moment of thought, he slapped the table.

"I see what this is about. That's when the prick died. Yeah, I read his obituary." When the deputies didn't respond, Middleton shook his head. "I was home, watching a movie."

"Can anyone corroborate your whereabouts?"

"I'm divorced."

"So that's a no?"

"Look, I didn't kill Lincoln Ramsey. Besides, didn't the newspapers say he died from emphysema or COPD?"

"Lincoln Ramsey suffered from COPD," Aguilar said.

"Then that's what killed him."

"Perhaps."

Middleton checked his watch.

"Well, your time is up, deputies."

"Just a moment, Mr. Middleton," Thomas said, scanning his notes as Middleton released a frustrated breath. "Where were you Tuesday evening between six and eight o'clock?"

"Tuesday? I thought the newspaper said Ramsey died Sunday evening."

"You're friends with Garrick Tillery."

The man moved his eyes from Aguilar to Thomas.

"What's this about?"

"Garrick Tillery fished at the river Tuesday evening. Around the same time, Cecilia Bond's body ended up dead in the water. Did you accompany your friend, Mr. Tillery, to the river?"

"This interview is done. You'll direct future questions through my lawyer."

Middleton stormed from the office.

"Where are you going?" Aguilar asked when Thomas stood.

"To make a phone call."

At his desk, Thomas scrolled through his internet browser and located the phone number for St. Mary's church.

"St. Mary's church. How may I help you?" the woman asked.

"Father Fowler, if he's in."

"May I tell him who's calling?"

"Deputy Shepherd from the Nightshade County Sheriff's Department."

Five seconds of silence followed.

"Please hold."

Thomas sifted through Carl Middleton's statement while he waited. Fowler answered his call a minute later.

"Deputy Shepherd, to what do I owe this unexpected pleasure?"

"Forgive me for bringing this up now. I need information about an altercation you witnessed between Carl Middleton and Lincoln Ramsey."

"Is that why you called, Deputy Shepherd. Is this an interrogation?"

A chuckle escaped Fowler's throat and broke the tension.

"I understand Middleton rammed his truck into Ramsey's bumper on the way out of your parking lot."

"Yes, and an argument ensued. An ugly moment for all of us. It seems awfully late for either party to press charges over a fender bender."

"Carl Middleton claims Lincoln Ramsey turned belligerent."

"That's not the way I remember it," Fowler said, lowering his voice. "Mr. Middleton threatened Mr. Ramsey. Had I not intervened, I shudder to imagine how far he might have gone."

"So Carl Middleton lied about Lincoln Ramsey causing the fight."

"Mr. Middleton is to blame. And for that reason, he's no longer welcome inside my church."

"Yet God forgives all."

Fowler cleared his throat.

"God does. But I do not."

"You're quiet today."

Raven glanced around her monitor at Chelsey, who clicked her mouse and released frustrated groans every few minutes.

"Just trying to catch up. I wasted yesterday afternoon and evening chasing after Damian Ramos."

Raven sipped from her water bottle and set it on the desk. She'd offered to follow Damian. But Chelsey insisted.

"What did you learn?"

"Nothing. Damian didn't show up at the gym, and his car wasn't at his house. I backtracked to the trading firm in Syracuse, cruised past Ellie Fisher's apartment, and gave up after sunset. Something tells me he's on to us and gave me the slip."

"So what did you do with the rest of your night?"

Chelsey narrowed her eyes.

"Nothing. Why are you so interested in what I do after work?"

Raven swallowed an argument. When Chelsey came into work in a difficult mood, there was no chance of knocking her out of it. It was clear what this was about.

"You could have come to the party. Everyone asked about you."

"Like I said, I spent the day searching for Damian Ramos. I don't have time for parties and cake, and whatever else."

"First, we ate sweet potato pie for dessert, and it rocked. Second, if you want to avoid people and sulk because you're alone—"

"I'm not sulking."

"You kinda are."

The door opened and Chelsey pulled her mouth tight.

"We can't take on another client. I'm swamped."

"I'll see who it is."

"No, I'll get the door. You keep doing...whatever it is you're doing."

Raven tugged her braid and promised herself she wouldn't smack the attitude out of Chelsey's mouth after the visitor left. She eyed the clock. Almost noon. Today was the perfect day to drive home and eat lunch with her mother. Either that or spy on Damian at the trading firm. Anything sounded better than spending another hour in the office.

When Chelsey returned, she folded her arms and said, "You have a visitor."

Darren Holt followed Chelsey into the office. He wore blue jeans and a navy blue Syracuse PD t-shirt that showed off his arms. He held a paper bag in his hand, and Raven whiffed lettuce and onions.

"Darren, what are you doing here?"

"Hope you don't mind. I was driving through the village and thought you might want lunch."

He brought her lunch? A flutter moved through her heart. Across the room, Chelsey hid behind her computer and typed far too hard on the keyboard.

"Wow. You didn't have to do that."

"Yesterday, you mentioned getting together for lunch sometime, so I figured today was as good a day as any."

"That's very thoughtful." She reached for her wallet. "How much did it come to?"

"Put your money away," he said, holding up a hand. "My treat."

"Well, thank you. We have a kitchen down the hall, if you want to eat where it's quiet."

"No, stay," Chelsey grumbled. "You don't have to leave on my account."

"I brought an extra sub," Darren said, glancing at Chelsey.

"No thanks. I have a yogurt."

"You sure?"

"Yeah, yogurt is my life."

Darren scratched his head and turned to Raven.

"You do like subs, I hope."

"Yum. What kind did you get?"

"One roast beef, one turkey, and a veggie sub. I, uh, wasn't sure which you'd prefer."

"All three are fine. But I could go for turkey."

"Turkey, it is. And I'll take the roast beef. You said something about a kitchen?"

"Stay here. I'll grab plates."

He handed her the bag.

"Put the veggie sub in the refrigerator," said Darren. He nodded at Chelsey. "If you change your mind, feel free."

Chelsey grunted something indecipherable.

Raven boosted herself onto the counter to reach the top shelf. Her heart pounded as she rummaged through the cupboards for plates. Ever since LeVar got Darren and Raven talking, she couldn't get the state park ranger out of her mind. She grabbed two sodas from the refrigerator, closed the door, and muttered to herself. She yanked the door open again and snagged a third soda. Inside the office, she set the extra soda on Chelsey's desk. Her boss swiveled her eyes to the can.

"Thanks," Chelsey said under her breath.

Raven gave her a love tap on the shoulder.

"Brighten up, sunshine."

The sandwich tasted wonderful and sure beat the salad she would have built at home. Still, she worried about her mother alone in the house. She couldn't call LeVar to check on her. Her brother worked this afternoon at the Broken Yolk.

Darren gazed around the room.

"I always wondered what it was like to work at a private investigation firm."

Raven chewed her sandwich and dabbed her mouth with a napkin.

"Considering a career change?"

"I'm happy at the state park. Peaceful days, no one staring over my shoulder, and good company."

He met her eyes, and she felt her face flush.

"I enjoy hanging out with good company."

"How's business?"

"We can't keep up," Raven said, glancing toward Chelsey. Her boss was too immersed to reply. "One case after another."

"What are you working on today?"

Raven sipped her soda.

"An infidelity case, but it's turning into something larger."

"Oh?"

"A client hired us to monitor her fiance, Damian Ramos. The guy is young enough to be her kid."

"That's always a bad sign."

"I caught him flirting with a cute blonde at Benson's Barbells in Kane Grove. You know the place?"

"I've heard of it."

"The girl turned out to be Ellie Fisher, from Wolf Lake."

Darren's forehead creased.

"Why do I know that name?"

"She's the girl on the news who went missing."

Chelsey glared at Raven through the tops of her eyes. Whatever goodwill Raven earned by offering her boss a soda flew out the window when she talked shop with Darren.

"Wow. Did this Damian Ramos character kidnap Ellie Fisher?"

"That's what we're trying to find out."

"I trust you're keeping the sheriff's department in the loop."

Raven looked at Chelsey. Her boss shoved her chair back and stomped toward the kitchen.

"Was it something I said?" Darren asked.

"Don't worry about her. She's in one of her moods."

"Sorry. I spoke to Thomas this morning. The cookout was such an enormous success, he wants to have one every week, at least while the pleasant weather lasts. He's hosting next week. We should invite Chelsey to the grill-fest."

Raven bit her lip.

"That's the last thing we should suggest." Raven leaned toward Darren and lowered her voice. "Chelsey and Thomas won't acknowledge their history together. They're still hung up on each other. But neither will admit it." She blew out a frustrated breath. "If I had my way, I'd lock them in a room and force them to talk."

"You're sure Thomas still has feelings for Chelsey? He's getting pretty chummy with his neighbor."

"Naomi Mourning?"

"You bet."

"Wow. That happened fast. I mentioned Naomi and Scout the other day, and Chelsey got sullen."

"You mean she's not always this way?"

"She's fun to be around. Most of the time."

Raven coughed into her hand when Chelsey returned to the room. Darren leaned back in his chair.

"What will you do about Damian Ramos?"

"Follow him from work, see what he's up to when he's off the clock. Flirting isn't cheating, and we can't prove he had anything to do with Ellie Fisher going missing. But if he's guilty, I'll nail him to the wall."

"You shouldn't spy on Damian alone. There's no telling if the guy is dangerous."

"I'm good at not being seen."

Darren gave her an unconvinced grunt. She wished he'd offer to accompany her. But she didn't expect Darren to abandon his post at the state park, and she barely knew the man. He finished his sandwich, crumpled the wrapper, and tossed it into the garbage.

"Be careful."

"I promise."

"Text me after you arrive. It's a smart idea to share your position with people, just in case the surveillance mission goes south."

"Roger that."

"I'm serious."

"So am I."

He brushed his hair back.

"We should do this again. Lunch, I mean."

"Maybe next time I'll drive to the park," Raven said. Chelsey didn't look up. "Anyway, I can't thank you enough for bringing me lunch. I'll call you later, okay?"

"I'll be around. Just me, three families camping, and a few dozen squirrels." He stopped in the doorway. "Nice to see you again, Chelsey."

"You, too," said Chelsey.

Raven rolled her eyes over the half-hearted reply.

A part of her wanted to take the afternoon off and spend the day at the park with Darren. And it wasn't only to avoid Chelsey's mood swings. Something about Damian Ramos made her flesh crawl. Like waking at midnight and finding a scorpion on the pillow.

"**A**re you sure about this? I don't want to offend her," said Naomi as she opened the truck door.

Thomas helped Naomi down from the cab. He'd parked the F-150 a block from the Broken Yolk where shoppers enjoying their lunch hours hustled through the village, the afternoon straight out of a Norman Rockwell painting.

"Ruth will be more offended, if we don't offer to help and she loses her shop. You have ideas for turning her business around?"

"They're all up here," Naomi said, tapping a finger against her head.

A nervous tremor rolled through her body.

"You'll do great."

"There's so much on the line. The Broken Yolk means a lot to you and the community."

Naomi's orange and yellow dress fluttered around her shins like liquid sunshine. She held the bonnet to her head when a gust of wind whipped along the sidewalk. A bell rang when Thomas pushed the door open. LeVar glanced up from behind the counter and raised his thumb.

"Ruth is in the back. I'll tell her you're here."

Thomas surveyed the shop. As was the case this morning, they were the only guests. Sweet confectionery scents hung in the air, and rows of donuts awaited customers behind glass. Ruth emerged from the back room and wiped her hands on her apron.

"Ruth Sims, this is my neighbor, Naomi Mourning."

The shopkeeper offered her hand hesitantly.

"Nice to meet you. Is this really necessary?"

Thomas set a hand on Ruth's shoulder.

"Are you ready to retire?"

She brushed flour off her apron.

"Well, no."

"Then listen to what we have to say. Please."

"I guess you're right. I can't close my eyes and hope the shop will survive until winter."

"Naomi worked with small businesses while she lived in Ithaca. She has great ideas for keeping the Broken Yolk solvent."

Ruth gave each of them a doubtful glance, then she lifted her hands.

"What do I have to lose?"

They chose a table in the back. Naomi slid into the chair beside Thomas while Ruth sat across from them.

"Let's begin with your strengths and build off them," said Naomi.

Ruth motioned at the empty seats and lack of customers.

"What strengths? I offer nothing the competition can't beat me at."

"That's not true. Thomas, who makes the best donuts in Nightshade County?"

"That would be Ruth Sims at the Broken Yolk. I worked in California for a decade and never ate a donut or drank a coffee that compared to what I get here."

"Ruth, would you give me your donut recipe?"

Ruth placed a hand over her heart.

"You want my recipe? I'm sorry, but I can't do that."

"Why not?"

"Because it's a family secret."

"That's where we should start. Your donuts are homemade, and nobody else has the recipe. Anyone who's eaten here will vouch for their originality and tastiness. You need to put that front and center in the window. Or write it on a sign and hang it behind the wall. When someone visits the Broken Yolk, they're enjoying an experience they can't get anywhere else."

"Okay, but I'm not sure it will make a difference. What else?"

"The cafe on Main Street is fair trade, and the younger crowd flocks there for coffee and pastries."

Ruth scowled.

"I bought a pastry from them last spring. It wasn't nearly as good as I'd been led to believe."

"It doesn't hold a candle to yours. But fair trade means a lot to young adults."

"The Broken Yolk has always paid fair prices to its suppliers. We source our ingredients from local farms."

"Then you qualify for certification. Apply. Once the Broken Yolk is certified, let everyone know you run a fair trade business that supports the local economy."

The light returned to Ruth's eyes, and she nodded along with Naomi's ideas.

"All right. Is there anything else I can do?"

"Get younger. A lot younger."

"What do you mean?"

"Your loyal customers are over fifty, and many are much older than that. When they leave the area, you don't replace them with new customers."

"I can't attract youth to the Broken Yolk. They come in once, buy a decaf to go, and never return."

"We can do something about that. Play music over the speakers. Something modern they would enjoy relaxing to."

"I listen to Sinatra and easy listening songs from the seventies. I know nothing about new music."

"But LeVar does," Naomi said, waving to the teenager.

"What did I do?" LeVar asked.

"Nothing, we're throwing around ideas for music to play over the speakers. But no hardcore rap."

LeVar raised his hands.

"You think Imma suggest gangster rap for a cafe?"

"You also need Wi-Fi," Naomi said, turning back to Ruth. "Give people a reason to visit, even if they're not hungry. They need comfortable seats and larger tables. Allow them to spread out with their computers and iPads and phones. Let them study, read, and call the Broken Yolk home."

"What if they come for the Wi-Fi and don't eat?"

Naomi inhaled and closed her eyes.

"Ruth, it's impossible to visit the Broken Yolk and not eat. Just get them in the door. Your baking is all the magic you need."

Ruth sat back in her chair. Thomas could see the possibilities brimming in her eyes.

"These ideas of yours might just work." She rubbed her chin and pointed at the open wall beside the register. "I could place a book shelf along the wall and fill it with reading material."

"Now you're getting the right idea."

"But how do I attract young people?"

"I suggest starting at the community college," Thomas said. "Print out menus and hang them on the walls around campus. LeVar is there three days a week. I'm sure he could drop the pamphlets off for you."

"Just say the word, Deputy Dog," LeVar said, wiping down the counter.

"That's a terrific idea," Naomi said. "Once you attract a few, word of mouth will bring the rest."

"It wouldn't hurt to expand your seating area," Thomas said.

"Remodeling is beyond my means," Ruth said. "I barely earn enough to pay the bills."

"Fortunately, I know two remodeling experts who work on the cheap. Isn't that right, LeVar?"

LeVar set the cloth on the counter and walked to the window.

"Yeah. It wouldn't take much. Another few yards of space, and customers could have a lounge area." LeVar squinted up at the strip lights. "Gotta do something about this lighting too. Tone it down a little, make it relaxing." They all stared at the teenager. He raised his palms. "What 'choo looking at? A former gangster can't remodel a cafe?"

With Ruth's mood elevated, Thomas and Naomi purchased pastries and coffee and walked back to his truck. The sunlight spread fiery streaks through Naomi's hair, and the woman wore the satisfied smile of a major accomplishment.

"That went better than I expected," she said, climbing into the truck.

He closed her door and circled to the driver's side.

"You should be proud, Naomi. Your ideas saved her business."

"Let's not put the cart before the horse. She has a long road ahead."

"I have a good feeling about the Broken Yolk."

As Thomas pulled into the road, Naomi yelled. He slammed his brakes before a 4x4 whistled past, almost tearing off his side mirrors.

"Who was that driving like a maniac?"

Thomas drummed his fingers against the wheel.

"That was Carl Middleton."

Wherever Middleton was going, he was furious and in a hurry.

FRIDAY, JULY 17TH, 4:55 P.M.

"No, Ambrose. I don't want you to come over."

Kay Ramsey brushed the unkempt hair out of her eyes and shuffled to the kitchen. Sauce-stained dishes filled the sink, and a bowl of half-eaten oatmeal congealed on the granite.

"You shouldn't be alone, Mom. Especially after what happened last night."

"Father Fowler exaggerates, dear. Yes, I was upset. But I don't need twenty-four-hour monitoring. Besides, you have your family to tend to."

"You're our family."

"Let me be. Give me time to clear my head."

"I'm uncomfortable with this."

"If I need someone to talk to, I'll call. I promise."

A glass shattered in the background.

"Shit."

"What happened?"

"I dropped a glass. Sorry, Mom."

"I'll let you go, Ambrose. If I need anything, I'll call."

Ambrose was in mid-sentence when Kay ended the call.

With the curtains drawn, the downstairs drowned in shadow. If Kay opened the drapes and let the sun inside, it would make her feel better. But she preferred the darkness now, waited for night to fall. The pain and loneliness lessened while she slept.

She scanned the mess in the sink and sighed. Turning on the faucet, she retrieved a rag from the drawer while the water warmed. She shoved aside dishes until she located the drain stopper, then she squeezed dishwashing liquid into the stream and filled the sink. Halfway through the stack, Kay's back stiffened when someone pounded on her door.

She turned the water off and listened. The pounding started again, irate and unrelenting. Kay eyed the phone and considered phoning Ambrose. But her daughter had her hands full, and the person couldn't get inside the house with the storm door locked.

A fist struck the door hard enough to shake the floor and jiggle the glassware. Kay crept to the curtain and peeked through the slit.

"I know you're in there, Mrs. Ramsey. Open the damn door!"

She touched her mouth and backed away from the window. Carl Middleton. What was he doing at her house? The audacity of the man to stand upon her stoop after he'd made Lincoln's final years miserable. Kay wanted to rip the door open and scream in his face. But the unhinged shouting pushed her deeper into the shadows, away from his ferocity.

And still the man bashed the door. The force of the blows squeezed sunlight between the door and jamb.

"You went to the sheriff's department and told them I threw a brick through your window! Open the door and face me, you old bitch!"

Kay didn't know what Middleton was talking about. She hadn't told the sheriff Middleton broke her window.

"Go away, Carl, or I'll call the police."

It became quiet outside the door. Kay's body trembled as she rubbed the goosebumps off her arms. She closed her eyes and counted to ten, praying she'd scared him off. That's when she heard footsteps moving along the house, arrowing toward the backyard.

She rushed to the kitchen and snatched her phone off the granite. The backyard was empty. Kay peered through the kitchen curtains and searched her neighbor's driveway. No vehicles. Nobody to help if the madman punched a hole in the glass and broke into the house. If Middleton was brazen enough to harass her in the light of day, how could she sleep at night, knowing he was out there, seeking his twisted revenge?

The window in the downstairs bathroom jostled. Someone was trying to open the screen.

Kay dialed 9-1-1 and ran down the hallway, her breaths coming quick as she stood outside the door.

"9-1-1 operator," the man said. "What's your emergency?"

"Someone is breaking into my house."

"What's happening?"

"A man is trying to climb through the bathroom window."

"I'm sending a patrol car to your location now."

"Thank God."

"Do you recognize the man?"

"I believe it's Carl Middleton. He owns Middleton Construction." A truck motor fired outside. Kay rushed to the living room and threw the curtains back. "Hold on. Something is happening."

Middleton's 4x4 squealed down the street.

The moment Thomas set Jack's food dish below the table, the big dog devoured his meal. He scratched behind the dog's neck and sipped his ginger beer. Outside the window, Naomi wheeled Scout toward the lake, his neighbor moving with a bounce to her step that hadn't existed before she helped Ruth Sims. While Jack ate, Thomas paged through the Cecilia Bond and Lincoln Ramsey case files, searching for something he'd missed. Scout's warning about an angel of mercy killer kept ringing inside his head. It was a long shot. But if another serial killer was loose in Wolf Lake, he needed an expert opinion.

Thomas snapped his fingers and scrolled through his contacts. When he located the phone number for the Behavioral Analysis Unit, he called the FBI.

"Please put me through to Agent Neil Gardy," he said.

The receptionist told him to hold, and the phone began ringing. Thomas had worked with Agent Gardy in Los Angeles after a series of child abductions convinced the LAPD to call the FBI.

"Agent Gardy," the familiar voice said.

"Neil, it's Thomas Shepherd."

"Detective, how is life in Los Angeles?"

"It's Deputy Shepherd now, and I work for the Nightshade County Sheriff's Department in New York State."

"Talk about a career change. Nightshade County. That's close to Syracuse, correct?"

"That's right. We're on the edge of the Finger Lakes." Thomas glanced through the window. LeVar returned home from work, and Scout met him outside the guest house. "It's a quieter life than DC and LA."

"Working at Quantico is a far cry from life in Los Angeles. I've got a little place by the coast. My town's population rose to three-thousand, according to the last census. Remember what I told you last time we spoke."

"I'm not FBI material, Neil."

"Who wants to work full time with the FBI?"

"You do."

Gardy chuckled.

"But I'm crazy. We have a consulting position open. Reasonable hours and travel. Good perks. And none of the pressure full-time FBI agents deal with. After your work with the DEA task force, you'd be a shoo-in for the position."

"I'm flattered, but it's not for me."

"You sure? I'd put in a good word for you."

"And I appreciate it. Neil, I don't want to take up too much of your time. We've had two unusual deaths in the last week. I'm worried we're dealing with a murderer, and I'd like to tap your expertise."

"What's happening up there?"

Thomas recounted the Lincoln Ramsey and Cecilia Bond deaths.

"You're certain Lincoln Ramsey didn't die from natural causes?"

"I'm not sure of anything, Neil."

"The Bond death is curious, though I can picture a scenario in which she lost her balance and hit her head."

"So can I."

"It troubles me that the deaths occurred in rapid succession. We're shooting in the dark, but it's possible you're dealing with a serial murderer."

"Like an angel of mercy killer."

"Exactly. Or an angel of death killer, as we often refer to them."

"Lincoln Ramsey was on his death bed, and Cecilia Bond wasn't far off."

"Have you ruled out Bond's spouse?"

"He gave me a bad vibe, and he became a religious fanatic after his wife fell ill."

"Interesting. Fanaticism ties into the angel of death theory. My partner, Agent Bell, is the top profiler at the BAU. She's out of the office today. I'm not a profiling expert. But I'm happy to lend my opinion."

"Who am I looking for?"

"Someone who knew both victims and encountered them regularly. Given both victims faced death, Ramsey and Bond might have sought counseling or a psychologist, someone who could help them cope."

Dr. Mandal's face popped into Thomas's mind. Though he hadn't mentioned Ramsey and Bond by name during therapy, he'd spoken about the cases and the difficulty he experienced watching Kay Ramsey and Ambrose Jorgensen struggle after Lincoln passed. In a small village like Wolf Lake, Mandal would have learned the names of the victims.

"Then there is the obvious choice—a medical doctor," Agent Gardy said, continuing.

"Wolf Lake only has a handful of doctors. Ramsey and Bond were patients at the same practice."

"That's a start. Many angel of death killers work in the medical field. Viewing tragedy every day drives them over the edge."

"What about clergy? Ramsey and Bond attended the same church."

Gardy considered Thomas's theory for a moment.

"I wouldn't rule it out. You have a potential suspect in Bond's husband. Can you link him back to the Ramsey case? Like you said, Wolf Lake is a small village."

And Bond had a weak alibi at the time Cecilia died.

Thomas had more questions than answers after the call ended. He tugged his hair as he ran through the suspect list. Was he off base this time? Lincoln Ramsey's death appeared tied to COPD, and Cecilia Bond was in no condition to hike along the river without supervision.

The phone rang and jolted him out of his thoughts.

"Sheriff?"

"Carl Middleton harassed Kay Ramsey a half-hour ago," Gray said. "I'm heading to Middleton's house now. Lambert is at the Ramsey residence."

"Do you need me to come in?"

"We have it handled. But Middleton blamed Kay Ramsey for ratting him out over the broken window."

"She had nothing to do with it."

"You and I understand that, but try to convince a jackass like Carl Middleton."

"Are you bringing him in?"

"Ramsey claims Middleton attempted to break into her house. I'll interrogate Middleton while Lambert dusts for prints." Gray groaned. "I wonder if this guy had something to do with Lincoln Ramsey's death. He can't let go of a grudge."

"Sheriff, I don't want you to think I went over your head. But

I called an old contact at the FBI. When I mentioned the possibility our killer was a priest, his ears perked up."

Gray paused.

"That bastard, Fowler. I don't trust him, Thomas."

"He knew both victims."

"The prayer jar," Gray said with a growl. Thomas recalled a glass jar in the vestibule. Until now, he hadn't understood its purpose. "When someone wants Fowler to pray for a loved one, they slip a note into the jar. As if the good Father has a direct line with God."

"Did Kay Ramsey enter Lincoln's name into the prayer jar?"

"Only one way to find out."

"Keep me in the loop. I'll call Kay Ramsey."

The first call to Kay Ramsey's phone dumped into her voicemail. He called again, and this time she answered after two rings.

"Mrs. Ramsey, this is Deputy Shepherd with the Nightshade County Sheriff's Department. I stopped by your house this morning."

Kay Ramsey's voice trembled, tugging at his heart strings.

"I remember you, Deputy."

"I understand Deputy Lambert is with you."

"Yes, he's here," Kay said, her voice devoid of hope.

"Then you're safe. I need to ask you an important question."

"I'll do my best to answer."

"While your husband battled COPD, did you enter his name into Father Fowler's prayer jar?" Kay didn't reply. "Mrs. Ramsey, are you there?"

"Faith is a private matter, Deputy Shepherd."

"Please, Mrs. Ramsey. It's critical you tell me if you entered your husband's name into the prayer jar."

"I did," she said after a long pause. "A lot of good that did us."

"Did Father Fowler speak to you about your husband's condition?"

"Many times. But I fail to understand what this has to do with Lincoln's death, or why Carl Middleton is harassing me."

"We'll speak with Mr. Middleton. That's all I needed, Mrs. Ramsey." Thomas gave Kay his phone number. "If anyone bothers you again, call me. You're not alone."

His pulse raced as he sat inside the quiet house. Jack cocked his head, sensing Thomas's consternation.

Thomas looked up Duncan Bond's number and entered it into his phone.

"Mr. Duncan, this is Deputy Shepherd calling."

Asking if Duncan Bond put Cecilia's name in the prayer jar was a formality. Thomas already knew the answer. But he needed to hear it from Duncan Bond.

"Every day, Deputy Shepherd."

Thomas jotted *prayer jar* on his memo pad and circled the words. Two gravely ill victims, and Father Fowler prayed for both.

30

"It's that goddamn Fowler," Gray said, slapping his coffee mug on the desk and splashing black liquid over the sides.

Thomas, Aguilar, and Lambert convened with Gray in the sheriff's office, the four of them squeezed together in close confines.

"All we know is Fowler prayed for Lincoln Ramsey and Cecilia Bond," Aguilar said, sitting on the edge of the desk. "That's hardly unusual, and it doesn't implicate Fowler for murder."

Gray swung his eyes to Thomas.

"You said it, yourself. This is an angel of mercy killer. Isn't that what the FBI agent called him?"

Thomas plucked at his shirt cuff.

"All I'm saying is we need to handle this delicately. We can't storm into Fowler's office and accuse him of murder."

"These murders have Fowler's stench all over them. He always considered himself above the law."

"So let me speak to him."

"I can handle Fowler."

"You're already upset."

"I'll be professional."

Lambert shook his head behind Gray and said, "Sheriff, why don't we work together and link Carl Middleton to the Cecilia Bond case."

After interviewing Middleton for an hour last evening, Gray had sent Middleton home. Lambert hadn't found fingerprints on Kay Ramsey's bathroom window, so they couldn't prove Middleton tried to break inside the Ramsey residence. The neighbor across the street confirmed Middleton pounded on the door and yelled. But Kay Ramsey was the only person claiming Middleton tampered with the window.

"Let's link Duncan Bond to Lincoln Ramsey," Aguilar added. "We need everyone working together."

The sheriff huffed and turned to Thomas.

"Fine. Interview Fowler at St. Mary's. But I want a full report after you finish."

Thomas drove across the village in silence. The morning had dawned gray and foreboding. Clouds hung low over Wolf Lake as he turned into the church parking lot. The announcement for Cecilia Bond's memorial service, set to begin in ninety minutes, greeted him at the door. A flurry of congregation members hustled through the church, making preparations. A robed teenage boy with a bowl haircut glared at Thomas as he crossed through the vestibule.

"Where's Father Fowler's office?"

The boy pointed at the stairs.

Thomas descended the steps to the basement. Gloom shrouded the lower level, and tables stood at regular intervals beneath the shadows. They looked like coffins in the dark. Light spilled from the room at the rear of the basement. The clicks of fingers running over a keyboard broke the silence.

Thomas peeked his head inside the room. A tall, black-haired woman with a sharp nose leaned over the keyboard. He recognized her as the woman who helped Fowler usher Kay Ramsey into the church Thursday evening. When she didn't notice him, Thomas cleared his throat.

"May I help you?"

"I'm looking for Father Josiah Fowler."

"Father is in his office, completing his sermon for today's service. It would be better if you returned after the ceremony."

"I'll only be a few minutes."

Thomas rested his hand against the jamb and blocked the doorway, an obvious message he wouldn't leave without speaking with Fowler. She tensed and set her palms flat on the desk.

"One moment."

She rapped her knuckles on Father Fowler's door. After squeezing her head inside the opening, she spoke to Fowler in a hushed voice, though Thomas caught the severity in her whisper.

"He'll see you now," the woman said, motioning Thomas inside.

Father Josiah Fowler's office looked more like a prison than a place to relax. Concrete walls with no windows, a prominent cross hanging behind his chair, a bookshelf overflowing with bibles and tomes Thomas didn't recognize. Except for the phone on the desk, it seemed Fowler had no contact with the world once he entered this strange sanctuary. Thomas closed the door.

Fowler's eyes widened. He'd expected someone else when his assistant told him a representative from the sheriff's department wished to speak to him.

"Deputy Shepherd," Fowler said with a gleam in his eye. "We meet again."

"I'm sorry, but this isn't a social call."

"Oh. I'd hoped you enjoyed Thursday's service enough to join the church. God will always welcome you, Deputy."

Thomas sat in the chair across from Fowler's desk. A cross hung from the priest's neck and reflected the lamp light. He'd been busy scribing when Thomas entered. Now he turned the papers over.

"Carl Middleton denies starting the fight with Lincoln Ramsey outside your church. He claims you're lying."

Fowler sniffed.

"Mr. Middleton is a child in a man's body, and if I had to guess, I'd say he's a dangerous child."

"Why do you say he's dangerous?"

"You weren't there, Deputy Shepherd. Had you seen the hate in that man's eyes, you'd understand. He would have harmed Lincoln and Kay Ramsey, and I'm unsure I could have stopped him without several people stepping in."

"You're a large man, Father Fowler. You'd handle yourself in an altercation."

"I'm not violent," Fowler said, glancing away.

"Garrick and Suzanne Tillery attend your masses."

Fowler's mouth twisted for a brief second. But Thomas noticed.

"They do."

"Garrick Tillery lives in the same neighborhood as Lincoln and Kay Ramsey, and he's an acquaintance of Carl Middleton."

"Acquaintance, or drinking buddy? That's the appropriate term, yes?"

"Do you believe Garrick Tillery is dangerous, as you say Carl Middleton is?"

Fowler's eyes squinted and tracked along the ceiling.

"When he drinks, he's not himself. Garrick Tillery is a very sick man. I fear he's beyond help, though I've tried to reach him."

"Sick enough to hurt Cecilia Bond or Lincoln Ramsey?"

"Perhaps."

"I spoke with Duncan Bond. The night Cecilia passed, Duncan claims he was here, at the church, and you saw him."

Fowler rocked back in his chair with his fingers interlaced behind his head.

"Yes, I recall passing Duncan as I entered the church." Fowler tutted. "Poor, poor man. He was here every day, praying for Cecilia."

"Can you verify the time you saw Duncan Bond?"

"It was fifteen minutes before nine. I remember because I lock the doors at nine. And Duncan was still in the church, praying for a donor. Understand I wouldn't have thrown him out of the building at closing time. Besides Duncan, the only person more concerned with his wife's suffering was me. Which is why today's service is dedicated to Cecilia."

"Do you know how long he spent inside the church?"

Fowler pursed his lip.

"Unfortunately, no. There wasn't anyone upstairs to confirm his whereabouts."

"Not even your assistant?"

"Ms. Barlow's day ends at four o'clock."

"So you leave the doors unlocked and the church unattended for hours at a time. Anyone could come inside and vandalize the church."

"I have more faith in people than you, Deputy. Most people, that is. And no one hides from the eyes of God. Besides, the youth church council met downstairs between the hours of seven and nine. If a troublemaker entered the church, we'd catch him."

Thomas scanned the time line in his notes.

"Where were you during this time?"

"Where was I?"

"Yes. You claim Duncan Bond passed you on your way into the church."

"Where I spend my evenings is my business. If you must know, I like to walk to clear my head. I'm closer to God when I feel relaxed."

"Would you describe yourself as a troubled man?"

"You're twisting my words. If you heard the stories I listen to everyday, you'd require time to unwind."

"Do you walk through the village park along the river?"

"I didn't murder Cecilia Bond, if that's what you're implying. You sound like Sheriff Gray, Deputy. Did he put these ideas in your head? I'm sure he told you I murdered Lana. That I crossed the center line and drove the poor woman into a tree. Isn't that the rumor? I can assure you, I never lost control of my vehicle."

"Had you been drinking that night?"

"No. And there isn't a witness who will claim otherwise. If I may be frank, Deputy, I pity your sheriff. He lost the love of his life, and he needs to blame someone so he can sleep at night. I'm the convenient fall guy. But I'm no murderer. And I wouldn't harm Duncan Bond's wife."

"I can't rule out anyone without an alibi. Were you at the river the night Cecilia Bond died?"

"No. I walked the side streets through the village."

"Can anyone vouch for your whereabouts?"

Fowler's lips curled into a hyena's grin.

"You're welcome to knock on doors and ask. Would you like me to map my route, Deputy?"

"That won't be necessary. Tell me about the prayer jar."

"Whatever for?"

"Were Lincoln Ramsey and Cecilia Bond's names in the prayer jar?"

"That's none of your business."

"I'd like the names of the people in the jar today."

"I trust you brought a warrant? The contents of the prayer jar are private. I won't violate anyone's confidence." Fowler rose and swept his robes behind him. "Will there be anything else, Deputy Shepherd? I have mass."

Thomas slipped his notes into his pocket.

"That's all for now, Father. I'll be in touch."

31

The murder board hung in the interview room as Thomas, Gray, and Lambert moved their eyes between the photographs. In the kitchen, the blender whirred. Aguilar entered the room with two pink protein shakes. The muscular deputy handed one to Thomas and the other to Gray. The sheriff sniffed the concoction.

"What in God's creation is this?"

"Protein powder, frozen berries, and a greens supplement."

"It smells like a hamster cage."

"It's good for you. Drink. You ate donuts all week and need to purge the toxins swimming through your system."

The sheriff raised the glass and touched the lid to his lips before twisting his nose.

"You first," he said, glaring at Thomas.

With a shrug, Thomas gulped the smoothie as Lambert grinned.

"Not bad."

Gray made a noncommittal grunt and sipped the protein drink. Aguilar wore a smug smile.

"Now, that didn't kill you, did it? Treat your body well, and it will return the favor."

Gray set the smoothie on the table and wiped his mouth on his sleeve.

"Enough with the health lesson. Get to work."

The murder board included photographs of a younger Lincoln Ramsey and Cecilia Bond, as she appeared after Thomas and Gray dragged her out of the river. The bloated corpse haunted Thomas when he closed his eyes at night. Facing it again, he wondered how bad the nightmares would be tonight. The sheriff arranged pictures of Garrick Tillery, Father Josiah Fowler, Duncan Bond, and Carl Middleton on the murder board. Colored strings connected each suspect to a victim, signifying a link.

"Start with Carl Middleton," Gray said.

Aguilar set her hands on her hips.

"He's at the top of the list."

"Why?"

"He lied about the altercation outside the church, and he threatened Kay Ramsey and tried to break into her house."

"Nobody witnessed Middleton circling the house and breaking through the window," said Thomas. "Kay Ramsey is going through a rough time, and Middleton pounding on her door threw her off. She might have been confused."

Aguilar shook her head.

"He all but admitted to breaking the window. If he hadn't, why would he encounter Kay Ramsey two years later? And what kind of psychopath throws a brick through a rival's window?"

"All right. Let's say he's our murderer. What's his trigger?"

Aguilar scrunched up her face in thought.

Lambert said, "The bank denying his loan."

"Middleton Construction survived. His team is all over the village, working on projects."

"It could be desperation. Middleton Construction is a small

outfit and can't handle the amount of projects he's taking on. That tells me the guy is having financial trouble."

Thomas hadn't considered the possibility, but it made sense.

"So why would Middleton murder Cecilia Bond?"

Aguilar lifted herself and sat on the edge of the table, her legs hanging over the edge.

"If Middleton went off the deep end and murdered Lincoln Ramsey, he wouldn't need a reason to kill Cecilia Bond. He's crazy."

"That doesn't convince me. Middleton is a bully. I need more proof, if I'm to believe he's murdering people in Wolf Lake."

"He attended church with Lincoln Ramsey and Cecilia Bond."

"Not recently. Father Fowler expelled Middleton from the church."

Gray tapped his forefinger against Garrick Tillery's photo.

"What about Garrick Tillery?"

"A witness placed him at the river around the time Cecilia Bond walked past," Lambert said. "His shirt was covered with blood, and he had a gash across his hand."

"When do we expect the DNA test?" Aguilar asked.

"It won't return for another three to five days," said Gray.

"I can't believe we let him walk," Lambert said, tracing the connecting strings with his eyes. "He lives a few houses from Lincoln Ramsey, and he was at the river when Cecilia Bond died."

Aguilar bobbed her head.

"He also attended church with both victims."

"Don't forget he has a sexual assault on his record."

"Tillery claims the underage girl he had sex with told him she was eighteen," Thomas said. "But you're right. It's another strike against him."

Gray released a breath and tapped a pen against Duncan

Bond's picture.

"Cecilia Bond's husband. He turned stir crazy after his wife's diagnosis and became a religious fanatic."

Thomas considered Duncan Bond's demeanor during the interview.

"He admits to fighting with Cecilia. He rubbed me the wrong way during the interview. Something about Duncan Bond seems unhinged. He wasn't beyond physically abusing Cecilia."

"The bruising on her body could have come from Duncan," Lambert said. "Or from falling into the river. Given her medical condition, she bruised easily."

Aguilar narrowed her eyes at Bond's picture.

"I suppose we won't have Bond's DNA test any sooner than Middleton's."

Gray tugged at his mustache.

"We'll have it as evidence if the case goes to court." Gray glanced at Thomas. "What did Fowler say?"

"Father Fowler saw Bond in the church around eight-forty-five. Bond's alibi is weak. If he stalked his wife between six-thirty and seven, he had time to murder Cecilia, clean himself up, and drive to the church before Fowler arrived."

"Now, do we include Ellie Fisher and Damian Ramos in this web?"

"We have no evidence linking the cases, and we're not even sure someone harmed Fisher. Her roommate claims she takes off without telling anybody when she wants to get away."

Gray turned on his heels and paced.

"Which leaves Father Josiah Fowler, who nobody saw inside the church until he ran into Duncan Bond."

"He doesn't have an alibi."

"Father Fowler knew both victims, and Kay Ramsey and Duncan Bond say they placed their spouse's names inside the prayer jar. That's not a coincidence."

Lambert glanced at Aguilar from the corner of his eye. Sheriff Gray couldn't assess Fowler without bringing his bias into the investigation.

"Fowler doesn't have a history of violence," Thomas argued.

"Unless you count vehicular homicide."

"Which we can't prove."

Gray pounded his fist against the table, causing them to jump.

"It has to be Fowler. The FBI agrees with Thomas—we're searching for an angel of mercy killer, someone with a God complex. In his twisted mind, he pretends he saved Ramsey and Bond from suffering." Gray stomped to the murder board and moved Fowler's picture to the center. "No alibi, a history of violence, and he knew both victims. The prayer jar is the trigger. Face it. All the evidence points to Father Josiah Fowler."

Thomas rounded on Gray and blocked him from marching out of the room.

"If you barge into the church with half-baked evidence, we won't be able to hold him. Fowler will walk. The wiser plan is to convince him he's in the clear while we accumulate evidence."

Aguilar dropped off the table and stood beside Thomas.

"How will we prove Fowler was at the river?"

Lambert strolled to the group.

"We go door to door through the neighborhoods Fowler claims he walked through. If he's telling the truth, somebody saw him. In the meantime, we canvas the area around the park. Fowler is a recognizable figure. Find a witness who will place him inside the park Tuesday evening."

"Then it's agreed," Thomas said, drawing a scowl from Gray. He'd usurped the sheriff. But Gray was too biased to offer an opinion on Fowler. "We keep a low profile and dig up everything we can on Fowler. Then we take him down."

32

Raven watched Damian Ramos enter Benson's Barbells with a gym bag slung over his shoulder. Running shorts showed off his muscular legs, and the gray tank top already dripped with sweat, evidence he'd exercised before driving to the gym. After a four-hour surveillance mission in which Damian never left the house, Raven worried she was wrong about the boy toy. The ropes and duct tape in his trunk might be explainable. Beyond a little flirtatious conversation, she hadn't connected Damian to Ellie Fisher. At least she'd found evidence Damian was cheating on Sadie Moreno, even though Raven served as the guinea pig.

After Damian disappeared inside the gymnasium, Raven grabbed her gym bag off the backseat and locked the doors. She spied a security camera angling off the roof and wondered if the owner, Mark Benson, was inside, staring at her on the monitor. Patting her pocket for her wallet, she jogged across the parking lot and pulled the door open.

The warm, vinegary stench of sweaty bodies hit her the moment she entered. Grunts and heavy bars dropped onto racks, drowning out the heavy metal blasting through the speakers. At the greeting window, a disinterested teenage girl stretched her bubble gum and ignored Raven until she knocked on the glass. The girl rolled her eyes when Raven asked for a one-day membership.

"Sign here and here," the girl said, tapping her red nails on the signature lines.

Once inside, Raven scanned the interior until she spotted Damian on the far side of the gym, racking the weight for a heavy set of bench presses. Not wanting to run into Damian immediately and raise suspicion, she located the stair machine and hung her bag on a rack. She set the machine to low speed and warmed up. After she broke a sweat, she increased the intensity and spied Damian between the safety bars. Good. He hadn't noticed her.

A sexy woman with auburn hair took the bench beside Damian. His eyes undressed the woman when she wasn't looking, and Raven caught Damian's tongue rolling across his lips as he assessed the woman's physique. After ten minutes on the stair machine, Raven moved on to free weights. Hoping to draw Damian's attention, she loaded two twenty-five pound plates on an Olympic bar and set up for shoulder presses. Halfway through her first set, her phone rang.

Chelsey.

"Is Damian inside the gym?"

"That's an affirmative," Raven said, using vague replies in case anyone eavesdropped. "Can I call you back, Mom? I'm in the middle of a workout."

"I ran full credit checks on Damian Ramos and Mark Benson, the jerk who harassed you. Damian came back clean, except he was denied a car loan two months ago."

"That's odd. His house lists for three-hundred grand, and he dresses to the nines."

"You know the old saying about rich people turning house poor."

Raven switched the phone to her other ear.

"Okay, so he's having money difficulties. That explains why he's marrying...your cousin."

"Right," Chelsey said, playing along. "Then I ran Benson's credit check, and things got more interesting."

Raven searched the gym for the burly owner and couldn't find him. He hadn't been inside the office when Raven signed up for a gym pass.

"So what's the story with Uncle Ben?"

"Get this. Benson's credit score is bottom of the barrel. Multiple loan defaults. It's amazing he still has his business. But that isn't all. He's Damian's client at the trading firm."

Raven's eyes moved to Damian. He was staring right at her, his chest heaving as he caught his breath.

"I gotta go."

"Damian saw you?"

"That's right, Mom. I'll check with Uncle Ben and call you after my workout."

"Something doesn't feel right, Raven. Be careful."

By the time Raven ended the call, Damian was strutting across the gym with an impish grin.

"So you took me up on my offer?"

Raven tilted her head, playing the role of a clueless girl.

"Oh, ha-ha. I forgot you wanted to train with me."

He lifted his chin at the barbell.

"You're moving serious weight. I'm impressed."

"This isn't my first time inside a gym."

"I can tell. You want a spotter?"

She didn't, but she nodded.

"That would be terrific. I might need your muscles to pull me through this set."

She forced her way through three sets until her shoulders screamed at her to ease up. She wanted to draw his interest, not enter a bodybuilding competition. If she played her cards right, he'd try to coax her into bed. Then she'd have the ultimate piece of evidence she needed to prove Damian was unfaithful to Sadie Moreno. Ellie Fisher's smiling face kept interrupting her concentration. How could she broach the subject and bring up Ellie's name without raising suspicion? If Damian had something to do with Ellie's disappearance, he'd know she was on to him.

"Damn, you have nice delts," he said, rubbing her shoulders. "You didn't strain your muscles, did you? I give a mean massage."

She sat with her elbows on her knees, head hanging low as she pretended to catch her breath.

"I'm just a little out of shape."

"Not from where I sit. You're a machine. I bet you go all day and night."

He'd taken her by surprise. Were it not for Chelsey's phone call distracting her, she would have started her voice recorder before she spoke to Damian. Which gave her an idea.

"I need to use the restroom."

He pointed to the doors behind the rows of elliptical machines and treadmills.

"The women's locker room is the door on the right. I'm gonna knock out a set of back squats. Meet you at the squat rack after?"

"Sure. I'll be back in a second." She winked. "Save those muscles for me."

Watching Damian in the mirrors, Raven waited until he turned his back and placed two plates on either side of the barbell. Then she scrolled through her phone and found the voice recording app. After she started the recorder, she slipped the phone inside her gym bag, leaving the top unzipped so voices would come through clearly. The women's locker room was empty when she set her bag on a wooden bench. Four walls of gray lockers boxed her in, making her claustrophobic as she toweled the sweat off her upper body.

A thud brought her head around. She couldn't determine if the sound came from inside the locker room or the gymnasium. She paused and listened, one eye fixed to the phone peeking out from below the zipper. When the sound didn't come again, she brushed off her nervousness and strolled to the sink. She turned on the faucet and splashed water against her face, washing sweat into her eyes. She squinted and ran the faucet on high, cupping water with her hands and clearing her stinging eyes until her vision cleared.

The door behind her whipped open before she could react. Something clubbed the back of her head.

Raven's legs gave out. She felt someone dragging her through the doorway before she lost consciousness.

33

The irate car horn knocked Thomas out of his daze. He glanced up at the traffic light, now green, and rolled through the intersection after being lost in thought, remembering the frustrating afternoon he spent knocking on doors with Aguilar. Nobody in the neighborhood near the church recalled seeing Father Fowler walking Tuesday evening, leaving the priest without an alibi at the time of Cecilia Bond's murder. Yet according to Deputy Lambert, nobody spotted Fowler in the park, though two people confirmed Garrick Tillery had fished off the banks within a quarter-mile of where Gray and Thomas found Cecilia's body.

When the thoroughfare opened to four lanes, the car passed him and sped past at twenty miles over the limit. The driver lifted a middle finger out the window, and Thomas wondered why people lost their minds over an extra second or two at stoplights. As he cruised into the heart of the village, the sidewalks choked with shoppers, he pulled to the curb outside a French restaurant and phoned his parents. They were ignoring his calls again. He hadn't spoken to his mother since she left the church Thursday night.

The call went to a recorded message. He redialed and waited. This time, his mother answered.

"I wanted to check on you and make sure you're all right."

"Why wouldn't I be?" Lindsey Shepherd asked with a contemptuous cough.

"You left the church without talking to me, and you haven't answered your phone."

"Why are you really calling, Thomas? Unless you're prepared to take over Shepherd Systems, your father and I have nothing to discuss with you."

Thomas swallowed an angry reply. He'd reached out to them since his father revealed his cancer diagnosis, and they'd slammed the door in his face every time. But Lindsey mentioning Shepherd Systems gave Thomas an idea.

"Let me speak to Father."

"Your father is resting in his study."

"Please, it's important."

Quiet. Then a huff, as Lindsey transferred the call to the study. Mason Shepherd answered.

"How are you feeling today, Father?"

"I'm reading, Thomas. Why are you bothering me?"

"I'd like to discuss the company."

"Then speak. I'm listening."

"I have someone who's a perfect fit for Shepherd Systems. She'd be an invaluable asset to the company."

"*She?*" The word rolled off his lips with derision. "Who is this woman, and what makes you think my company needs her?"

"Her name is Naomi Mourning."

After Thomas explained her background, Mason chuckled in his ear.

"She had success in Ithaca, not New York City or Chicago. We work with clients all over the world. There's nothing in her background to convince me she's fit to work for Shepherd Systems."

"If you'd been there when she spoke with Ruth Sims... Naomi's ideas saved the Broken Yolk from—"

"That hole in the wall isn't worth saving. But then you could never say no to their cheap treats. You're still a child, concocting fantasies where you save all your friends. Grow up. The real world is about utilizing superior ideas to squash the competition. If this woman friend of yours was worth her salt, she wouldn't be unemployed."

Thomas ground his teeth. His father didn't know what Naomi had gone through.

"You're playing with people's lives. She has a paralyzed daughter and can't pay her medical bills. Shepherd Systems has a first-rate benefits package, and she—"

"Tell you what, Thomas. Quit your job and run the company. Then you can hire all the friends you want."

The line died. Thomas stared at the phone in disbelief, hands trembling. He wanted to whip the phone through the glass before his shoulders wilted. Seeking attention from his parents sapped his strength and stole his will.

He shifted into drive and swung the truck into traffic. A drive around the lake would clear his head. As he angled toward the lake road, his phone rang. Thomas suspected his father had called back, seeing his error in judgment. But his parents were only reasonable with Thomas in his fantasies, and Mason Shepherd wouldn't speak to Thomas for weeks unless he retired from the sheriff's department. LeVar's name popped up on his phone.

"Deputy Shepherd."

That LeVar hadn't called him Deputy Dog or even Thomas gave him pause. The teenager's voice carried a smile whenever he spoke, and had so since he left the Harmon Kings and moved into the guest house. Thomas didn't hear that smile now.

"Is everything all right, LeVar?"

"Raven was supposed to pick my mother up for therapy at four. She never showed."

"That's no problem. I can swing by the house and drive Serena to her appointment."

"No, that's not the issue. I can drive her. It's not like Raven to forget Mom's sessions."

"Your sister is working a case in Syracuse and Kane Grove. It's conceivable she lost track of time and is on her way to Wolf Lake now."

"Maybe, except she ain't answering my calls."

That was strange. Possibilities flew through Thomas's head —Raven was trailing Damian Ramos and needed to keep her phone silenced, she got stuck in traffic and lost cell coverage, her battery died. None of the theories held water. Something was wrong.

"Have you called Wolf Lake Consulting?"

"Nah, I don't call that place. Not since her boss accused me of killing that girl in Harmon."

Thomas shifted his jaw. Chelsey hadn't accused LeVar. But the teenager had sat at the top of her suspect list before Thomas proved Jeremy Hyde was the killer. He couldn't blame LeVar for holding a grudge. How do you accept an apology from someone who investigated you for murder?

"Tell you what. I'll phone Wolf Lake Consulting. Chelsey must know where Raven is. Then I'll call Darren Holt at the ranger's station and find out if Raven contacted him today."

"All right, I appreciate it. I'm picking Mom up in five minutes. If Raven shows her face before then, I'll call you."

"Thanks for letting me know. Hang in there, LeVar. I'm sure your sister is fine."

Thomas hung up the phone and let his lie simmer. LeVar didn't buy it, and neither did Thomas.

34

D arren hoisted the ax over his head and brought it down, splitting the log. It was too hot to stack firewood. But the chilly air of winter was never far away in upstate New York, and he'd be running the new wood stove before Halloween. He carried the halved log behind the cabin and set it on the stack. With a satisfied grin, he estimated he'd accumulated a full cord. He needed two more to get through winter.

He tossed his gloves aside and slipped into the cabin, the breeze making the curtains dance at the windows. From the refrigerator, he grabbed a pitcher of lemonade and poured a tall glass. A green sofa he'd purchased at a garage sale sat beside a window overlooking the neighboring cabins. As he relaxed his fatigued muscles, he watched a couple with twin six-year-old girls build a fire behind cabin three. The sisters scavenged for sticks, choosing pieces long enough for roasting hot dogs and marshmallows.

This was a good life. Better than slumping over a desk at the Syracuse Police Department, or responding to a fight at the local bar. He'd spent the day trimming the plant life encroaching on the trail. It got lonely at the state park sometimes, though the forest was a natural nirvana. It seemed empty without someone to share it with, and the campers kept to themselves.

Loneliness made him think of Raven, the private investigator he couldn't push out of his thoughts. Not that he wanted to. Darren never stopped grinning when he was around Raven. What did she see in a forty-two-year-old ex-cop? The irony was he'd never had a serious conversation with Raven until her brother got them talking at the cookout. Before then, he'd looked sidelong at the former Harmon Kings gang member. Now that he'd gotten to know LeVar, guilt suffocated him for prejudging the boy's character. He should have listened to Thomas after the deputy vouched for the teenager.

No sooner did Thomas pop into Darren's head than the phone rang, the deputy's name displayed on his screen.

"Darren, have you spoken to Raven today?"

"Not since yesterday at lunch. I was about to call her."

"Well, she isn't answering her phone or responding to texts, and she was supposed to pick her mother up for an appointment forty-five minutes ago."

Raven had a strained relationship with Serena. But she supported her mother and wouldn't forget Serena's therapy session.

"Did you call her office?"

"I tried. It might be better if you call. Chelsey won't answer the line if she sees my name on the screen."

Darren paced from one window to the next.

"Let me try. Do you know what Raven was working on today?"

"I'm sure it's the Damian Ramos case."

"That's what I'm afraid of. I'll check with Chelsey and get back to you. Thanks for the heads up."

Darren glared at the phone after the call ended. He dialed

Raven's number and got her voice-mail. Outside, flames shot through the grates after the father added too much lighter fluid.

"It's me...Darren. Call me back when you get this. Just checking in since your family hasn't heard from you since morning. Talk to you later."

He followed up the call with a text. Raven didn't write back. His stomach roiling with a heavy sickness, Darren found the number for Wolf Lake Consulting. Chelsey Byrd answered.

"Chelsey, it's Darren Holt at the state park. I'm trying to reach Raven. Her family can't contact her, and I'm getting a little worried."

"Raven was in Kane Grove this afternoon," Chelsey said.

"Checking on Damian Ramos?"

Chelsey hesitated, and Darren knew she didn't want to discuss the case.

"Last I heard."

"When exactly did you last speak to Raven?"

"A little before one. She worked out at Benson's Barbells in Kane Grove so she could monitor Damian."

Darren was beginning to feel angry with Chelsey.

"And you aren't worried?"

"Raven sent me a text a half-hour after her workout. She said Damian showered and drove home, and that she would clean up, grab a late lunch, and swing past his house before she quit for the day."

That explained why Chelsey brushed off Raven's disappearing act. But the story didn't compute. Raven never mentioned taking Serena to therapy in the text. She was too organized and responsible to forget family obligations. Had Raven written the text, or did someone have her phone?

"Has she messaged you since?"

"Well, no. What's this about, Darren?"

Chelsey liked to hide behind a tough girl persona. But Darren caught a tremor of worry in her voice.

"It might be nothing. If Raven's vehicle broke down and her phone died, she wouldn't receive our messages. But I want to be sure. You think this Damian guy would hurt Raven?"

"Let's not assume a worst-case scenario. I'll drive past Damian's house and look for Raven."

"Thanks, Chelsey. I want to stay ahead of this situation, so I'm calling the sheriff's department. I'd rather feel embarrassed for overreacting than regretful if something happened to Raven."

Silence followed, and Darren pictured Chelsey at her desk, frozen with indecision.

"Okay, I'll call you after I arrive in Kane Grove."

"Perfect. And Chelsey?"

"Yes?"

"With the sheriff's department getting involved, you need to work with Thomas should he call."

"I understand."

"Do you? Because this is bigger than the two of you."

"Raven's my best friend," Chelsey said, snapping. "If you think I'd let anything happen to her..."

She lowered the phone and sobbed.

"Chelsey?"

He gave her a moment to compose herself.

"Sorry for yelling. I'll find her, Darren."

Darren slipped the phone into his pocket and yanked the closet door open. He kept a *go bag* packed for emergencies. Unzipping the bag, he tossed his LED flashlight and binoculars inside and strapped on his shoulder holster. Butterflies winged through his chest, and his heart hammered as it had when he'd entered unsecured buildings during his police career. Now someone he cared about was in danger, and that ramped up his anxiety as he loaded his gun. Tonight, Darren didn't care about rules and regulations. He wasn't a cop anymore, and if he was honest with himself, he was nothing but a vigilante. If Damian Ramos harmed Raven, Darren would force the truth out of him.

On his way to the truck, a baseball cap slung low over his brow, Darren dialed the sheriff's department. He couldn't sit still until he confirmed Raven was safe. And if she wasn't safe, he needed to find her before it was too late.

35

SATURDAY, JULY 18TH, 8:50 P.M.

The jukebox inside Hattie's blasted the same Deep Purple song someone had played a half-hour before. The ruckus of raised voices, clinking glass, and rock-and-roll gave Garrick Tillery a splitting headache, the kind that started behind his eyes, snaked down his neck and spine, and kindled pins and needles in his toes. When the headaches were this bad, he got confused. Forgot things he'd done.

His bottle tipped over, spilling beer into the stinging wound across his hand. He winced and cursed into his forearm, scrambling for napkins. As he dabbed the wound dry, the alcohol bit and seared his flesh. He wondered about the gash. Had he hurt himself with the fishhook as he told Suzanne and the sheriff's deputy? He couldn't recall much about Tuesday evening, except that he drank himself into a stupor at Hattie's, somehow drove to the river without crashing into a telephone pole, and carried his fishing rod to the bank.

That was it.

And now the deputies thought he'd hurt that Bond woman.

What if he had? No, that wasn't possible. He refused to believe he attacked Cecilia Bond and tossed her into the river.

Yet horrors drifted through his head. He pictured himself as
Frankenstein's monster, tossing a little girl into the pond after
she offered him flowers. What had he become? A killer? A devil?

He leaned his head back and guzzled the last of his beer.
Then he caught the fat waitress's eye and snapped his finger
over his head. She rolled her eyes and stomped to the bar for
another bottle.

As Tillery waited for the server to return, a dark figure
blocked his view. He squinted up at the lights and recognized
Carl Middleton looming over the table. Without asking,
Middleton sat across from Tillery and set his meaty forearms on
the table, jiggling two empty bottles. Tillery considered
Middleton a friend. But he didn't appreciate the man's hard stare
or the challenge in his eyes.

"You've been talking to the sheriff's department, Garrick."

It wasn't a question.

The fat waitress set his beer on the table, took one look at
Middleton's glare, and got the hell out of there.

"Who told you that?"

Middleton snatched Tillery's beer and twisted the cap off the
bottle. He took a long sip.

"Everyone around town is talking about it. Did you tell the
cops about the brick, Garrick?"

"What brick?"

"Don't play stupid. The sheriff's department grilled me about
the brick. Seeing as you're the only person I told, that makes me
think you're the one who ratted me out."

Garrick remembered. Two winters ago, Middleton threw a
brick through Lincoln Ramsey's window after the banker turned
down Middleton's loan. Middleton had been damn proud of
himself, and Garrick got a laugh out of it, until the deputies
banged on his door, wondering if Garrick had anything to do
with the vandalism. Garrick never liked Lincoln and Kay

Ramsey. A couple of snooty assholes for neighbors. But he wouldn't shatter their front window over money.

"Your little stunt almost got me arrested."

"All the more reason for you to go to the cops."

"Two years later? You're not making sense, Carl. What's gotten into you lately?"

"I'll tell you what's gotten into me. That prick, Lincoln Ramsey, made my life a living hell. And I've still got the sheriff and his deputies accusing me of harassing him. You know what I'd like to do? I'd like to dig that old bastard out of his grave and see if he has any blood left to spill."

Middleton pushed the beer across the table, and Garrick slid it back to him. He wasn't about to drink it after Carl slurped from the bottle.

"He's dead. Let it go."

"The son-of-a-bitch got everything he had coming to him."

What did that mean? The rumor around town said Lincoln Ramsey hadn't died from COPD. Someone killed him. Tillery narrowed his eyes.

"Wait, did you—" The server set another beer in front of Tillery, interrupting him. Suddenly, Tillery lost his taste for alcohol. "I didn't order this. Take it back."

"Compliments of the lady," she said, pointing toward a brunette woman at the end of the bar.

Middleton turned to look and whistled.

"Wow, get a load of that one."

Tillery rubbed the grit from his eyes. The woman wore a black leather miniskirt that barely touched her thighs. Her makeup matched the pitch of her hair and skirt, and her low cut top angled past her breasts and stopped just above her navel. She had the body of a fitness model, the face of a goth angel. There was something familiar about the woman. Someone from high school? A woman he hooked up with and forgot? She kept her back to Tillery and concentrated on her cocktail.

"Hey, Garrick. Stop staring at the bitch." Tillery swung his eyes back to Middleton. "We're not finished here. What did you tell the cops?"

"Nothing."

"Nothing? You spent the night in jail. Call it a coincidence, but the deputies accused me of stalking Lincoln Ramsey after they released you. I'm guessing you cut a deal. Is that what happened, Garrick? Because if it is, you and I are gonna have this out."

Tillery shook the cobwebs out of his head.

"You're insane. All this bullshit is in your head. Whatever you did to Lincoln Ramsey, leave me the hell out of it."

Middleton shoved the table into Tillery's belly. Pinning Tillery between the table and chair, Middleton rose and pointed a meaty finger into Tillery's face.

"If I find out you're lying, you're a dead man. You got that, Garrick? I'll fucking slit you from ear to ear. And you better not run to the cops again."

Middleton strode away, carrying the bottle he'd stolen from Tillery. The music stopped. Everyone was staring at Tillery, expecting a fight. He wanted to throw the table aside and go after Middleton. Tackle him from behind and drive his head against the floor. Instead, he stayed glued to the chair, stunned Middleton would turn on him.

His eyes trailed back to the bar. He pounded the table when he realized the woman was gone. Tillery hadn't even gotten her name. He waved down the waitress and motioned her to the table.

"The woman who bought me the beer. Where did she go?"

The server chomped her gum. The fruity stench did little to cover the cigarette smoke on her breath.

"How would I know?"

As the woman turned to leave, Tillery snatched her arm. She scowled at his hand and shrugged it off.

"You didn't get her name?"

"She paid cash. I don't give a shit what her name is. That's for you to figure out, honey."

Tillery slapped his money on the table and shrugged into his jacket. On his way out, he scanned the crowded bar one last time, searching for the sexy stranger.

The night thickened with humidity as he staggered through the parking lot. He punched the air, imagining it was Carl Middleton's face. Everything sounded muffled, as if someone stuffed cotton in his ears. His shoes scuffed through gravel as he pulled the keys from his pocket. Inside his truck, he shook his head like a wet dog and cleared the haze from his head. He was fifteen minutes from home, and he gave himself even odds of making it back without wrapping the truck around a tree.

The truck rolled out of Hattie's parking lot at turtle speed and bucked over the curb. He giggled at the oversight and righted the truck after it swerved into the oncoming lane. Trees angled over the curving road and extended their branches downward like the grasping claws of monsters. It took him a full minute before he worked up the courage to drive faster than fifteen mph. Driving too slow would attract the deputies, and there was no way he'd pass the sobriety test. The truck weaved over the centerline, and he jerked the wheel back.

As he rounded the bend, his headlights glistened off the tire spikes. There was no time to react.

He slammed the brakes. The tires issued a banshee's shriek as the truck fishtailed. All four tires blew with sonic bangs when the spikes dug into the rubber.

The truck spun and careened onto the shoulder, missing the

guardrail by inches. He sat with his heart jumping into his throat. Who would throw tire spikes in the middle of the road?

Climbing down from the cab, he moved from one tire to the next, assessing the damage. The tires sat flat against the paved shoulder. Well, this was the perfect end to his night. He cursed and kicked a rock into the guardrail.

Tillery couldn't call the police in his drunken state, and he sure as hell wouldn't call Suzanne. He wasn't in the mood for a lecture.

A scenic overlook sat a quarter mile up the road. With nothing better to do, he stumbled along the shoulder toward the overlook. As he crossed through the grass, headlights seared the back of his neck. The vehicle stopped along the shoulder, the engine rumbling as the brights shone in Tillery's eyes. He cupped a hand over his forehead. A door opened, and a shadow cut through the lights as he struggled to make out the approaching figure.

"Who's that?"

Footsteps echoed through the night. The silhouette grew closer until the stranger stepped out of the shadows. A relieved grin softened his face.

"Oh, it's you," he said before the knife plunged into his belly.

36

The house creaked and issued a wretched groan. Like old bones awakening.

Raven's eyelids flickered. Her head felt trapped between a vise, some madman wrenching on the handle and cracking her eggshell skull. Her body dragged her toward unconsciousness, a whirlpool pulling her into a watery grave. What happened?

At-once, her eyes popped open, chest heaving as she remembered. She'd entered the locker room inside Benson's Barbells and washed up at the sink when someone struck her from behind. What happened next, she couldn't recall, though she'd awoken later inside a cramped, blackened space, the thick scent of rubber and oil boxing her in. She'd been inside a trunk.

Had Damian Ramos kidnapped her?

The stabbing pain in her head made it difficult to think straight. And she needed to, if she wanted to figure out where she was and plan an escape. She sat inside an empty room with scuffed hardwood floors. Drapes hung over a window, and a slit of darkness spilling between the curtains told her it was night-time. The door stood closed, the house silent except for her beating heart.

And something else. A whispering, breathing noise that sent a chill down her spine. Someone was behind her.

She jolted at the realization and rose. Ropes pulled her down. Until now, she'd been too groggy to notice the bindings clamping her wrists to the chair arms. A second rope snaked around her ankles. She assessed the ankle knot and noted the kidnapper hadn't wrapped it around the chair or attached it to her wrists. Nor had the kidnapper gagged her. A sloppy job. Whoever her kidnapper was, she doubted he'd done this before. The lack of a gag suggested the kidnapper held her in the country. Someplace where nobody would hear her scream.

The breathing continued behind her. Raven twisted her neck. Couldn't locate the source.

Maybe it was her kidnapper, stalking her, toying with her.

"Why are you doing this to me?"

No answer.

Angered, she nudged the chair sideways. A woman sat in a chair against the wall, bound as Raven was. Her head hung to her chest, a blonde ponytail dangled over her shoulder. Raven didn't need to see the woman's face to know it was Ellie Fisher.

"Ellie. Ellie Fisher. Wake up."

The woman didn't move. Had it not been for the rise and fall of Ellie's shoulders as she breathed, Raven would have worried the woman was dead.

Before Raven raised her voice, a noise sounded inside the house. Footsteps.

She clamped her eyes shut and lowered her head until she realized the footsteps weren't outside the door. They came from deep in the house. On a lower floor, she assumed. A door squealed open and closed with a hollow thump.

"Is the black girl awake?"

That voice, so gruff and arrogant. She recognized it from somewhere.

"Why the hell did you bring her into it? What good does she do us?"

Raven squinted her eyes and concentrated. The second man was Damian Ramos. And the first man had to be Mark Benson, the gymnasium owner. Benson must have attacked her in the locker room. Only Benson could unlock the rear entrance and enter unannounced.

"She was onto us. Why the hell do you suppose she signed up for a gym pass? It's not a coincidence she ran into you in Syracuse. She's following you."

A hesitation, then—

"How did she figure out we kidnapped Ellie?"

"I told you. I caught her on camera taking photographs. You're an idiot, Damian."

"That makes zero sense. I didn't grab Ellie until I left the gym."

"Put two and two together. Someone hired a private investigator to follow you. Think. Who would want information on you?"

Damian sighed.

"Sadie, my fiance. Shit."

"Christ. This was a stupid idea." One of the kidnappers paced with nervous indecision. Raven pictured Mark, his hand tugging at his graying hair as Damian stared at the floor. "I shouldn't have agreed to this."

"We need the money, Mark. If we don't come up with another two-hundred thousand, we'll lose our houses, our cars. You'll lose the gym."

"Who do I have to thank for that? Dammit, I can't believe you convinced me to short that stock."

"It was a can't miss opportunity," Damian pleaded. "I have a source on the inside. The company is going bankrupt."

"Then why did they announce record earnings? The stock shot from three dollars to fifty-eight in one week."

"It can't go any higher."

"Admit it, Damian. You got screwed. We both got screwed. What if the stock opens at seventy on Monday? Or it doubles? All you needed to do was place a stop order above the short price. Anything to cap our losses."

"It was a guaranteed win," Damian said, defeated.

So that explained why Damian and Mark kidnapped Ellie Fisher. Using insider information, Damian convinced Mark to bet against a company, and the investment blew up in their faces. How much money did they owe their broker—a hundred-thousand, half a million or more? From Chelsey's conversation with Lizzie Todd, they'd learned Ellie Fisher inherited almost a million dollars.

"You left me no choice," said Mark. "That bitch investigator took photographs of you and Ellie before the kidnapping."

"What should we do with the private eye? We won't get much from ransom."

"Kill her. Put a bullet in her head and bury her in the woods."

"Jesus. We never discussed killing anyone."

"She saw our faces, Damian. We'll go to jail."

The voices trailed away, and Raven scooted the chair toward Ellie Fisher, careful to be as quiet as possible. When she was inches from Ellie, Raven leaned into the woman's ear and whispered.

"Ellie, wake up."

The girl jumped as though electrocuted. Her head swung to Raven, the woman's eyes twin moons of panic. Recognition crossed Ellie's face, and her shoulders relaxed.

"I was awake when they brought you into the room. Who are you?"

"My name is Raven Hopkins. I'm a private investigator with Wolf Lake Consulting."

Ellie's brow shot up.

"What do they want with a private investigator?"

"I figured out they kidnapped you."

"Why would Damian do this to me? Is it because of the money?"

"Your grandmother's inheritance. Damian Ramos swindled a rich woman into getting engaged, and now he's after your money. He means to place a ransom on your head. They're in financial trouble."

Ellie shivered.

"I never trusted Mark Benson. He always strolls out of the office when a pretty woman enters the gym. Scumbag."

Raven held Ellie's eyes.

"Do you know where they're holding us?"

Ellie's head shook, and a tear crawled down her face.

"It's a farmhouse in the country, that's all I know." The woman went quiet when the front door opened and someone stepped outside. "That must be Mark. He's a heavy smoker, and Damian won't allow him to smoke inside."

Which left Damian alone in the house. Raven tested her bindings and felt wiggle room around her wrists. Given enough time, she believed she could break free. But how long would Mark and Damian wait before they killed her?

37

A half-mile from Hattie's bar, two state police officers manned a roadblock and turned an irate driver around. When Thomas flashed his badge, the larger of the two officers touched the brim of his hat and waved Thomas around the barricade. He pulled his truck behind Aguilar's car. His fellow deputy dressed in plain clothes like Thomas.

"What do we have?"

Aguilar nodded toward the ditch.

"Twenty-five minutes ago, a driver reported a truck stopped along the road and a man lying in the ditch. It's Garrick Tillery, Thomas. Somebody stabbed him."

Surreal shock rolled through Thomas as he glanced around the deputy. Earlier today, he'd considered Tillery a suspect in the murders of Lincoln Ramsey and Cecilia Bond. He could see one leg covered in blue jeans, the cuff tucked inside a beige work boot. Blood pooled in the ditch, black and silver under the moonlight as Gray glared down at Tillery. Virgil Harbough arrived. The medical examiner's hair stuck up in opposite directions, as if he just woke up.

Thomas groaned when Gray spotted him. The sheriff strode to them with fury tattooed to his face.

"We can rule out Garrick Tillery as our killer," Gray said. "Pretty soon, we'll be down to one suspect. Isn't it obvious Josiah Fowler is behind the murders?"

"What makes you believe Fowler killed Garrick Tillery?"

"Tillery attended church with the Ramsey and Bond families. We made the mistake of linking Tillery to the victims because he had contact with them."

"And a sexual assault conviction," Aguilar added, trying to reason with the sheriff.

"All we did was waste time. It was Father Fowler all along. He's the only link between our victims."

Thomas tugged at his collar. Damn, it was humid tonight.

"You agreed Fowler is an angel of mercy serial killer, using the prayer jar to choose his victims."

"And?"

"Lincoln Ramsey was on his death bed, and Cecilia Bond needed a kidney. Why would Garrick Tillery's name appear in the prayer jar?"

The sheriff swatted a mosquito, painting a bloody smear across his neck.

"So he doesn't use the prayer jar. I guess he's a wolf picking sheep from his flock. What does it matter how he chooses them?"

Thomas wanted to scream. Though he loved the sheriff and appreciated everything Gray had done for him, Thomas recognized Gray was in over his head and tainted with bias. He hated Father Josiah Fowler and ignored evidence pointing toward other suspects.

"I'm going after Fowler," Gray said.

Thomas shifted his body to block the sheriff.

"No, you're not. You don't have proof Fowler did this."

"Every second we waste gives Fowler time to hide the knife and dispose of the evidence."

"Let me investigate the scene before you pound on the church doors."

"I'll give you fifteen minutes," Gray said, turning in a huff.

Aguilar shook her head at Thomas. It frustrated him that the killer kept striking and they couldn't narrow the suspect list. But Gray made the case unbearable with his vendetta against Fowler. At what point did Thomas call the sheriff out for shoddy investigative work?

"I'll dust the truck for prints," Aguilar said.

Thomas slid gloves over his hands, clicked the flashlight, and lit the blacktop, pulling out the cracks and disrepair that would turn the road into a minefield by winter. Skid marks trailed from the center line to the guardrail, ending beneath Tillery's flattened tires. Did the killer stab Tillery, then slash the man's tires in case he survived and tried to drive away?

"Aguilar," he called over his shoulder.

"Yeah?"

"Are Tillery's tires slashed?"

She moved from one wheel to the next, crouching to examine the flattened tires.

"They're torn up, like he hit something in the road. It almost looks like Tillery drove over a spike strip."

Thomas swept the light down the road. Something flickered along the far shoulder. Crossing to the other side, he bent to examine the object.

"I found a tire spike," he said, slipping the spike into an evidence bag.

Aguilar jogged to Thomas.

"One spike wouldn't take out four tires."

"The killer must have collected the spikes before he fled the scene."

"Except he forgot one." Aguilar lifted the bag to eye level. "I doubt I'll pull a print off the spike."

"Keep looking."

For the next five minutes, Thomas and Aguilar walked up and down the curving road.

"That's the only one I found," he said, handing the evidence bag to Aguilar. "What else do we have?"

She cocked her head toward the truck.

"I found two sets of footprints leading from Tillery's truck to his body."

Thomas and Aguilar followed the trail, one weaving while the other arrowed straight down the bank. When they reached Garrick Tillery's body, Thomas compared the tread on the dead man's boots with the footprints.

"Those prints belong to Tillery," Thomas said, pointing at the twisting indentations. "Given the erratic gait and weaving, I'd say he was drunk."

"The other guy wasn't."

No, the killer wasn't drunk, judging by the straight path he took from Tillery's truck to the shoulder.

"The killer's prints end on the pavement. He didn't follow Tillery into the ditch."

"So he stabs Tillery, then Tillery stumbles off the shoulder and lands in the ditch."

"That's the way it appears."

The splash of blood on the shoulder suggested the killer gutted the drunk man along the road. Had someone driven past and witnessed the murder?

"Deputy." A tall state trooper left his post at the barricade and approached Aguilar. "My partner interviewed a server at the bar down the road."

"Hatties?" Aguilar asked.

"That's the one. The server remembers the deceased stopping in this evening. She says Tillery drank too much and left the bar around nine."

"Was he with anyone?"

"Negative, but he got into an altercation with a man named Carl Middleton."

Aguilar's eyes shot to Thomas.

"What happened?" asked Thomas.

"No punches thrown. The argument ended when Middleton shoved a table into Tillery and drove off."

"We need to find Carl Middleton," Thomas said.

Aguilar agreed.

"I'll follow up with Harbaugh and meet you at Middleton's place." Aguilar glanced at her watch. "Give me half an hour."

"Gotcha."

"Don't knock on Middleton's door before I get there. We don't know how dangerous he is."

Thomas climbed into his truck as Virgil's team arrived to take Tillery's body to the county morgue. Gray knocked on Thomas's window.

"I'll notify Suzanne Tillery," Gray said. "Better to do this in person. It's gonna be a long night."

A third person dead, and nobody could find Raven Hopkins.

38

The woman stumbling through the cemetery gates might have been a ghost from the way the moonlight bathed her in ethereal light. She barely stayed on her feet, the mental exhaustion crippling her as she searched the graveyard through a haze of tears.

Kay Ramsey tripped and caught herself on a tree. The gravestones glowed like hundreds of broken teeth sticking out of the earth. Above her, an oak tree extended a long bough. Under the light of day, the tree would have appeared protective. In the dark, it seemed grotesque and misshapen, the tentacle of a monstrous beast.

Confused, she spun one way, then the next. Lincoln's gravestone should be just up the incline. But she didn't see it.

Her husband's funeral felt surreal Saturday morning. It seemed half the village attended, everyone with a kind word to say about the man she loved. Memories from school and work. All those memories were pages torn from a book, left to the wind to scatter. She'd nodded and shared tears and hugs, and when it was over, Ambrose drove her home and sat with her inside the empty, gaping house.

Yet it never hit Kay that Lincoln was dead, that Virgil Harbough wouldn't call her in the middle of the night to announce Lincoln miraculously sat up. They'd made a mistake, and he was going to be fine. Not until she climbed the stairs to the guest bedroom, still unwilling to sleep in the bed she shared with Lincoln, did the reality crash down on her. After staring at the ceiling for an hour, she'd risen from bed, climbed into her clothes, and donned a dark jacket. She couldn't sleep without speaking to Lincoln one last time. She'd staggered to her vehicle and driven across the village to the cemetery without a single memory of the trip.

"Where are you?"

She swung her eyes across the gravestones, reading the names, searching for her lost husband. Is this what heaven was like—an endless exploration for the people you lost?

Now she stood in the dark, alone and afraid, as the night made sounds around her. Some sounds she expected—cricket songs and the hoot of an owl somewhere in the trees. Others, like the whispers of footsteps through the grass, she did not.

She wasn't alone in the night. Someone was in the graveyard. A caretaker? Another soul grieving a lost love?

Kay stumbled against a headstone and recoiled when her hand came away with a crushed slug. She shook her hand and slung the dead thing into the grass, a yelp escaping her throat as she turned in a circle. She was lost. As crazy as that seemed, she had no idea where she was in the cemetery.

Then she spotted his headstone. It stood fifteen feet away, nestled amid flower arrangements. Grief rushed at her, and she dropped to her knees and cried into her hands, her forehead leaning against the headstone, as if Lincoln, himself, supported Kay in her time of need. Her face reflected in the polished stone and looked cruelly aged.

"I can't do this without you," she cried. "Nobody told us it would be this hard."

In Kay's head, his comforting voice spoke to her. She was strong, and their family needed her.

As she curled beside his grave, not caring if she fell asleep and the caretaker found her in the morning, she glanced at the empty plot beside his. This would be Kay's someday.

The moon shone a spotlight upon her. This was the first time she'd experienced true comfort since the night the ambulance took Lincoln away. She closed her eyes and hummed as she did when Ambrose was sick as a child, and Lincoln sat beside her on their daughter's bed. The night sounds grew faint and blended with her own breathing until she didn't hear them anymore.

She imagined Lincoln whispering in her ear. Telling her not to fear death. That they'd be united soon.

Only it wasn't Lincoln's voice.

Her eyes snapped open to the dark. Heart thundered inside her chest. She grasped hold of Lincoln's headstone and dragged herself to her feet. The moon was wrong. Its location in the sky seemed too low, the glow almost to the tree line. And something hid inside the dark.

"Is someone there?"

Her eyes swept the grounds as footsteps skittered among the trees.

Kay placed a hand over her heart and realized she didn't want to die. A tree branch snapped. Then a shoe crunched brittle grass. The noises came from all directions, the sounds echoing through the graveyard as she held a defensive hand in front of her. She remembered the phone inside her pocket and pulled it out, fingers trembling and stumbling over the keypad. Before she could call the police, a figure emerged from the shadows. It slithered from stone to stone. A wraith come to life, intent on dragging her into a shallow grave.

"Don't cry, Kay. It will all be over soon."

That voice. She recognized it from somewhere.

Kay punched in the last number for the sheriff's department when the killer strode into the clearing. The phone rang. A man answered on the other end before she dropped the phone.

"Not you," she said in disbelief as the knife glistened in the moonlight.

She stood quivering, her feet cemented to the ground, as the killer approached.

"I'm sorry for what I did to your husband. But he no longer suffers, and you don't have to suffer, either."

The knife slashed across Kay's throat as she plunged into the dark. The night was forever, and its depths were black and endless.

39

F ive minutes until midnight.

Thomas sat beside Aguilar in the cruiser, thinking about his F-150 in the Nightshade County Sheriff's Department parking lot and how tired he was. He wanted nothing more than to curl up under the covers with Jack lying at the foot of the bed.

The lights were off inside Carl Middleton's cardinal-red ranch house. The pickup that almost ran Thomas off the road, parked in the driveway and collected moths. The moon fell behind the tall pines, darkening the neighborhood, and a dog barked down the road. Headlights flashed at the end of the block as a car turned down a side street.

"How many people murder their best friends and sleep soundly?"

Aguilar glanced across the car.

"I bet Jeremy Hyde slept well after he murdered Erika Windrow."

"You're probably right," Thomas said, shifting in the passenger seat, unable to get comfortable.

They'd surveyed the house for fifteen minutes. No lights shone inside the house. It was dead quiet.

"Let's wake him up," Thomas said, checking his weapon.

Their shoes scratched along the cement walkway to Middleton's front stoop. A wilted flower leaned in the corner, and the mailbox regurgitated bills and catalogs. Were it not for the Middleton Construction truck in the driveway, Thomas would have guessed Middleton fled Wolf Lake days ago. Aguilar radioed their position to dispatch as Thomas pressed the buzzer. Thirty seconds later, he jammed his thumb against the button again, listening as the bell rang through the house. A light flashed in the bedroom. Aguilar's hand drifted toward her gun. It took a full minute for Middleton to drag himself to the living room. The door opened, and Middleton rubbed the grogginess out of his eyes.

"Carl Middleton," Thomas said. "Were you at Hattie's bar between the hours of eight and nine o'clock?"

Smelling like a distillery, Middleton glanced between the two deputies, still half-asleep.

"Hattie's?" He massaged his belly and stifled a burp. "I guess so. Why?"

"We understand you had an altercation with Garrick Tillery inside the bar."

Suddenly awake, Middleton raised his hands at the deputies.

"Now, hold on. You can't arrest me for shouting at Garrick. It was just two friends disagreeing."

"The server says you shoved a table into your friend," Aguilar said.

"I don't recall."

"Where did you go after you left Hattie's?" asked Thomas.

Middleton glanced behind him, as though the living room furniture would provide an answer.

"Home. I came home and crashed."

"Did you take Marcellus Street?"

The construction worker scrunched his face in thought.

"That would have taken me to the opposite side of the village."

"So you had no contact with Garrick Tillery after you left Hattie's."

"None."

A pair of work boots sat on a mat inside the door. Dirt flecked off the treads and littered the entryway.

"Those your boots, Mr. Middleton?"

He stared down at the work boots.

"Yeah, why?"

"Could you show them to me?"

"I'm not giving anything without a warrant. Those are Timberland Pro work boots, and they don't come cheap."

"Just pick them up and show me the treads."

Middleton shot Thomas a doubtful stare before he bent over and hoisted the boots. He turned them around to display the bottoms, his head cocked to the side, as if to say, "Are you satisfied, asshole?"

Aguilar glanced at Thomas in question. He shook his head. This wasn't their killer. But Middleton was the last person seen with Tillery, and a witness verified he'd argued with the murder victim.

"I need you to come to the station and answer a few questions," Thomas said.

"Am I under arrest?"

"Not at this time."

"Then why the hell should I go with you?"

"It will be a lot easier for you, if you come with us. We need you to tell us about your argument."

"Why are you so interested?"

"Because Garrick Tillery died after he left Hattie's," Aguilar said. "Someone stabbed him on Marcellus Street and left him to bleed out in the ditch."

The color drained from Middleton's face. His bluster and arrogance vanished, and he gripped the jamb to hold himself upright.

"Somebody murdered Garrick? Why would anyone...are you sure?"

The door opened. Middleton staggered on stiff legs onto the stoop and stared into the night as though the two deputies weren't there.

"You might want to put on shoes," Thomas said, prompting Middleton to stare down at his bare feet.

"Right."

"And bring your work boots."

During the ride back to the sheriff's station, Middleton sat in the cruiser's backseat, wearing a thousand-yard stare. The blood hadn't returned to his face, and his eyes watched the neighborhoods shoot past like pictures in a movie. Aguilar kept glaring at Thomas. He couldn't tell her in front of Middleton that the boots were the wrong size. The footprints following Tillery's had been three or four shoe sizes smaller.

The deputies led Middleton into the interview room where Lambert waited. After Thomas briefed Lambert on Middleton, their radios flared to life. Gray's voice, almost hysterical with grief, came over the radio.

"The caretaker at St. Mary's cemetery just found Kay Ramsey dead beside her husband's grave. Someone slashed her throat. I don't think she's been dead more than half an hour."

"I gotta meet Gray at the cemetery," Thomas said.

Lambert pulled Thomas aside.

"Aguilar and I will handle the interview. But Thomas, something is wrong with Gray. Get the sheriff under control and stop him from doing anything stupid."

Thomas replied with a grim nod. As he climbed into the cruiser, he sensed the case unraveling. Kay Ramsey was the fourth body found, and Carl Middleton couldn't be responsible.

40

"It's easy," Mark Benson said, aiming the gun at Raven's temple as he mocked pulling the trigger. "One bullet to the head, and it's over."

Raven knelt in the grass outside the farmhouse with Damian and Mark standing over her. Her eyes pleaded with Damian, but the market analyst turned away.

"If it's so easy, then why don't you do it?"

"This is your mess. Clean it up."

Mark slapped the pistol into Damian's hand and made a sweeping gesture toward the woods. The moon hid behind the trees, making the forest appear as a black, craggy wall. Damian grasped Raven's elbow and hauled her up. Mark had untied her ankles, but the ropes still held her wrists behind her back. She gave Damian an imploring look.

"You heard the man," said Damian, hauling her toward the forest. "Start walking."

"You won't regret this," Mark called behind them. "When you get back, we'll make the ransom call. By this time tomorrow, we'll be on a beach in the Caribbean."

The footing became treacherous when they entered the

woods. Raven couldn't see two steps in front of her, and branches whipped at her face.

"Don't do this," she said.

He ignored Raven, dragging her through dead leaves until the forest engulfed the light spilling out of the farmhouse. Damian didn't wear gloves, and Mark's fingerprints were all over the pistol. Had they thought this through? These men weren't killers. Well, at least Damian wasn't, she prayed. There was still time to talk sense into him.

"What if he shoots you after you're finished with me?" she asked. In the deepening gloom, Damian pressed his lips together. "He'll make you do all the work. Then he'll kill you and leave your body beside mine."

"Shut up and walk."

"I overheard your conversation about the stock trade. He's desperate. Don't think he won't kill you and keep the ransom money for himself. Even if he doesn't kill you, your prints will be on the weapon when the cops figure this out. They'll arrest you for murder, and Mark will get away with the cash."

If she'd gotten through to him, she couldn't tell. He pulled her with renewed determination, his fingers digging into her biceps and shooting pain through her arm. He pulled up when the trees rustled. Something big hurried through the dark. She used the pause to regain her bearings. They were a hundred yards from the farmhouse. Listening, she discerned a creek trickling to her left. She'd seen the water glistening in the distance while Mark held her at gunpoint. If she escaped in the forest, the creek would lead her back to the farmhouse.

"Get moving," he said.

Raven stumbled onward. The forest floor snagged her sneakers and tripped her every few steps. Somehow, Damian stayed upright and kept hold of her arm. She wondered if he possessed a preternatural ability that allowed his eyes to penetrate the darkness. But as he tugged her over a rise, she felt the bindings loosen around her wrists. She'd almost broken free. All she needed to do was distract Damian while she worked her arms out of the ropes.

"Hey, loosen up on the arm, will ya? There's no reason to torture me before you pull the trigger." He didn't respond. "Ow. That really hurts."

"Cry all you want. Nobody will hear you out here."

Another animal burst through the brush. Raven used the distraction to wrestle her arm free as Damian stood with the gun aimed into the unknown, his foot tapping with indecision. Twisting her wrists together, working up a sweat in the humid night, Raven slipped one hand halfway out of the bindings.

"What was that?" he asked with wide eyes.

"There are bears out this way."

"Shut up."

"I'm not kidding. A bear took out my bird feeder last fall, and I only live two miles outside the village."

She hoped she could trick him into giving up their position. Damian didn't take the bait.

"It wasn't a bear. Walk, or I'll squeeze the trigger and let the coyotes make a meal out of you."

They descended a ridge. Damian kept looking around, as if he'd gotten lost. Raven stayed attuned to the trickling creek. The water lay straight ahead. Damian had veered left.

"So what's the plan? Shoot me, then put a ransom on Ellie's head?"

"Something like that."

"How will you pick up the money?"

Damian glared at Raven.

"What do you care?"

"The cops will set up surveillance and take you down. You

can't trust them to hand over the money. And even if you pull it off, you'll be on the run for decades. Ellie saw your face."

"Mark and I have it handled."

"So you intend to shoot Ellie too."

"Why would I kill her? She's a friend."

"A friend who wants you arrested."

She spied the uncertainty on his face.

"I could handle the pickup for you."

"Fat chance, since you'll be dead."

Raven stopped. He turned on her with a threat in his eyes.

"Untie my wrists and let me go. Tell Mark you shot me in the woods, then I'll take him down from behind. With Mark out of the picture, you can keep all the money, and I'll pick it up for you."

"You want me to kill my best friend?"

Raven laughed.

"He doesn't act like your best friend. The way Mark calls the shots and talks down to you, he thinks he's running the show."

Damian jammed the pistol into her temple.

"No more talking. I see what you're doing."

He shoved her from behind and got her moving again. Now he paced behind her, and she worried he'd look down and notice her hand slipping out of the ropes.

"All I'm saying is he doesn't respect you. You're the brains behind the operation, Damian. Mark runs a lousy gym, and you're a market analyst. In my book, that makes you the smart one."

"That's another thing. I don't appreciate you snooping around and digging into my background. Sadie put you up to this, didn't she?"

Raven talked over her shoulder as she stumbled between the trees.

"Can't blame her for being careful. Anyhow, you won't need

Sadie's money. Not after you snatch Ellie Fisher's inheritance. I can't believe her grandmother left her fifty-thousand."

Damian froze. Raven walked several steps before she realized he wasn't behind her.

"No...no." He yanked his hair. "Ellie Fisher is worth a million dollars."

Raven turned to face him, wiggling her wrist past the last binding as she screwed her face up in shock.

"A million? Is that what she told you?" Raven giggled. "Honey, she played you. If Ellie Fisher was worth a million dollars, do you really believe she'd flaunt it to a guy she met at the gym?"

"It's not like that. We've worked out together for two years."

"Damian, listen to me. I have Ellie's finances on my laptop. The grandmother left her fifty-thousand. Combine that with her savings, and Ellie is worth sixty. Minus the loan she took out on her car."

"Shit."

"Why so glum? Fifty-thousand is a lot of money. That should take care of your margin call, right? Plus enough to disappear with until the cops give up on finding you."

Damian placed his hands behind his head and paced in a circle with the gun dangling off his thumb.

"You're screwing with me. That's all this is. Ellie Fisher has a million in her bank account."

"How much do you owe your broker?"

His head fell back, and he stared up at the canopy.

"Too much. This can't be happening."

"All right. Plan B. It doesn't matter if you can't pay your broker. The police will seize your funds the second they figure out you kidnapped Ellie. So take the money and disappear—no Mark, no cops breathing down your neck. Just you living on the coast under a different name."

"You make it sound so easy."

"It is easy, Damian. That's where I come in. As a private investigator, I know how to make somebody vanish. Trust me. I'll get you out of this."

Raven's hand popped free. The rope unfurled, and she grasped it between her fingers before it fell to the ground and gave her away. Bringing her legs together so he wouldn't see the rope, she drew his gaze. Thinking fast, she bent down and grimaced.

"What the hell is wrong with you?"

"I have to pee. Like really bad."

"So go in your shorts. I don't care."

"Come on, Damian. I'll make you a promise. If you do me a solid and unbutton my shorts, I'll take care of the rest. You don't need to untie me. I'm talented."

"I don't trust you."

"What are you afraid of? I'm in the middle of nowhere, my hands are tied behind my back, and you have a gun."

He shook the pistol at her.

"No funny business, or I swear I'll shoot."

Raven bounced on her toes, playing up her need to relieve herself. He edged closer, the gun aimed at her forehead. She wondered if he had the stomach to pull the trigger. His fingers curled over her waistband and took liberties. As he grinned, she felt his fingertips pluck at her panties.

Raven dropped the rope and whipped her arm around, striking his forearm with her palm. The force jolted the gun from his hand and knocked it to the forest floor. Raven dove for the weapon with Damian's weight crashing down on her back. The air rushed from her lungs as she grasped for the fallen pistol. His fists pummeled the back of her head while he sought to control her. She swung back with her elbow and struck his temple. Stunned, Damian toppled over and landed in the brush.

He was almost on his feet when her hand closed over the pistol. At the moment he lunged, she whipped the gun against his head. His legs gave out. Damian lost consciousness before he crumpled.

A hum came from inside his pocket. His phone.

Wincing, Raven fished the phone from Damian's jeans, terrified his hands would snap up and wrap around her neck. Little good the phone did her without his code. Noticing the phone used facial recognition, she turned the screen toward his face and unlocked the phone.

He mumbled under his breath as she stepped away. Her body thrumming with adrenaline, she dialed Chelsey.

"Raven, we've been looking everywhere for you," Chelsey said.

"I don't have time. Damian Ramos and Mark Benson kidnapped me and locked me in a farmhouse with Ellie Fisher."

"Just tell me where you are."

"I have no idea where I am. Somewhere in the country, surrounded by forest. I disabled Damian, but Benson still has Ellie."

"Do you recognize any landmarks?"

"None."

"Okay, let me—"

The phone died. Raven stared at the black screen. Damian hadn't recharged his phone.

"Dammit."

With no other choice, Raven slipped the phone into her pocket and caught her breath. It was only a matter of time before Mark sensed something was wrong and fled with Ellie. Raven retraced her path until she spotted the creek. The clock ticked toward one in the morning as she raced to the farmhouse.

41

SUNDAY, JULY 19TH, 12:55 A.M.

Yellow crime scene tape flapped in the wind. Kay Ramsey lay flat on her back, legs akimbo, a deep gash across her neck. Lights whirled across the graveyard as an ambulance followed the winding road into St. Mary's cemetery. Virgil Harbough's car trailed the ambulance.

"A woman walking her dog heard a scream and called the department," Gray said, standing over Kay's corpse. "I was two miles from the cemetery and responded. Found her like this, her throat slit from ear to ear."

"Nobody saw anyone leave the graveyard?"

"No. What in God's name was Kay Ramsey doing in a graveyard in the middle of the night?"

Cricket songs swelled around them as Thomas assessed the scene.

"She had trouble sleeping. My guess is she couldn't stay away from her husband."

"The poor woman. Lincoln's funeral must have torn her apart."

Thomas glanced at Gray and recognized the injured stare of a man who understood loss too well.

"You still believe Father Fowler committed these murders?"

"I'll tell you who didn't kill Kay Ramsey. Garrick Tillery and Carl Middleton. Like I said on Marcellus Street, we're narrowing our suspect list every hour, and it keeps coming down to Fowler."

Thomas popped the cruiser's trunk and removed his investigation kit. As Gray videotaped the scene, Thomas donned yellow glasses and shone an alternate light source over the grass, then swept it over Lincoln Ramsey's headstone. The blue wavelength filtered out external light and revealed evidence the naked eye missed. Blood splatter covered the ground and sprayed the gravestone.

"I found a shoe print," Gray said, directing the camera toward an indentation in the dirt.

Thomas knelt in the grass, snapped a photograph with his phone, and placed a yellow evidence marker beside the print. The scale on the evidence marker told Thomas the shoe print was too small for Carl Middleton. Thomas gave Gray room to compare the scale and print.

"Fowler's a big man, right?"

Gray nodded.

"Couldn't tell you his shoe size, though."

"Men's size seven?"

"It's possible."

Thomas ground his teeth. Who were they looking for? All this time, he'd focused on Tillery and Middleton.

"I wonder where Duncan Bond is tonight."

Gray turned off the camera.

"You believe Duncan Bond is capable of this?"

The sheriff swept his arm over Kay's body.

"Carl Middleton has five inches and fifty pounds on Duncan Bond, and Father Fowler is a big guy too. This print is too small to belong to Middleton or Fowler."

Gray scoffed.

"Shoe size doesn't always match physical size. And anyhow, this might be Kay Ramsey's print."

Thomas set a second evidence marker beside Kay Ramsey's foot.

"No chance. Kay's shoe size is smaller."

Virgil strode through the grass, hunched over as if he hadn't slept a wink in the last week. The sheriff turned his attention to the medical examiner.

"I'm sorry you have to see this, Virgil. Everyone in Wolf Lake loved Kay Ramsey."

"Seems we keep burying our neighbors," Virgil said, dabbing his forehead with a handkerchief. "You better catch this guy, Sheriff. The village can't survive another week like this one."

"I'm pretty certain I know who did this. All I have to do is prove it." Gray's eyes held Thomas's. "Speaking of which, I have a door to pound on."

"Maybe you ought to think this through," said Thomas, as Virgil glanced worriedly between the sheriff and his deputy.

"If I'd followed my gut after we found Garrick Tillery, Kay Ramsey would still be alive." Gray packed his investigation kit. "Stay with Virgil's team. Find me a fingerprint or anything that proves Fowler did this."

Before Thomas stopped him, the sheriff stomped to his cruiser and slammed the door. The engine roared to life, and the cruiser kicked up stones as the tires spun.

The farmhouse glowed in silver moonlight. Two lamps burned inside the home, one in the living room, the other upstairs where Mark and Damian held Ellie Fisher.

Raven stood behind the tree line and parted the branches. No sounds came from within the house, and no shadows moved past the windows. The driveway led to the garage. The door was closed, but Raven discerned the silhouette of Damian's Audi beyond the windows. Were the keys inside the house?

Sometimes batteries recovered enough life to power the phone. Crouching amid the shadows, Raven tested Damian's phone. No juice.

She was due a run of good luck. If Mark left Ellie alone to search for Damian, Raven could free the kidnapped woman. Raven scanned the backyard, then sprinted out of hiding and moved along the wall. She discovered a back door beneath a roofed porch. The steps appeared rickety, but they held her weight without squealing as she climbed onto the porch and tested the knob. Unlocked.

Without making a sound, Raven stepped into the darkened

kitchen. Light bleeding out of the living room ended at the threshold. The ancient refrigerator in the corner rumbled, causing enough clamor to cover her steps as she crossed the room. A white cable extending from an outlet caught her eye. Damian's phone charger. She wrestled with indecision while she listened for Mark. The coast clear, she plugged the charging cable into Damian's phone and turned the screen face down so it wouldn't draw attention. She'd give the phone a minute to recharge before she called the sheriff's department.

A floorboard groaned on the upper level. Raven pressed her back flat against the wall and waited until the house fell silent.

"Come on, come on," she begged the phone.

The screen flickered to life as the phone rebooted. She hid beside the jamb with Damian's gun in hand. After another thirty seconds, she crept to the counter, cringing when the floor squealed beneath her weight. She dialed 9-1-1. Raven sighed in relief when she recognized the dispatcher's voice. She was still in Nightshade County.

"I'm inside a farmhouse with Ellie Fisher, the kidnapped girl from the news," she whispered.

The dispatcher couldn't understand Raven. She was about to raise her voice when a thump came from somewhere down-stairs. Mark was near.

Raven darted away from the phone, knowing the dispatcher would assume the caller was under duress after she didn't respond to his questions. If she was lucky, the sheriff's depart-ment would locate the phone using GPS coordinates. That she'd called with Damian's phone gave her added hope the sheriff would recognize the name and act quickly.

As she edged out of the kitchen with the gun trained at the empty living room, she wondered where Mark was. She swung the weapon and directed it up the staircase. Light from Ellie's room spilled across the upper landing.

Raven froze when the gun barrel pressed against the back of her neck.

"Drop the gun," Mark growled.

She never considered he carried a second gun. Raven contemplated swinging a blind elbow at Mark's head. But unlike Damian, Mark held his weapon with confident certainty. If she fought back, he'd pull the trigger. Defeated, Raven let the gun slip from her fingers and smack against the floorboards.

"That's good. Now raise your hands above your head." After Raven complied, he gave her a shove from behind. "Climb the stairs. We're taking Ellie and getting the hell out of here."

43

Thomas stomped the gas and pushed the cruiser to seventy mph on the open road, as the night flew at the windshield. By now, the sheriff would be at St. Mary's church, interrogating Father Josiah Fowler, and if Gray was right about the priest, the sheriff was in danger.

"Gray, come in."

The sheriff didn't respond to radio calls. Thomas's heart pounded as the church came into view. The rectory next door housed Fowler. The lights were off.

He stopped behind Gray's abandoned cruiser and radioed his position. After dispatch confirmed Aguilar was en route, Thomas jogged up the church steps, stopping when he noticed a glow behind a stained glass window. The door stood open a crack.

At the sound of shouting, Thomas shoved the doors open and entered the vestibule. The worship area was empty, the pews spreading into darkness. He followed the light down the stairs and retraced the path he'd taken when he interviewed Father Fowler.

"I didn't kill anyone. What is wrong with you?"

Thomas found Gray standing over Fowler, who cowered behind his desk. The sheriff waved his gun at the priest.

"Show me your hands and step out from behind the desk."

"Not until you tell me what this is about." Fowler's eyes swung to Thomas when he entered the office. "Deputy, tell this man he can't arrest me without provocation."

"You were at the cemetery with Kay Ramsey," the sheriff said, ignoring Thomas's presence.

"Kay Ramsey? I was here all night."

"You killed Lincoln Ramsey and Cecilia Bond."

"This is ludicrous."

Thomas turned and glared at Gray so Fowler couldn't see his face.

"Put the gun away," he whispered, holding Gray's eyes. "We don't have the evidence to hold him."

He'd never seen Gray like this. The sheriff knew no boundaries. Possessed by rage, he was prepared to fire his weapon if Fowler twitched.

"He's guilty. I spoke with Suzanne Tillery. She put Garrick's name in the prayer jar."

Thomas felt his stomach drop. He glanced over his shoulder at Fowler, the priest staring at the sheriff and deputy in disbelief.

"What's this about the prayer jar?" Fowler asked, rising.

"I told you to show me your hands," Gray said as the priest's hands hung beneath the desk. "We know Duncan Bond entered Cecilia's name into the prayer jar, and Kay Ramsey did the same for Lincoln."

"And?"

"It's funny how they both ended up dead within days of each other. How did you do it, Fowler? Did you climb through Ramsey's window and cover his face with a pillow, making it look like the COPD killed him?"

"You have no right to question me in God's house."

"You don't have an alibi for the night Cecilia Bond died. You claim you walked through the neighborhoods surrounding the church. But nobody remembers seeing you." Fowler's jaw shifted. "Suzanne Tillery gave up on Garrick because she couldn't control his drinking. She asked you to pray for her husband. Then you stabbed him."

The priest's face went slack.

"Garrick Tillery is dead?"

"That gave you time to cross the village and murder Kay Ramsey in the cemetery. You knew she'd visit Lincoln's grave, didn't you? You're sick, Fowler, and you're going to prison."

Fowler faltered. He grasped the desk as his knees buckled. Thomas rounded the desk and caught the priest before he fell.

"Kay? Why would someone hurt that wonderful woman?"

As Thomas supported Fowler, he frisked the priest and confirmed he didn't conceal a weapon. But as Thomas glanced down, he noted Fowler's shoe size looked about right for the prints at the two murder scenes. Dirt marred his black shoes and covered the floor beneath his desk.

"Where did you pick up the mud?" Thomas asked.

Fowler stared back at Thomas with hazy eyes.

"What?"

"You claim you were here all night. But your shoes are covered in dirt."

The priest looked down, then back to Thomas.

"The rose garden. I watered the roses outside the rectory before sunset."

Gray shook his head and said, "We'll match the soil to the cemetery. Come clean, Fowler. You murdered Garrick Tillery and Kay Ramsey. Did you believe you were saving them from suffering? Do you think you're God?"

Fowler's legs collapsed. Thomas caught the priest and

guided him to the floor. Fowler's breaths came too fast and sounded shallow. Thomas checked the man's racing pulse.

"He's going into shock. Call an ambulance."

Gray glared at the fallen priest.

"He's faking. Cuff the bastard."

"Listen to yourself!" Thomas's shout reverberated off the walls and knocked Gray back on his heels. "All this goes back to your wife's death. You're convinced Fowler is a murderer because you can't forgive him for running Lana off the road."

Injury clouded Gray's eyes, and Thomas harbored guilt for snapping at the sheriff and bringing Lana into the case. But he couldn't separate Lana's mysterious death from the Fowler investigation.

If the priest understood the sheriff's accusation, he gave no indication. He blinked at the ceiling, confused by his surroundings.

Thomas radioed dispatch and requested an ambulance for the priest. This wasn't right. Thomas had witnessed bad acting by criminals over his career. He'd yet to see someone fake shock.

"Father, can you hear my voice?" Fowler blinked twice. His eyes followed the walls before falling to the deputy's face. "You fainted, but you're doing fine. Breathe and focus on my voice."

"I didn't hurt anyone," Fowler said, his voice weak and fading. "All I wanted was to help Kay and Cecilia and support their families. That's the role God chose for me."

Thomas met Gray's eyes and motioned him behind the desk. The sheriff complied, and Thomas tilted his head at the carpet beneath Fowler's chair.

"There's red mulch mixed with the dirt," Thomas said. "That didn't come from the cemetery."

A vein pulsed in Gray's neck.

"Doesn't mean he wasn't there when Kay Ramsey died."

Ignoring Gray, Thomas directed Fowler's eyes to his.

"Who has access to the prayer jar besides you?"

Fowler swallowed. Sweat trickled down his forehead.

"I don't allow anyone to read the contents. There's a lock on the lid, and I have the key."

"Where do you keep the key?" When Fowler didn't answer, Thomas set a hand on the priest's shoulder. "It's important you tell me everything. Where do you hide the key?"

Fowler's eyes drifted to the desk, and Thomas pulled the drawer open. Three keys hung from a ring. Donning gloves, Thomas removed the keyring.

"Which key unlocks the prayer jar?"

"The bronze one in the middle."

"And you keep the keys inside your desk at all times?"

Fowler blinked again, composing his thoughts.

"Yes, and I always lock the office. Nobody opens the door except for me and..." The priest's jaw hung open. "No, it can't be."

The reality hit Fowler and Thomas at the same time. Thea Barlow had access to Fowler's desk. All evening, Thomas had wondered why the footprints at the crime scenes were smaller than Middleton's.

"Does Thea Barlow bring the prayer jar to you?"

"Yes."

The possibility Barlow killed Garrick Tillery and Kay Ramsey worked across Gray's face. Thomas faced the sheriff.

"Barlow was there Thursday night when Kay Ramsey said she no longer wanted to live."

"An angel of mercy killer," Gray said. He shook his head to clear the cobwebs. "I'll call Lambert and have him track down Thea Barlow."

"That won't work. Lambert released Carl Middleton and responded to a call, and Aguilar is on her way to the church."

Two murders in one night. Thea Barlow was escalating. A chilling thought crossed Thomas's mind.

"Father, give me the names from the prayer jar."

The request grounded Fowler and gave the priest something to focus on.

"I already told you. The contents of the prayer jar are private. They belong to the family and me."

"If Thea Barlow is our killer, I need to know who she's going after next."

Fowler covered his face with his hand. A moan rolled out of the priest.

"Talk to me, Father. Who did you pray for tonight?"

The priest's eyes locked with Thomas's.

"I prayed for Mason Shepherd. Your father, Deputy."

44

Ignoring Deputy Lambert's warning to wait until he arrived, Chelsey stomped on the gas pedal and pushed the Honda Civic faster. The rural road on the northern fringe of Nightshade County undulated and cut through forestland. She couldn't drive safely at these speeds during the day, let alone in the middle of the night.

Twenty minutes ago, the sheriff's department had triangulated the location of Damian Ramos's phone. Chelsey promised Lambert she'd let the deputy handle Raven's rescue. But she was at least two minutes ahead of Lambert, the cruiser's lights pinpricks in her mirror.

She scanned the terrain as she tugged the wheel. Tires screeched while she rounded a sharp curve. Where was the farmhouse? It seemed she'd left humanity behind when she exited Wolf Lake.

Chelsey checked her GPS. The house had to be close. A glow through the trees caught her eye, and she pulled hard on the wheel and whipped the car to the right. A two-story farmhouse rose beside a dirt road. But it was the dust hanging in the air that pulled her attention.

Straightening the car, she accelerated down the road, the
dust growing thicker. Then she spotted the glowing eyes of taillights in the distance and the source of the dust storm. Mark
Benson was fleeing with Raven and Ellie Fisher.

The cruiser's headlights grew in size in her mirror. Her
phone rang, and she recognized Lambert's name on the screen.
No chance she could control the car if she answered.

It was a minor miracle she'd located Raven tonight. Chelsey
knew the sobering statistics. Once she lost sight of Raven and
Ellie, the chance of a happy ending dropped like a stone in a
bottomless river.

"You're not getting away," she muttered through gritted teeth.

Chelsey punched the accelerator and closed the distance on
Mark Benson's SUV.

DARREN GRIPPED the door handle inside Lambert's cruiser as the
deputy glared ahead, his vision razor-focused on Chelsey's
Honda Civic. They had to find Raven and Ellie Fisher before
Mark Benson did something crazy. Darren refused to accept the
possibility the women were already dead.

The cruiser flew down a dirt road, choked with dust. It was
impossible to see a hundred feet in front of the vehicle, and
Darren never spotted the farmhouse until Lambert slowed
outside the driveway.

"Benson must have fled with Raven and Ellie," Darren said.

The farmhouse appeared abandoned. Chelsey must have
been chasing Benson.

"Hang on," said Lambert a second before he shot down the
road.

The dirt road ended at a T-intersection. The deputy paused

at the stop sign and glanced both ways before Darren spied two sets of taillights to the right.

"There they are."

Lambert nodded and turned right. On the paved road, it didn't take long for the deputy to raise his speed and close on Chelsey's car. He flashed his lights, a signal for Chelsey to let them pass. Chelsey's car rode the SUV's bumper, the private investigator pacing Benson's vehicle as the kidnapper tried to shake her.

"Why won't she pull over and let us pass?"

Darren had no answer. He just stared through the windows into Benson's SUV, searching for a sign the women were inside and alive. He didn't see anyone except the driver.

Chelsey swerved into the passing lane. Benson matched her speed, aware Chelsey wanted to cut him off. Lambert took advantage of the opening and accelerated until the cruiser rumbled a foot behind Benson's bumper.

The Civic and SUV drove in lockstep at over seventy mph down the dark roadway. Lambert's knuckles turned white as he gripped the wheel. Benson rocketed ahead, but Chelsey pushed her car over eighty and caught up. Darren could see the back end of the Civic shimmying, Chelsey on the verge of losing control.

Before Darren recognized Benson's intentions, the SUV drifted left. The heavier vehicle clipped the Civic. Darren cried out. Chelsey's car skidded and launched off the road, disappearing into the trees.

Lambert struck the SUV near the wheel. The SUV spun and came to rest when the back end fell into a ditch. Tires squealed as Lambert brought the cruiser to a stop. Darren was first out of the vehicle. The door to Benson's SUV flew open, and the burly gym owner limped down the rural route.

"Let Benson go, and help Ellie and Raven!" Lambert called over his shoulder. "I've got Chelsey."

Benson's footfalls echoed down the lonely roadway as Darren rushed to the SUV, searching for the kidnapped women. Where were they? The backseat lay empty. A cold thought gripped his spine. What if Benson had already murdered the women and dumped them in the farmhouse?

A thud pulled Darren's attention. The trunk.

He pulled the release and opened the hatch. Raven and Ellie lay on their sides with ropes binding their ankles and wrists. He released a breath when Raven groaned in pain.

The rear windshield had shattered in the collision, and a minefield of safety glass littered the trunk. Blood trickled down their bare legs and arms. The cuts appeared superficial.

"Are you injured?"

Raven shook her head.

"Check on Ellie. She hit her head when Benson spun out."

Ellie couldn't focus her eyes as Darren untied the blonde woman's wrists and ankles. He helped her out of the trunk and sat her beside the wheel, careful to avoid the broken glass. Next, he freed Raven and supported her as she climbed down from the SUV.

"Stay here. I'll check on Chelsey with Deputy Lambert."

Raven's head shot up.

"What's wrong with Chelsey? She's here?"

Darren didn't have time to explain. He leaped the shoulder and ran toward the woods where Chelsey's Civic had vanished, praying she'd survived the crash. The hollow pit in his stomach burned with worry.

When he reached the crash site, the car's wheels continued to spin. Smoke curled out from beneath the hood. The car lay upon a tangle of brush, and the crumpled front bumper hung like a broken wing. Darren knew moving Chelsey carried a heavy risk. But they had to remove her from the car before the fire spread. Darren radioed for an ambulance as Lambert lifted Chelsey. Her neck hung limp, the woman's eyes closed. A lightning bolt gash cut across her forehead and oozed blood.

"Is she breathing?"

Lambert nodded.

"Help me get her away from the car."

When the deputy set Chelsey on the shoulder, Chelsey's eyes flicked open. Darren threw his head back in relief.

"Thank God."

Chelsey eyes swiveled between the two men. Darren noted she hadn't moved her neck.

"What happened?"

"You crashed your car," Darren said, brushing matted hair off the woman's cheek. "Lie still."

"My car? I don't remember anything after the farmhouse." Worry lit her eyes. "Where's Raven and Ellie?"

"They're back at the SUV and doing fine."

Two pairs of footfalls approached. Raven had Mark Benson's arm wrenched behind his back as she walked him back to Lambert and Darren.

"Ellie's still at the SUV," Raven confirmed, answering the question in Darren's eyes. "Don't worry about me. I can take care of myself. And I can certainly handle apes like this guy."

Lambert slapped the cuffs on Benson and walked him back to the cruiser. Raven's eyes stopped on Chelsey, and she dropped to her knees beside the crumpled woman.

"My God, what happened to you?"

"I'm not sure," Chelsey said. "Darren says I lost control of the car."

Raven glanced at Darren, and the sick feeling in his stomach grew. Memory loss was common with concussions. But Chelsey hadn't moved since Lambert set her down.

"I can't believe you found us," Raven said, locking eyes with Chelsey.

"Did you expect anything less? I'm the best P.I. you've ever worked with."

"Girl, you're the only P.I. I've ever worked with. Are you all right?"

Chelsey closed her eyes and winced.

"I can't feel my legs."

Darren saw the flashing lights in the distance before he heard the approaching sirens.

45

Thomas jogged up the walkway outside his childhood home with Aguilar by his side. The moon lingered on the horizon, the house blanketed in darkness as he stared up at the windows. He'd phoned his parents three times while he crossed the village. No answer.

Now he moved to the door and slipped his key into the lock. The door slid open on its own. The knob hung askew as if someone had taken a hammer to it.

"We go in slow and careful," Aguilar said, holding his eyes until he acknowledged her.

He stood in the entryway and listened to the grandfather clock tick. All was silent inside the cavernous home, the shadows long and menacing. Aguilar reached for the light switch, and Thomas shook his head and placed a finger against his lips.

"Barlow is already here. Take her by surprise."

The quiet was tainted. Like a sarcophagus with the lid sealed. The kitchen and study stood near the end of a long hallway. Stairs off the living room led to the upper landing and the master bedroom. Something shifted upstairs. A subtle movement.

Thomas rushed to the stairs before Aguilar snatched his arm. She pointed toward an open door at the top of the landing. Thomas's old bedroom. His mother kept the door closed at all times, as though he'd died and his ghost haunted the upstairs.

Lined with pile carpet, the well-constructed staircase concealed their steps as they climbed. Thomas stared at the open doorway, then shifted his attention to the master bedroom at the end of the hall. His father was a heavy snorer. No sounds came from the bedroom.

Thomas spun inside his old room and motioned Aguilar through. The closet door was closed. His chest tightened as he opened the door and swept his gun through the darkness. When he turned, he noticed the disturbed blankets and bedspread. Neither of his parents would have climbed into his bed.

A sound came from down the hall. Inside the master bedroom.

Aguilar raised her eyes to Thomas before a floorboard groaned. They crept into the hallway with their guns drawn. The landing lay empty before them.

A moan came from inside his parents' bedroom. Thomas and Aguilar hurried to the door and stood to either side. On Aguilar's nod, Thomas twisted the knob and opened the door. Curtains blocked out the starlight. Two lumps beneath the blankets marked his mother and father. But Thomas sensed something wasn't right. The moaning sound came again. It sounded muffled and faraway, as if it came from another room. Or the closet.

As Aguilar trained her gun on the closet and crept across the room, Thomas approached the bed. His father's head lay on the pillow. He was certain Mason Shepherd wasn't breathing until his father's eyes popped open. He threw the covers off and sat up.

"Thomas? What is the meaning of this?"

"There's someone in the house," Thomas said, urging his father to be quiet.

Mason Shepherd creased his brow.

"You break into our house in the middle of the night, and you expect me to believe there's a prowler?"

Thomas stared at the unmoving form beside his father.

"Mother?"

Lindsey Shepherd didn't reply. Her body lay beneath the blankets with the covers pulled over her head.

Mason glanced between his wife and Thomas.

"Wake up, Lindsey," Mason said, shaking her. "Your son is out of his mind."

When Lindsey didn't awaken, Mason's mouth fell open. Panic twisted his face, and he jostled Lindsey with increased vigor.

The covers flew back. Thea Barlow sat up beside Mason Shepherd with an unhinged grin. Mason cried out and scurried from the woman. She produced the butcher's knife before Thomas could react and stabbed the mattress just as Mason twisted away.

Thomas raised the gun.

"Drop the knife!"

Barlow lunged at Thomas, hissing like a feral cat as he opened fire.

The gunshots tore gaping holes in the woman's chest and threw her against the headboard, where she slumped over and lay still. Her eyes never left Thomas as he shielded his father and helped him off the bed.

～

"Jesus," Aguilar whispered, walking Thomas's mother out of the closet.

The deputy supported Lindsey Shepherd as the older woman clutched her forehead. Lindsey's scalp clotted with blood, and she wore the dazed look of someone who'd just awoken. Thomas snatched a towel from the bathroom and handed it to Aguilar, who pressed it against Lindsey's head.

Mason's legs trembled, and he stumbled twice as Thomas led him to his wife. The father's body hummed with tension, as if he wanted to throw Thomas off and walk on his own. But he couldn't support himself without his boy to hold him up.

Blood droplets stained Lindsey's hands and shirt as Mason draped an arm around Lindsey and cried into her shoulder. She kept rubbing the towel over her bloody shirt and hands, desperate to rid herself of tonight's memories.

When she saw Thea Barlow's dead body in the bed, Lindsey screamed for a very long time.

46

"*You're still in love with her.*"

It's not a question. Dr. Mandel's statement causes sweat to trickle down Thomas's brow. The room seems smaller today, the little office confining. Like his personal prison.

"*Yes.*"

One word. Hearing himself say it aloud is a punch to his gut.

"*Does she know?*"

Thomas lowers his head and studies his hands.

"*I don't think so. We haven't spoken since the morning after I shot Jeremy Hyde.*"

Dr. Mandal sets the pen and paper aside and sips her tea. When she stares at him like this, he's unclothed, exposed. The secrets he conceals from himself, he cannot hide from her.

"*Perhaps she wishes to move on and leave the past behind. It's a challenge for people with Asperger's to see the world from another's perspective.*"

"*I don't blame her for moving on.*"

"*And yet you still pursue this woman, despite her indifference toward you. Does that sound familiar to you?*"

He chews his cheek until the coppery warmth of his own blood touches his tongue.

"Should it?"

She fixes her skirt and taps her fingers on her thigh.

"When you were a child, you believed you could control your own fate. You tossed coins into fountains and wished upon stars."

Thomas nods.

"What did you wish for?"

With a shrug, Thomas says, "Nothing important, I suppose."

"I doubt that's true. You wished your parents would love you and show you affection."

His eyes rise to hers.

"How did you..."

"Why else would you chase the only person who showed you love when you were young?"

THE WORLD SPUN TOO FAST.

Thomas couldn't process the news as he rushed into the hospital. The words *accident* and *paralyzed* kept flying through his head as he rushed through the lobby. Lambert hadn't told him about Chelsey's crash until they crossed paths in the office, both deputies almost twenty-four hours into their workdays. His stomach lurched as he stood inside the elevator, tapping his foot as the floors scrolled by.

The doors opened to the trauma unit. He scanned the room numbers and hurried down the corridor. Room 712.

When he entered the room, Raven sat beside Chelsey's bed and held her hand. A confusion of wires trailed from Chelsey's body to machines with digital readouts. He released a breath when Chelsey's eyes fell to his.

Raven rose from the chair.

"Thank you for coming," she said, hugging Thomas.

"I came as soon as Lambert told me about the accident. How's she doing?"

"She's awake. I'll let the two of you talk." Raven turned to Chelsey. "I'll be back in twenty minutes."

Chelsey's eyes fell to her hands. Bandages circled her head, and a laceration trailed down her left arm.

"You shouldn't have come," Chelsey said, fiddling with the blanket.

"Why wouldn't I? Lambert said you lost feeling in your legs."

She waved a hand through the air.

"The crash gave me a concussion, and that's what caused the numbness. I'm not paralyzed, if that's what you're worried about."

As he reached to brush the hair from her eyes, she pulled her head away and threw him an irritated look. Thomas settled into the chair.

"Don't take a concussion lightly. The recovery time ranges seven to ten days in mild cases, and yours isn't mild."

"I don't want to talk about it."

She folded her arms and glared at the wall. The monitors beeped, and conversation from the medical staff filtered down the corridor.

"I'm relieved you're all right." His eyes held concern as he touched her arm. "Lambert told me what you did. You could have killed yourself."

"That was my best friend in that SUV. I did what I needed to do."

"You should have backed off and let Lambert rescue Raven and Ellie. Racing into the oncoming lane...that was reckless, Chelsey."

"What do you care about Raven?"

"She's my friend too."

"Well, you had a more important case to solve. So it was up to me."

Thomas took a breath. Why was she fighting him?

"The important thing is, everyone is all right. Rest and heal up. Take some time off. Raven can run the show while you recover."

"There's a backlog of cases piling up on my desk."

"Don't put yourself at risk by returning to work too soon. After the shooting, I returned before my doctor cleared me. My stubbornness set me back months."

"Well, maybe you should have quit."

Thomas shifted. Chelsey impatiently tapped her hand on the mattress.

"You think I should have quit law enforcement?"

She'd avoided his eyes until now. When Chelsey turned to him, her cold, uncaring glare stunned him.

"Why would you come back to Wolf Lake and accept a deputy position? You should have listened to your parents and taken over the business." She swept her arm toward the window. "There's no future for you here. Stop wasting your talent and do what you were meant to do."

"Where's all this coming from?"

"For as long as I've known you, you've fought your parents. Stop and listen, for once. You're killing yourself, and they're offering you a better life."

She looked away. Now that she'd lobbed the grenade, she hunkered down inside her bunker.

"I didn't come here this morning to talk about my job or Shepherd Systems."

"Then what? Did you come here to talk about *us*, Thomas? Because if you did, you should go. There is no *us*. There hasn't been since we were too young to know better."

He took a quivering breath. His chest tightened.

"I'm not here to rekindle failed relationships and live in the past. I came because you're family, and you're hurt. Family members support each other."

"I'm not your family."

"That's where you're wrong. In my heart, you will always be family." He leaned over the bed and kissed her forehead. "Take care of yourself, Chelsey. I hope we cross paths again one day." Her eyes swung to him when he stood. "Goodbye."

He was halfway to the elevators when the first tear rolled down his cheek.

CHELSEY FLICKED a tear off her eyelid and turned away when she heard Raven's footsteps approach. What had Thomas meant about crossing paths someday? She hadn't meant to hurt him, didn't understand where the vitriol had come from. Since she was eighteen, she'd pushed people out of her life and hurt the ones she cared about, every decision wrong and full of regret. She couldn't do this anymore. She was numb.

Swallowing the lump in her throat, Chelsey closed her eyes and pretended to be asleep.

"You're not fooling anyone," Raven said, sliding into the chair. "You're awake."

Raven held a cup of coffee. The aroma enveloped the room and mixed with the heavy scents of cleaning solutions.

"Let me be. I haven't slept in twenty-four hours."

"I'll let you sleep all day, if that's what you want. But you're gonna listen first."

Chelsey groaned.

"No talking. It makes my head hurt."

"You're a mule, Chelsey, and it's about time someone gave you a smack on the rear."

"Go ahead. Everyone's taking shots at me this morning."

"What's wrong with you, girl? The greatest guy to enter your life came to see you, and you drove him away. Again."

Chelsey flipped over and glared at Raven.

"The greatest guy in my life? He was my high school boyfriend. That was forever-ago. Get real."

"I'm the only one in this room getting real. Every time the two of you are together, I see longing in your eyes." She leaned forward. "And I see fear."

"Oh, very poetic."

"He's doing everything he can to win you back, and you slammed the door in his face. One of these days, you'll wake up and realize he's gone and not coming back. You'll spend your life wishing you'd hung on to one good thing and allowed yourself to be happy for a change."

"I'm happy, Raven. What more can I ask for? I have friends and a successful business...too successful, judging by our growth."

"You have one friend. Me. Not that you couldn't have more, but you never leave the house. And Wolf Lake Consulting allows you to hide behind your work and push people away."

Chelsey bit her lip. She wanted to scream, to tell Raven to get the hell out and never come back. Chelsey's hidden fears and frustrations wilted her. Where did the tears come from? It seemed she'd held them back for years, and now the dam burst.

"You don't understand what it's like," Chelsey said, choking out each word. "I didn't want to live anymore. You think I asked for my depression, that I wanted to lose my friends and family, and go to sleep at night wishing I wouldn't wake up again?"

"My mother used to get her fix from a pusher outside the news stand in Harmon. Now she won't read the newspaper when I bring it home, because in her cluttered head, she relates newspapers to heroin addiction."

"What does this have to do with me?"

"You're afraid, Chelsey. I don't know why I didn't recognize it until now. You associate Thomas with the nightmare you lived through. The same way you associate your high school friends and family with depression. It's not fair what happened to you. But you let depression win with every pig-headed decision you make. In that stubborn head of yours, you believe letting Thomas into your life will open the door to depression again. That the medication and years of therapy won't stem the tide."

Chelsey's head fell to her chest. It became difficult to hear Raven over her sobs.

"But you don't need to be afraid. I'm here for you, and I sure as hell won't let depression attack you again. Not on my watch."

"I won't go back to those days. I'm not strong enough to beat it a second time."

"Give yourself a little credit. You're stronger than anyone I know. But you don't have to face the enemy without an army standing behind you. Let us in, Chelsey. We love you."

Raven patted Chelsey's hand and stood.

"It's late...or early, I suppose. I'm going home and getting some sleep. Think about what I said. See you this afternoon, all right?"

"Sure."

Raven paused at the door, indecision and a sense of duty preventing her from leaving.

"You're not alone."

"I know."

But after Raven turned down the hallway, Chelsey hadn't felt so alone in years.

The sun snapped Raven's eyes open. She glanced around in confusion, expecting to see her bedroom and not recognizing the surroundings. For a fleeting second, she thought she was trapped inside the farmhouse with Damian Ramos and Mark Benson.

Then Darren emerged from the kitchen with two mugs of coffee and set hers beside the bed. He'd brought Raven back to the cabin after an endless night. After she'd ensured Chelsey would make a full recovery, Darren drove her to the sheriff's department. Two hours of questioning later, the sun was up, and all she wanted was to crash in the closest bed.

"What time is it?" she asked, rubbing the sleep from her eyes.

"Almost noon."

She jolted and sat up.

"Why didn't you wake me? My mother has been alone since—"

He set a hand on her shoulder.

"Calm down. After you fell asleep, I drove to your house and drank coffee with your mother. She's fine."

"Thank goodness," she said, setting a hand over her chest. She tilted her head at his mug. "How much coffee did you drink today?"

"Too much. I'm so wired, I could power half the village."

"You didn't tell Mom what happened, I hope."

"She would have heard about it on the news. Don't worry. I made it sound less scary than it was."

Raven picked at her nails. Battling the ropes and smacking Damian across the head hadn't done her manicure any favors.

"I assume Ramos and Benson didn't murder Cecilia Bond and Lincoln Ramsey."

"No. But while you were at the farmhouse, the killer struck again. Twice. She murdered Kay Ramsey and Garrick Tillery."

"She?"

"Thea Barlow."

"I don't recognize that name."

"She works at St. Mary's church and knew the victims. Thomas shot Barlow after she broke inside his parents' house and tried to kill Mason Shepherd."

Raven leaned her head against the pillow and closed her eyes.

"Good lord, that's horrible. Thomas must be a mess."

Darren pressed his lips together and glanced away.

"You see how he is. He's the first to help anyone in need. But he hides his emotions."

"Reminds me of someone we know. If Chelsey and Thomas don't work out their issues, I'm gonna slap them silly."

He laughed and touched her face.

"I was so worried about you."

Her hand closed over his.

"Well, you found me. And you better not let me get away next time."

He waggled his eyebrows.

"Sexy."

She punched his shoulder.

"Speaking of getting away, whatever happened to Damian Ramos?"

"State police caught him wandering back to the farmhouse. He had a fat lump on his forehead after you rocked his bells. Once they put the spotlight on him, he sang like a bird. He's locked inside the county jail with Mark Benson."

"Good. He's a creep, and Sadie Moreno deserved better."

Darren held Raven's hand and stared into her eyes. His stubble was a few days old now, and she wanted to press her cheek against his and stay in bed all day. But she couldn't leave her mother alone.

"Can I make you breakfast? Or lunch?"

She swung her legs off the mattress and stepped into her shorts.

"I'd better get back to Mom." After he gave her a disappointed stare, she put a hand against his chest. "How would you like it if I stopped by later?"

"I'd like that a lot."

Their lips met and lingered as Raven did the math in her head. Take a quick shower, check on Mom, and drop her off at the guest house with LeVar. If she hurried, she'd be back in ninety minutes. That gave them all day to make up for lost time. When his tongue flicked against hers, she pulled away before she ended up in bed all day.

"Hold that thought," she said, pressing a finger to his lips. "I'll call you when I'm ready."

Glancing back at the state park ranger, she felt herself falling in love.

Thomas stared at the Nightshade County Sheriff's Department building through the windshield of his Ford F-150. Puddles soaked the parking lot and reflected billowing clouds. After last night's downpour, the world seemed bathed in green grass and leaves, almost other-worldly. Sunlight simmered behind the clouds and struggled to burn through the dense overcast.

His fingers drummed the steering wheel with indecision before he lifted the phone and replayed his messages. Neil Gardy with the FBI's Behavioral Analysis Unit had left two voice-mails. The consulting position was his. All Thomas had to do was say yes.

Three months ago, when he'd returned to Wolf Lake, the future was bright with promise. Now the village seemed unre-pairable, damaged beyond reconstruction. How could he give up Uncle Truman's A-frame? And what would become of LeVar and the Mourning family, if he packed his bags and left? Since he'd plastered the town with lost dog signs, nobody had claimed Jack. The loyal dog was his, and he'd accompany Thomas to Virginia.

But nothing compared to the life Thomas could offer Jack beside Wolf Lake.

Inside the office, Sheriff Gray moved past the window. Someone needed to convince Gray to step down. As much as it pained Thomas, the sheriff wasn't fit to hold his position. At sixty, Gray remained as sharp as when Thomas first met him. Tragedy had ruined the sheriff and tainted his judgment. Thomas couldn't work under Gray another day. But he wouldn't be the one to tell his mentor he needed to retire. He'd sooner leave than tear the sheriff's heart out.

The walk across the parking lot felt like a death march. He pulled the door open and donned a painted-on smile. Maggie wasn't buying it.

The administrative assistant took in a sharp breath.

"Thomas? Did something happen to..."

"My father is recovering fine, Maggie. Thank you. I need to speak with the sheriff."

"He's in his office," Maggie said, fiddling with the stapler. "Go right in. Fair warning. He's in one of his moods this morning."

Thomas passed through the office. An open box of donuts sat in the break room, and Aguilar and Lambert were hunched over their computers. Aguilar's eyes followed Thomas as he marched toward the sheriff's office.

Seated behind his desk, Gray appeared a shell of his former self as he scribbled his signature on a form. The sheriff's clothes hung off his body like shedding skin, and the circles under his eyes ran deep. Had the man slept since Thomas gunned down Thea Barlow?

"Close the door," Gray said without looking up.

Thomas complied. With the window shut, the close confines amplified every noise in the room—the squeaky wheels of Gray's rolling chair, the desk clock ticking like a bomb. Gray set the papers aside and tossed the pen inside his desk drawer. His eyes were hard and bloodshot.

"You openly defied my orders inside the church. What's more, you questioned me at every turn during the investigation."

Thomas didn't reply. He forced himself to hold his chin high and ride out the storm. It would all be over soon.

"And you were right to do so," the sheriff said, glowering. Thomas blinked. "I was a fool. Since spring, I've committed too many judgment errors to count. If it wasn't for you, I would have arrested Fowler and exposed the department to a humiliating lawsuit. I'm positive the bastard killed my Lana. But he didn't murder Cecilia Bond and Lincoln Ramsey, and he was at the church when Kay Ramsey and Garrick Tillery died." Gray leaned back in his chair, removed his hat, and set it upon the desk. "I'm stepping down, Thomas. I'm no longer qualified to hold this position. Seems everyone acknowledges this truth except me."

"Sheriff?"

"Don't talk me out of it. I've made up my mind, and life is too short to torture myself for another year. My time has passed." He clasped his hands over his belly and assessed the deputy sitting across from him. "I'd like you to be sheriff."

Thomas swallowed.

"Me?"

"You were overqualified for the deputy's position when you came to me in April. A decade with the LAPD. Then you rose to detective and led a task force with the DEA. Nobody's more qualified to man the ship than you, which makes it even more ridiculous I didn't defer to your judgment during the Fowler investigation."

"What about Aguilar and Lambert? They've been here longer."

Gray glanced at the closed door and shook his head.

"Lambert is a great deputy, but he isn't a leader. And Aguilar doesn't want the job. She'd be out of her element dealing with politics."

Thomas's legs bounced below the desk. This was the last scenario he envisioned when he'd entered the building.

"You can't name me sheriff. The people of Nightshade County will decide who the next sheriff is."

Gray's eyes grinned at Thomas.

"I ran unopposed the last two elections, and you will too. Plus, you solved the Jeremy Hyde and Thea Barlow murders. The people won't forget what you did for Wolf Lake. The county commissioners will appoint you interim sheriff, if I put in a good word. My opinion still carries weight in this county, even if it shouldn't." Gray slid the chair forward and set his forearms on the desk. "You'd make the best sheriff this county has ever seen. Now, stop being a humble bastard and accept the position."

Thomas ran a hand through his hair. He'd never envisioned himself as sheriff. Was Gray's confidence in him misplaced?

"Allow me a day to mull this over. I'll give you an answer by four o'clock tomorrow."

The two men rose from their chairs. Gray clasped hands with Thomas.

"Nightshade County needs you, Thomas. Don't let us down."

49

Abe Fairbanks, the head lawyer for Shepherd Systems, was a tall, imposing man. His dark, thinning hair slicked across his head. The lawyer sat across the table from Thomas, while Mason Shepherd manned the head of the table. Lindsey Shepherd watched from the doorway with her arms folded. Mason cleared his throat.

"It's comforting you finally came to your senses, Thomas."

Without replying, Thomas sat in silence while Fairbanks sifted through a ream of papers. Assessing Thomas through the tops of his eyes, Fairbanks slid a form across the desk.

"If you will sign beside the red X, here and here," Fairbanks said, pointing with a pen. "The transfer will be complete."

After Thomas penned his signatures, his mother issued a relieved sigh.

"At last," Mason said. "You made the right decision. Shepherd Systems will enjoy a better tomorrow with my heir running the company."

"I'll do my best."

Mason sniffed.

"You must do better than your best, Thomas. This is a

cutthroat industry, and the competition will come for you after news spreads that I've stepped down. But I have faith in you."

Thomas couldn't recall the last time his father complimented him. The lawyer extended his hand to Mason, then shook hands with Thomas. After Fairbanks departed, Lindsey Shepherd strode to Mason's side, helping her husband out of the chair. Mason Shepherd's frailty grew each day. Yet he still carried an air of authority that intimidated anyone in the same room with him. The Thea Barlow attack had left his parents skittish, their eyes haunted. It would be a long time before Lindsey felt comfortable in her own home.

"When will you announce your retirement from the Nightshade County Sheriff's Department?" Lindsey asked. "Soon, I hope. It will take weeks to spin you up."

"I won't be retiring from the department."

Thomas's parents gazed at him without blinking.

"What do you mean, you won't retire?" Mason growled. "You can't work two jobs at once, foolish boy."

"I'm the owner of Shepherd Systems."

"Yes."

"And as owner, I choose who runs day-to-day operations. As I've told you many times, I'm not qualified to run the company. But I will ensure the right person does."

Mason's face reddened. His body shook.

"What is the meaning of this? Call Fairbanks into the room, and order him to tear up the contracts."

"The transfer is official, Father. I promised you Shepherd Systems will reach new heights. You must trust me to run the company as I see fit."

"You lied to me."

"No, I didn't. The best leaders delegate authority and admit when they're out of their element."

"You're the only Shepherd left. Nobody else is qualified."

"There is one. As CEO and owner, my first task is to name a new company president." Thomas turned to his mother. "I'd be honored if you accepted the position."

Her mouth agape, Lindsey glanced from Mason to Thomas.

"You're naming me president of Shepherd Systems?"

"Why not? You attended Union with Father and hold the same degree. In addition, you're the only person besides Father who watched Shepherd Systems grow from a tiny startup to a national power. You know all the inner workings." When Lindsey opened her mouth to protest, Thomas raised a hand. "And you'll ensure my decisions do justice to Father's legacy. I'll need your help if this is to work, Mother."

Lindsey glanced doubtfully at Mason.

"What do you think of this?"

"Our son pulled a fast one on me. But he's correct about one thing. You're the right choice for company president." Mason straightened his jacket. "Lindsey, you could have run Shepherd Systems in my place."

Thomas took his mother's hands in his.

"You'll make the best president this company has ever seen."

"But who will run day-to-day operations?" Lindsey asked.

Thomas smiled.

"You'll meet her soon."

50

MONDAY, JULY 20TH, 2:30 P.M.

C helsey's arms trembled as she ran the brush through her hair. Staring into the mirror, appraising the ugly gash across her forehead, she daubed makeup beneath her scalp and exhaled. For too long, she'd pushed away anyone who tried to help her, guaranteeing a solitary life.

Guilt clenched her throat when she recalled how she'd treated Thomas at the hospital. How could Chelsey tell Thomas the real reason she wished he'd quit law enforcement? She was convinced something terrible would happen to him and couldn't face life if Thomas died in the line of duty. Had she not intervened, Jeremy Hyde would have murdered Thomas inside the A-frame, leaving the madman free to stalk up the staircase and slaughter Naomi Mourning and Scout. A shiver ran down Chelsey's back. It was only a matter of time before Thomas's luck ran out on him. She refused to lose him again.

She loved him. God, she loved him, and had since they'd held hands at the high school football game—the night he offered his sweatshirt because she was cold, even though it left him exposed to the autumn wind. That was Thomas. Always thinking of others before he cared for himself. And that needed to change. Someone had to watch his back for a change.

She mussed her hair and questioned her reflection. Was she making a wise decision? Her body quaked with hesitancy.

Raven was right. Chelsey needed Thomas in her life. Today, she'd tell him the truth. If he spurned her, she had only herself to blame after the way she'd mistreated him.

Chelsey silenced her phone and slipped it into her purse, not wanting any interruptions. She grabbed the keys and limped to the red Kia Sorrento in the driveway, the rental she was driving until she replaced the totaled Civic. Inside the car, she rechecked her face in the mirror.

To hell with it. No more hiding her scars.

Amid a sea-blue sky, the sun shone upon the village as she turned the Sorrento toward the lake. For the first time in four-teen years, Chelsey was ready for a new beginning. And that started with correcting the worst mistake she'd ever made.

THOMAS COULDN'T REMEMBER the last time he'd felt this nervous. He wiped his hands on his pants, then set the tray of drinks and snacks beside the lake. The Pinot Noir was the best the Finger Lakes offered, and the cheddar cheese was farm-fresh and savory, not too sharp. Perhaps he overdid it with the presentation. But he wanted the moment to be special.

While he set the beach chairs along the shore, Naomi strolled down the concrete path. She wore a sleeveless paisley-print dress and sandals, her hair loose and blowing in the wind. His heart jumped. He'd never seen her without the ponytail. The cheese and wine caught her off guard, and she touched her heart.

"You said you had something important to ask me. Now I'm intrigued. What's the occasion?"

"Have a seat," Thomas said, inviting her to sit beside the lake. He lifted his wine glass and motioned for her to do the same. "A toast."

"What are we toasting?"

"A better tomorrow for all of us."

"I can drink to that." Naomi sipped the Pinot Noir. She closed her eyes as a smile spread across her face. "That's amazing. I'm in heaven."

Thomas shifted his chair to face hers. She crossed one leg over the other and watched him with curiosity. The lake breeze kept flipping the hem above her knees, forcing her to flatten it out.

"There's something I need to tell you."

She set the wine down. Uncertainty flashed in her eyes.

"Okay."

"I took my father up on his offer."

Naomi sat forward.

"You really did it?"

"Shepherd Systems is my company."

She popped out of her chair and wrapped Thomas in a hug.

"I'm so proud of you, Thomas. You made the right decision. But I never expected you'd leave the sheriff's department."

"I'm not." As she returned to the chair, her eyes questioned his. "As I told you, I'd be in over my head if I ran my father's company. It's not my area of expertise. The last thing I want is to ruin the business my father built and destroy his legacy."

"I don't understand."

"I'm bringing in an operations manager, someone with the requisite skills to push the company to new heights." Thomas leaned forward and set his elbows on his knees. "Naomi, I want you to run Shepherd Systems."

She choked on the wine and coughed into her hand. After she composed herself, she said, "I know nothing about Shepherd Systems. Don't you think you'd be better off finding someone with more experience?"

"I saw your eyes light up when you helped Ruth Sims. Your ideas are innovative and effective, and your track record in Ithaca speaks for itself. There's nobody more qualified to run my father's...to run my company."

Naomi touched her forehead as her eyes glistened.

"This is a lot to process. I don't know what to say."

"Say yes. Starting salary is one-hundred-seventy-five thousand, and that includes full medical, dental, and vision. We offer six weeks of paid vacation time, eight after three years, and unlimited sick and maternity leave, all paid. So what do you think?"

She was quiet for a long moment as the boats rolled across the lake. Then she sprang from her chair and threw her arms around Thomas.

Crying into his shoulder, she said, "This is the nicest thing anyone has ever done for my family. This morning, I wasn't sure how I'd put food on the table. And now you're offering me more money than I've ever dreamed of. How can I ever thank you?"

He uncertainly hugged her back, patting her shoulder as she continued to weep.

"You can thank me by stopping by the office Monday morning to fill out your paperwork. That is, if you don't need time to get your affairs in order."

"No, no. I can't wait to start." She bounced on her toes. "This is so exciting."

"The office opens at six in the morning and closes at eight in the evening. Unlike my father, all I care is that you put in a full work week. If you have to leave for a few hours in the afternoon to pick up Scout, or your caregiver flakes out and leaves you hanging, you'll adjust your hours. We're flexible."

She kissed his cheek.

"You don't need to convince me. I can't believe this is happening."

As they laughed and watched the blue waters slosh against the shore, Scout wheeled herself down the path. Thomas couldn't wait to share the good news.

THOMAS'S F-150 slumbered in his driveway when Chelsey parked at the curb. She glanced at the house and didn't see him inside. Reaching across the seat, she grabbed the bouquet she'd picked from her yard. It seemed awkward giving flowers to a guy. But she wasn't one for tradition, and she didn't want to arrive empty handed. Call it a peace offering.

Along the ridge, a shadow moved through the state forest. Her eyes stopped on the shape. The stranger seemed to be staring at the A-frame. As she stepped along the ramp to gain a better view, the person vanished.

An enormous dog watched her through the window, its tail thumping. Raven had mentioned something about a dog Thomas rescued from the woods. Chelsey climbed the wheelchair ramp installed for the neighbor's daughter and pressed the doorbell. After a minute, she pressed the bell again. The dog was closer now, its snout pressed to the glass and leaving condensation splotches on the window. The rescued animal appeared to be some sort of German Shepherd or Siberian Husky, but larger.

Her heart hammered as she waited for the door to open. She'd held the words inside for so long.

Maybe he was out back, working in the yard or hanging out at the guest house with LeVar.

Chelsey rounded the house and saw them. Thomas and Naomi embraced on the lake shore as Scout hurried to join them. They looked like the perfect family.

The sickness rolling through Chelsey's body doubled her over. The yard vanished behind a veil of tears. All around her, the wind off the lake shoved and pushed, driving her off the lawn as though she wasn't wanted. She'd been a fool to believe in new beginnings and fairytale endings.

She dropped the flowers and left them to die.

Two miles from Thomas Shepherd's backyard where the sheriff entertained Naomi, Scout, and LeVar on the deck, a storm cloud drifted over the state park. A single bolt of lightning forked earthward and tore a gap in the soil below Lucifer Falls. Rain fell, beginning as gentle patter, before it grew into a deluge and chased campers back to their cabins.

The falls surged from the storm and grew into an unholy roar. Flooded waters cascaded off the cliffs and crashed into the creek bed, scouring away years of hidden secrets.

From beneath the silt, a skeletal finger poked skyward. Almost accusatory. The creek swelled as the storm pounded the wilderness. Surging out of its banks, the water scoured the earth and buried the hand before anyone could see.

The secret would not stay buried for long. A forgotten ghost had returned to haunt Wolf Lake.

Thank you for reading!
Ready for the next Wolf Lake thriller?
Read River of Bones today

GET A FREE BOOK!

I'm a pretty nice guy once you look past the grisly images in my head. Most of all, I love connecting with awesome readers like you.

Join my VIP Reader Group and get a FREE serial killer thriller for your Kindle.

Get My Free Book

www.danpadavona.com/thriller-readers-vip-group/

SHOW YOUR SUPPORT FOR INDIE AUTHORS

Did you enjoy this book? If so, please let other thriller fans know by leaving a short review. Positive reviews help spread the word about independent authors and their novels. Thank you.

ABOUT THE AUTHOR

Dan Padavona is the author of the The Darkwater Cove series, The Scarlett Bell thriller series, *Her Shallow Grave*, The Dark Vanishings series, *Camp Slasher, Quilt, Crawlspace, The Face of Midnight, Storberry, Shadow Witch*, and the horror anthology, *The Island*. He lives in upstate New York with his beautiful wife, Terri, and their children, Joe, and Julia. Dan is a meteorologist with NOAA's National Weather Service. Besides writing, he enjoys visiting amusement parks, beach vacations, Renaissance fairs, gardening, playing with the family dogs, and eating too much ice cream.

Visit Dan at: www.danpadavona.com